KU-530-972

THE HEALER

SHARON SALA

THORNDIKE
CHIVERS

This Large Print edition is published by Thorndike Press, Waterville, Maine, USA and by BBC Audiobooks Ltd, Bath, England.
Thorndike Press, a part of Gale, Cengage Learning.
Copyright © 2008 by Sharon Sala.
The moral right of the author has been asserted.

ALL RIGHTS RESERVED
This is a work of fiction. Names, characters, places, and incidents are either the product of the author's imagination or are used fictitiously, and any resemblance to actual persons, living or dead, business establishments, events or locales is entirely coincidental.
The text of this Large Print edition is unabridged.
Other aspects of the book may vary from the original edition.
Set in 16 pt. Plantin.
Printed on permanent paper.

LIBRARY OF CONGRESS CATALOGING-IN-PUBLICATION DATA

Sala, Sharon.
    The healer / by Sharon Sala.
        p. cm. — (Thorndike Press large print basic)
    ISBN-13: 978-1-4104-0554-8 (alk. paper)
    ISBN-10: 1-4104-0554-0 (alk. paper)
    1. Healers — Fiction. 2. West Virginia — Fiction. 3. Large type books. I. Title.
PS3569.A4565H43 2008
813'.54—dc22   2008011227

BRITISH LIBRARY CATALOGUING-IN-PUBLICATION DATA AVAILABLE

Published in 2008 in the U.S. by arrangement with Harlequin Books S.A.
Published in 2008 in the U.K. by arrangement with Harlequin Enterprises II B.V.

U.K. Hardcover: 978 1 405 64500 3 (Chivers Large Print)
U.K. Softcover: 978 1 405 64501 0 (Camden Large Print)
20178886
MORAY COUNCIL
LIBRARIES &
INFORMATION SERVICES
F
Printed in the United States of America
1 2 3 4 5 6 7 12 11 10 09 08

When I was a little girl, my paternal grandmother, Katie, who hailed from the hills in Tennessee, always had a remedy of her own design for whatever ailment I had. Her rule of thumb was if it didn't kill a horse, it wouldn't kill a kid.

I used to pray not to get sick when I spent summers with her, because I didn't want horse liniment rubbed on my wounds any more than I wanted the tea she boiled up for me to drink.

Then one summer I showed up with a wart on my hand. Little did I know, but I was due for one of Grandma's spells. Just when I thought she'd forgotten about the offending knot, she dragged me out of bed in the middle of the night, took me outside, wrapped an old dishrag around the wart on my hand, then began to turn me in a circle beneath the light of the full moon.

As I turned, she began to chant. I've long since forgotten the words. All I remember is what happened when she was done. She took the dishrag, buried it under the back porch, then sent me to bed.

I lay there under the sheets scared out of my mind, uncertain as to my fate. I should have known not to fret. Within a week, the wart was gone. My grandmother thought nothing of it. She'd done what she intended to do. But for me, she was forever branded into my mind as a healer with astounding ways.

So it is with love and affection that I dedicate this book to the healer in my life: Kathryn Cooper Smith.

ONE

Snow Valley, Southern Alaska: 1977

The rangy gray she-wolf, still thin from the passing winter, paused at the edge of the tree line above the valley. As she lifted her nose and sniffed the air, the hair on the back of her neck rose. She could smell the danger. Every instinct she had told her to turn and run, but the pup beside her had needs she couldn't provide.

At that moment the pup whined. When she turned and licked its dusty face, it wiggled with pleasure. As much as she would like to lie down, time was not on her side. She nudged the pup gently until it latched on to her pelt. With a single whine of reassurance, she started forward, confident that it would follow as she started down the gentle slope into the valley below.

The spring sunshine in Snow Valley was a welcome respite from the bitter Alaskan winter and the months without sunlight. It took a special kind of people to be at peace with a world that had months without sunlight, then months without darkness, but the native Inuits were just such a people. It took more than funky geography and quixotic weather patterns to stagger them. They'd been here for centuries and were at peace with their world.

Today, a brisk wind was coming down from the slopes, whipping among the simple wood-frame buildings housing the hunting camp and the small contingent of people who lived there, popping and yanking at the fresh laundry the women had hanging on their clotheslines.

A bush pilot named Harve Dubois, originally from Biloxi, Mississippi, had a small house on the south edge of the tiny settlement, next to the landing strip, which was the only way in and out of the camp. He'd been in residence for almost twelve years now and considered himself a replanted Alaskan. During the different hunting seasons, he flew hunters in and out of the area with his Bell Jet copter. In the off-seasons, he had a propensity for hibernation, at which times he retreated to his cabin with a case of Jim Beam and a grocery sack full of paperback thrillers.

Doctor Adam Lawson lived on the other edge of the hunting camp. He'd been brought in more than six years ago on a mercy mission when an unfortunate hunter had met up with a pissed-off grizzly. The hunter's gun had jammed, and then the grizzly had jammed him up one side and down the other. By the time the doctor had patched the hunter up enough to be flown out, he'd fallen for the people and the place. He'd come back the next spring on his own and had been there ever since.

A man named Silas Parker was the owner of the camp and lived and worked in a small, two-story A-frame. The lower floor was devoted to a sort of grocery and dry goods store, in which he stocked a wide variety of ammunition and a lesser amount of canned and dry goods. The second floor, which amounted to two very small rooms, was where he lived and slept.

The rest of the residents of Snow Valley were mostly Inuit and had been here longer than God. At least, that was what Harve claimed. Adam Lawson figured it was just the opposite. God had put them here. They'd just had the good sense to stay. The Inuit men were good hunting guides, and a large number of them were often away from the camp with hunting parties for long

9

periods of time, which periodically left the women and children alone.

The recent good weather had spawned a flurry of expeditions, which meant the women were taking advantage of extra time alone to do a little spring cleaning. With the below-zero temperatures behind them, the good weather also allowed their children to play out in the fresh air and sunshine.

Some of the older children were involved in a game of softball. Others were playing tag or hide and seek. A pair of six-year-old twins who went by the names of Shorty and Bubba were sitting in the middle of the road that snaked through the village, drawing pictures in the dirt with sticks.

As they sat, a strong burst of wind lifted the dirt in which they were playing, blowing bits of grass and sand into their eyes. Shorty, the older twin, frowned and closed his eyes, while Bubba, the taller one, quickly turned away, shielding his face from the debris. As he turned, he happened to look up the road. Seconds later, he jumped to his feet, squinting his eyes against the sun, unable to believe what he was seeing. Then suddenly reality surfaced. He grabbed his twin by the hair, and started pulling on him and screaming, "Run, Shorty, run!"

Shorty reacted without question. Together,

he and Bubba ran full tilt for their house, which was less than fifty yards away, screaming as they went. Their screams brought not only their mother, Willa, running, but others, as well.

"Mama, Mama . . . wolf!" Bubba screamed as he pointed up the road.

Willa needed only one look to begin echoing his cries.

"Wolf! Wolf!" she screamed, and began shoving her boys toward the house as the other women began a frantic search for their own children, desperate to get them inside.

The she-wolf stopped. She heard the screams. She smelled their fear. It was all the warning she was going to get. She wanted — needed — to run in the opposite direction. But the pup's tug on her hair matched the tug of instinct that kept her from abandoning it to an uncertain fate. It was that fierce, motherly instinct that gave her the courage to continue on, moving slowly with her head lowered to accommodate the little brown pup now clinging to her ear.

Silas Parker heard the commotion. Curious, he put down the cans he was shelving and moved toward the front door. It didn't take him long to see what was happening. A big gray wolf was coming into the village. Her walk was slow, and sometimes she staggered, with her head low to the ground. There was only one reason he could think of as to why a wild animal like that would come into the camp.

Rabies.

Silas had once seen a man die from the disease and didn't want to ever witness such suffering again.

He ran behind the counter, lifted his rifle from the rack on the wall, grabbed a handful of shells from a box beneath the counter and began loading the rifle on the run.

"Get inside! Get inside!" he shouted, as he started down the road. He wasn't much of a shot, which meant he was going to have to get closer to ensure a hit, and he didn't want to have to be dodging kids and women to take aim.

Another woman came out of her house with her rifle as Silas ran past. He could hear the unsteady sound of her breathing as she struggled to catch up.

He was still shaking from the burst of adrenaline as he neared Harve's landing strip. The wolf was close, almost too close. Afraid to go any farther, he stopped, lifted the rifle to his shoulder and took aim.

Counting slowly backward from five to steady his breathing, he tightened his finger on the trigger and had started to squeeze when the woman who'd been coming up behind him suddenly screamed in his ear, then shoved the rifle up into the air.

"Don't shoot!"

He flinched. Marie Tlingtik's shout was not only startling, but confusing. He turned abruptly.

"What the hell, Marie?"

"Look," she said, pointing at the wolf.

Silas turned in the direction she was indicating. "Yes, damn it. It's a wolf and —"

The words froze in the back of his throat. He took a deep breath and then wiped his eyes, certain he was hallucinating.

"That is not possible," Silas muttered, then turned toward Marie. "Holy Mother of God, is that a baby? Is it? Do you see it, Marie? Is that a real baby beside that wolf, or am I crazy?"

Marie muttered something in her native language, then turned around and ran.

Silas wanted to follow her, but the sight of that thin sun-browned toddler held him fast.

The wolf yipped. Once.

The gun Silas was holding slipped from his hands and landed at his feet with a thud.

13

He stood, still staring in disbelief as the she-wolf also stopped. Separated by less than twenty yards, Silas watched as the wolf lifted her head. Even from this distance, he felt her gaze fixed on him.

"Jesus, Jesus, Jesus," he whispered as his legs went weak. He wanted to run, but he couldn't bring himself to move. Still, he had to do something. That little kid could barely walk and was frighteningly thin. He couldn't just turn away from this. Even if he didn't understand it, he couldn't let it go.

Without thinking of the danger to himself, he took a deep breath, and started waving and shouting at the wolf.

The she-wolf flinched at the sharp, frightening sounds. She felt the danger as vividly as she felt the wind on her face. It was time to go. She turned to the pup and nudged it forward. It toddled a few steps ahead of her, then stumbled and dropped into the dirt.

Every instinct she had told her to run. Now. But she was torn. The pup whined as it fell. When it began struggling to get up, her instinct was to go toward it, but then she looked up. The human was moving closer. Without looking at the pup again, she turned and began loping back toward the trees.

Left on its own, the pup began to cry in

earnest. She could hear it as she ran. But it was only after she reached relative safety at the tree line that she stopped and looked back. The place looked deserted. That was when she lifted her head and howled. The long, mournful sound spilled down into Snow Valley, then echoed off the surrounding hills.

But it was what happened next that sent the entire village of Snow Valley into shock.

Silas had the child in his arms and was heading for Doc Lawson's house as fast as he could go. He looked behind him more than once as he ran, making sure the wolf hadn't done a U-turn and nipped back on his heels. As he ran, he kept glancing down at the baby, feeling the little boy's long black hair blowing across his face and the heat emanating from his thin brown body. Silas thought the child looked Indian, but it was hard to tell how much was dirt and how much was true skin color.

Suddenly the long, mournful howl of a wolf rode the wind blowing down into the valley. The howl was disconcerting. Silas flinched as he looked over his shoulder one last time, just to assure himself that the wolf was gone.

At the sound of the wolf's howl, the baby grabbed Silas by his full, bushy beard, then

15

twisted in his arms so that he was now looking toward the mountain. The little boy's tear-filled eyes were wide with shock. But instead of crying, he opened his little mouth and wailed. The high-pitched sound was an almost perfect echo of the wolf's howl.

Startled, Silas gasped and came close to dropping the child. If the boy had not been holding on to Silas's beard with both hands, he would have gone tumbling down to the ground. But Silas quickly recovered and began patting the baby on the back, trying to give him comfort as he kept on going.

"Now, now," Silas muttered. "Don't cry, little fella, don't cry."

The sound of Silas's voice was as startling to the baby as the wolf's howl had been to Silas. For a few silent moments, their gazes locked.

It was then that Silas realized the baby's eyes were not brown, but amber, marked with flecks of a yellowish gold, more like the eyes of the wolf instead of the dark-eyed Inuits.

"Damn, kid . . . where did you come from?"

But the wolf couldn't talk and the child didn't know.

Two years later

Adam Lawson sat on the steps of his front porch with his nearest neighbors, Wilson and Patty Umluck, watching his little boy and their three children at play. He never would have thought that, at the unmarried age of forty-three, he would have agreed to raise an abandoned baby, let alone believe that such a child would become the center of his world.

But he had.

From the first moment, when Silas had come staggering into his house with the naked toddler in his arms, to this morning, when the little boy, who Adam had named Jonah Gray Wolf, had crawled out of his bed and helped himself to a messy assortment of crackers, peanut butter and honey, he'd been hooked.

At his best guess, Jonah was now about four years old and bright beyond his years. Despite such an ignominious beginning, he was remarkably self-assured. Jonah had a way of watching his surroundings without comment that made him appear shy, but he wasn't. Quite the contrary. To Adam's dismay, the child was afraid of nothing.

Sensing Adam's gaze upon him, Jonah abruptly stopped his play and turned toward his father. He met his father's gaze, and for

17

a few silent moments, stared back. Then he slowly smiled, as if they were sharing a secret.

Adam smiled back, but Jonah had already moved past the moment and was back on his hands and knees in the grass, helping with the miniature log house the kids were building with a set of toy building logs. There was a bird on the ground near Jonah's feet and another that flitted about his head. Every now and then, it would land on his shoulders for the sunflower seeds Jonah kept in his pocket.

The residents of Snow Valley were somewhat intimidated by the little boy. His arrival into their midst was already legendary, and no other child had such an affinity with animals. Camp dogs followed him everywhere, and even the wild animals in the forest were drawn to him. Animals showed him no fear and were forever crawling over him, as if he were one of their own. Oddly enough, for a child with no knowledge of his past, he was never alone.

Adam didn't know what to make of it and had long ago quit trying to explain it, but he knew his boy was special. By all counts, he should have perished in the mountains and been eaten by the very animal that delivered him to safety. They'd searched for answers as to where he'd come from. Despite months of diligent attempts by the authorities to locate a parent, the case was still unsolved. No planes had gone missing. No area residents, no tourists, no hunters of any sort had gone unaccounted for. There was nothing to explain his presence.

As the adults sat on the steps watching the kids play, Adam's old dog, Sun-Catcher, came loping into their yard with something in his mouth. Before Adam could react, Jonah cried out and bolted to his feet.

At the sound of Jonah's shout, the dog stopped as if he'd run into an invisible wall, lowered his head and opened his mouth. A small gray squirrel dropped in the grass, limp and bloody.

"Oh no," Adam muttered, foreseeing the inevitable sadness that would come when Jonah realized the little squirrel was dead.

"Jonah! Wait!" he shouted, as he ran toward his son, but he was too late. Jonah was already on his knees and cradling the squirrel in his arms.

Wilson and Patty stood up and gathered their children beside them as Sun-Catcher lay nearby with his muzzle on his paws, watching Jonah's every move.

Adam laid a hand on Jonah's back.

"It's dead, son. Old Sun-Catcher here was

only hunting. It's what dogs do, you know. Come on, put it down and let —"

"No, Papa. I will fix it."

Adam's heart hurt for his son's confusion. "No, Jonah. You can't —"

The air went out of Adam's lungs all at once as Jonah sucked in his breath, then exhaled on a moan. When his eyes lost focus and his expression changed, Adam almost panicked. He didn't know what was happening, but clearly his son was somehow traumatized by the little animal's death.

Jonah laid the small bloody squirrel on the ground and began running his fingers up and down the body.

Adam could see the puncture marks on its neck, as well as on its belly. Old Sun-Catcher had done his worst.

Jonah cupped the tiny head, then laid the palm of his hand on top of the belly.

"Jonah . . . stop, son. That's enough. The little fella is —"

The words froze at the back of Adam's throat as he felt himself being enveloped by something still and dark — something so heavy that he could no longer move.

There was a dull ringing in his ears, and he could no longer hear the sounds of the birds that had been singing, or the tap-tap of a woodpecker who'd been hammering on a nearby tree.

He watched in disbelief as his little boy bent over the squirrel. How could Jonah move when Adam felt unable to even take a breath? Then the air began to shift.

At first Adam thought it was a breeze; then he realized it was more like a vibration. The tremors rocked against his body from every direction, and even beneath his feet. Was this an earthquake — or the end of the world?

A faint light enveloped the child and the squirrel as Jonah's small, grubby fingers gently spread across the animal's belly. When the squirrel's back legs began to twitch, Adam thought he was seeing things. When the animal's tiny belly began to rise and fall, Adam heard his neighbors' swift, indrawn breaths. When the squirrel's black eyes opened and his nose began to twitch, Wilson's wife, Patty, groaned, then began to pray. Adam recognized the chant but did not understand the words. It didn't matter. At this moment, a prayer in any language seemed more than appropriate.

Suddenly Jonah rocked back on his heels and put his hands in his lap. As he looked up at Adam, the smile on his face was nothing short of beautiful. At the same time, Adam felt the air around them change, and the light that had enveloped the boy and the squirrel disappeared.

"Look, Papa, I fixed him. I did good, right?"

Adam didn't know he was crying until Jonah stood up and laid his hands on his father's cheeks.

"Don't be sad, Papa. The squirrel is okay. See? I fixed it just fine."

The squirrel was up and running as Adam began to come to himself. Old Sun-Catcher glanced longingly at the squirrel, then fixed his gaze back at Jonah, as if waiting for permission to move.

"Go on, Sun-Catcher. No squirrel today," Jonah announced.

The old dog jumped up and loped off as Adam reached for Jonah and pulled him close.

Wilson and Patty stared at Jonah without speaking. When their oldest boy started toward Jonah, they grabbed him, then took the kids and left without explanation.

Adam felt their fear, but there was nothing he could do to change it.

"Jonah . . . oh, Jonah . . . what did you do?" Adam whispered, still unable to believe his own eyes.

Jonah pulled back and stared at his father.

"Papa, did I do something bad?"

Adam sighed. He heard the tremble in his son's voice and saw the tears in his eyes, which was the last thing he'd meant to achieve. He hadn't meant to scare Jonah, but *he* was scared — as scared as he'd ever been.

"No, no, nothing bad, son. Not bad at all."

Jonah relaxed and then smiled as he blinked away tears. "Okay, Papa," he said, and sank into Adam's lap.

Silence lengthened as Adam sat with his arms around Jonah, trying to find words for what he'd seen. Finally, there was no way around it but to ask.

"Jonah?"

Jonah tilted his head so that he could see his father's face. "Yes, Papa?"

"How did you do that?"

"Do what, Papa?"

"Fix the squirrel. How did you do that?"

Jonah's eyebrows arched as his eyes widened. Adam found himself staring at his own reflection.

"I just fixed what Sun-Catcher broke, that's all."

Adam felt sick. This was so far out of his comfort zone that he didn't even know what to say or how to say it. Still, he had to know.

"Have you ever done this before . . . I mean, fix animals that were, uh, broken?"

23

"Sure, Papa. All the time. Just like you. I fix just like you."

TWO

West Virginia
Present Day
Thin wisps of smoke from the dying embers of a campfire spiraled upward through the skeletal limbs of the barren trees. Before morning, frost would cover the ground.

A man slept near the dying fire, wedged as tightly beneath the overhang of rock at his back as he could get. A large mountain lion lay stretched out on the outcropping of rock above, chewing on the haunch of a deer that it had taken down earlier in the day.

Suddenly, it stopped in mid-chew and lifted its head, sniffing the air. Its ears suddenly flattened against its head, and a low, warning rumble came up its throat.

The man was awake within seconds. He rolled out from under his covers and stood abruptly.

"Easy, boy," he said softly. "I hear it, too."

25

The cougar hissed.

The man turned and stared straight into the big cat's eyes. For the space of a heartbeat, he and the cougar were as one.

Go. Now.

The cat grabbed the deer leg it had been eating and disappeared into the darkness.

The man turned back around and fixed his gaze on a small opening in the stand of trees in which he'd taken shelter. His nostrils twitched once as scents were carried to him on the air.

One dog. One man. One gun.

He smelled skunk on the dog, filth on the man and gunpowder. The gun had recently been fired.

He kicked dirt onto what was left of the coals, then stepped back into the shadows.

Chock Barrett paused beneath a stand of pines to catch his breath. As he did, he pulled a small penlight out of his pocket and checked the compass on his watch. It was hard to stay true to a direction when going uphill through such a heavily wooded area. Not only was this part of the Appalachians wild and brushy, but the population of the mountain that walked upright was definitely in the minority.

Still, the last decent bit of information

he'd had on the man known as Jonah Gray Wolf was supposed to be good, and the bounty would be worth all the crap he had to go through to get it. The only problem with bringing the man in was that the authorities would view it as kidnapping, which meant staying under the radar, because it wasn't the law that wanted Jonah Gray Wolf. It was a man named Major Bourdain.

Bourdain — the only man Jonah regretted healing. But he'd done it, and Bourdain had been after him ever since, shelling out money to anyone willing to hunt for the man who dispensed miracle cures through his hands.

Barrett dropped the penlight back into his pocket, shifted his gun to the other hand and started forward, then suddenly caught a whiff of something completely out of order.

Wood smoke. The dog beside him whined.

He grinned, revealing a mouthful of tobacco-stained teeth. Maybe he was about to get lucky. He shifted the backpack off his shoulder and felt through a side pocket for the tranquilizer darts he was carrying, then slipped one into the rifle before pocketing the others in his coat. His step was softer, his stride slower, as he started forward, guided by stray beams of moonlight filtering through the tree limbs onto the forest floor.

The intruder was close now. Despite the chill of the night, Jonah Gray Wolf could smell sweat from the man's unwashed body. Seconds passed, and then he heard a twig snap a few yards to his left. His nostrils flared slightly. It was his only reaction to being stalked.

A leaf shifted somewhere above him.

The cougar.

It had sensed trouble and come back.

Jonah didn't understand the connection between himself and animals, but he had long ago accepted it; it was as odd and complicated as his ability to heal others.

The cougar huffed once — a soft, almost undetectable cough — as a message to Jonah that it was there. To the untrained ear, it would have sounded like nothing more than wind shifting the leaves on the floor of the forest.

Jonah glanced back at his camp. In the dark, it still appeared as if he were in the bedroll, asleep. If whoever was on the mountain turned out to be just a hunter who'd smelled the smoke of his fire, he would most likely pass by the camp without revealing himself. But if it was one of Bourdain's men . . .

A few more seconds passed, then Jonah saw a shape emerging from the shadows on the far side of his camp. From where he was standing, he could see the man, as well as his rifle. But then, any hunter would be carrying. It remained to be seen exactly what it was that this man was hunting.

Jonah saw him pause. As he did, the dog that was with him suddenly yelped as if it had been shot, then pivoted and bolted back into the trees. Obviously, the dog had smelled the cougar. Too bad the man's olfactory senses were not as keen. It might save him some trouble.

When the dog bolted, he heard the hunter curse softly. For a moment, he thought the man was going to leave, too. Instead, he watched as the hunter raised his weapon and fired straight at Jonah's bedroll.

Jonah flinched, but didn't move. At least now he had an answer. The end of the tranq dart was sticking out of the bedroll at the place where his chest would have been.

The hunter lowered the weapon and swaggered toward the bedroll, then used the barrel to lift the covers. His posture changed when he realized the bedroll was empty.

"What the —"

Jonah stepped out of the shadows.

"You missed."

Barrett jerked as if he was the one who'd been shot. He was already scrambling to reload his rifle with another tranquilizer dart as Jonah emerged.

"Stand back!" Barrett shouted, as he shoved the dart into the chamber and swung the rifle straight at Jonah's chest. "It's nothing personal, buddy, but a million-dollar bounty is too good to pass up."

"You're never going to collect it," Jonah said.

Barrett grinned. "I've got a rifle here that says otherwise."

Suddenly the cougar on the rock ledge above their heads made itself known with a scream that ripped through the night. Jonah had heard it before, yet it never failed to raise the hair on the back of his neck.

Barrett jumped back in panic as he looked up and saw the cougar. Cursing wildly, he swung the rifle toward the cat and was about to pull the trigger when Jonah spoke.

"You shoot that cat, and I will kill you."

Barrett shuddered, then nervously swung the rifle back to Jonah. As he did, the cat shifted position, readying to pounce.

"You shoot me, and the cat will kill you," Jonah added.

Barrett was sweating profusely beneath his hunting gear.

"Shut up! Just shut the fuck up!" he yelled.

The cat snarled warningly.

Barrett was shaking. This wasn't the way it was supposed to go. Suddenly the million dollars wasn't as appealing as it had been. He swallowed nervously and wished he'd left with the dog. Even though it was dark, there was just enough moonlight for him to see the cougar's powerful haunches and big head. Picturing the teeth and claws that came with it, he took a shaky step backward while thinking he needed to regroup. He lowered his rifle.

"Look. I'm leaving now. No hard feelings . . . okay?"

"Sorry, but I have all kinds of hard feelings," Jonah said. "How do I know you won't come back and try again?"

The answer died in Barrett's throat as the cougar suddenly leaped down from the ledge. When it crouched beside Jonah and fixed Barrett with a motionless stare, he began moving backward.

"No, no, oh, God . . . don't let it get me. Please, don't let it get me!"

"What's your name?" Jonah asked.

"Chock Barrett."

"So. Barrett. You need to shut up now."

Barrett obeyed. He was too scared to argue. Long silent moments passed while his gut tied itself into a knot. He was promising God and himself that he would be a changed man if he could just get out of this mess alive and in one piece.

Jonah pointed to the gun.

"Toss the weapon," he said.

Barrett tossed it toward the bedroll. "Now can I go?"

"Empty your pockets," Jonah said.

Barrett dumped the rest of the loaded darts beside the rifle.

"Everything," Jonah said.

Barrett started tossing things out, but he wasn't pitching his car keys, no matter what.

"That's all. Now can I go? I won't tell anyone where you are. I swear."

"You lie," Jonah said softly, and stomped on all the darts until they were in pieces.

Barrett began to beg. "I didn't know . . . they said the animals protected you, but I didn't think —" He shuddered. "You're supposed to be a healer. You can't let me die."

"Yes, I can," Jonah said.

The cat hissed warningly.

Barrett began to shake. "No, no, you heal people," he wailed.

"Not if I don't want to," Jonah said.

32

Flop sweat dripped from the tip of Barrett's nose, and he was shaking so hard he could barely stand. When Jonah began moving about the campsite, packing up his things, Barrett thought maybe this was over. He started to pick up his gun when the cougar screamed a warning.

"Oh! Crap! Call it off! Call it off," Barrett begged.

Jonah paused in the act of packing his bedroll to glance at the cat, then at Barrett.

"He's pissed," Jonah said. "If I were you, I wouldn't move."

"But you can make him —"

Jonah shrugged. "I told you. Not if I don't want to, and frankly . . ." He paused to pull the tranq dart from his bedroll and then ground it under his heel. "I don't have any warm feelings toward you whatsoever."

Barrett shuddered.

"What are you going to do?"

"Obviously, I'm leaving," Jonah said, then kicked some more dirt onto the smoky embers, shouldered his backpack and headed out of the clearing.

Barrett's heart kicked so hard he gasped. The son of a bitch was leaving him here with a wild animal? No way.

"Wait! Wait! The cougar. What about the cougar?"

Jonah paused to look back. The cougar was flat on the ground, readying to pounce.

"Like I said, I'd suggest you don't move," Jonah offered, then walked away.

Barrett couldn't believe this was happening. His rifle was too far away to use as a club, and the darts were all broken. The cougar didn't move, and neither did he.

Jonah was all the way off the mountain and down onto the highway by the time dawn broke. About two hours ago, he'd come upon a truck. Guessing it belonged to Barrett, he had let the air out of all four tires.

Unless Barrett did something stupid, the cougar would eventually leave to return to his feeding. In fact, Jonah figured that had already happened and that Barrett was probably on the way down, possibly to resume his hunt.

Of course, the four flat tires he'd just left on the truck were going to slow him down even further. Jonah didn't take chances. A million dollars was incentive enough to give anyone a second wind, make him say to hell with cougars and resume the hunt. Jonah was tired — so tired — of being the prey.

Jonah was correct in every assumption

34

except the one that Barrett might resume the hunt. Barrett was so terrified, he'd almost passed out. But it was also sheer terror that had kept him upright. He could only imagine what would happen if he was unconscious. Would the cougar consider him a midnight feast and start chewing on his head, or would it just take a bite right out of his belly and go from there? This was a nightmare, and he wanted to wake up.

When, after two long hours, the cougar suddenly got to its feet, Barrett flinched. Was this it? Was he going to have to fight for his life?

Instead of bared teeth, the cougar showed its disdain for Barrett by urinating on the gun. Then, in one leap, it disappeared from the campsite, leaving Barrett alone in the dark and almost afraid to believe it was over. He stood for a few moments more, listening, praying he wouldn't hear the sound of something moving on the leaf-covered floor of the forest.

Blessed silence.

Without a second look at his rifle, he turned and bolted out of the clearing, heading down the mountain the same way he'd come up. His legs were shaking and his chest was burning, but he didn't let up on the pace. Once he tripped on a tree root and went sprawling, plowing up dirt and rotting leaves with his face. He got up quickly, spitting dirt and leaves as he went.

By the time he reached his truck, he was crying like a baby. Even though the moon had disappeared behind gathering cloud cover, he saw the four flat tires. It didn't matter. If it meant leaving this mountain on four rims, that was the way he would go.

He dug in his pockets for the keys and hit the remote for the door before he even got them out of his pocket. As soon as he heard the lock release, he catapulted into the seat, slammed the door, then hit the locks. The distinct click signaled a shutdown of the adrenaline that had been racing through his veins. Within seconds, he began to shake.

"Oh, God, oh, God, oh, God."

His tremors were so violent that he found it difficult to catch his breath, and he kept looking out the window into the darkness, just to reassure himself he was still alone.

Long minutes passed before his nerves began to settle. At that point, he began to focus. The last time he looked, he'd had a flask in the glove box. A shot of the hard stuff would be a welcome distraction, but when he leaned across the seat and popped the small door open, he found nothing but papers.

"Shit," he muttered, then wiped tears and snot off his face with the back of his sleeve before reaching for his cell phone. He had a sudden urge to take a long vacation somewhere warm, but first, he needed to end some obligations.

Major Bourdain was participating in a casual bout of sexual intercourse with a leggy hooker he'd tied to the brass headboard of his bed, when his phone began to ring.

The first ring made him flinch, but he kept on pumping, not wanting to lose the impending climax.

At the second ring, the hooker's focus automatically shifted from his face to the phone. Distracted by her inattention to business, he was thrown out of sync. Within seconds, he lost his erection.

The third ring was a death knell for whatever sexual satisfaction he'd been expecting. With an angry curse, he rolled off the woman just as the phone rang a fourth time. His tone was choked and angry, as he answered.

"This better be good!"

Barrett flinched. Sounded like Bourdain wasn't too happy. *Tough shit,* Barrett thought. *He should have been in my shoes*

*tonight, then he'd really have something to be
pissed about.*

"It's Barrett. I quit."

Bourdain rolled over to the side of the bed
and sat up.

"No, you don't quit on me. Nobody quits
on me."

"I just did," Barrett said.

"But you said —"

"That was before your Indian stomped
my tranq darts into pieces and sicced a
cougar on me. Don't call me again — ever.
I don't want anything to do with someone
who's more animal than man."

The dial tone in Bourdain's ear was silent
proof of the seriousness of Barrett's intent.

"Damn it all to hell," Bourdain muttered,
as he turned around and unlocked the
handcuffs on the hooker. "Get out!"

Then he walked into the bathroom and
shut the door. From inside, he could hear
the hooker scrambling into her clothes, but
his taste for sex was gone. He stood in front
of the full-length mirror on the back of the
bathroom door and then ran his fingers
along the scars on his torso.

Ten years ago he'd been a dead man. The
moment he'd seen the grizzly, the Alaskan
hunting trip he'd been on had gone horribly wrong. The bear had come at him like

a bat out of hell and, with one deadly swipe of its massive paw, taken out most of his belly.

Blessedly, he'd passed out from the pain. The next thing he remembered was looking up into the face of a young Indian man and feeling a heat unlike anything he'd ever known flowing through every vein and muscle in his body.

He had tried to speak, but words wouldn't come.

At that point, he'd seen his friend Dennis Henry move into his line of sight. He'd known Dennis for years and had hunted with him on safari in Africa, gone deep-sea fishing with him in the Gulf of Mexico, and the day before yesterday, had flown into Snow Valley, Alaska, to hunt caribou with him and a couple of his friends.

Dennis was staring at Major's body with a look of such horror that Major knew it was over. The last thing he remembered thinking was: *So this is what it feels like to die.*

Instead, he'd woken up some time later in the helicopter that had flown them from Snow Valley into their camp two days earlier. Dennis and the other members of the hunting party were staring down at him as if they'd never seen him before.

"Dennis?"

"I'm here," Dennis said.

"Are we dead?"

Dennis masked a shudder. "No. We're on our way back to Seattle."

"But the bear . . . ?"

"The bear is gone," Dennis said.

Major felt his face, tracing the familiar lines and angles, then moved to his belly, expecting, at the least, to feel massive bandages. Instead, there were faint ridges beneath his fingertips that he didn't recognize.

"So . . . I'm not dead, after all . . . only . . . I don't understand. What about the wounds? The blood? The pain? My God, I never felt so much pain in my life."

Dennis looked at him oddly, then glanced away.

"What?" Major asked. "What the hell is it? Why isn't anyone talking?"

Dennis ducked his head. A couple of the other men tried to make small talk, but Major wasn't having any of it.

"Damn it! Somebody tell me what the hell is going on. The last thing I remember is being gutted. Is this hell and I just don't get it?"

"Shut up, Major. You're fine, okay? Just shut up," Dennis said.

Major shoved the blanket off his body.

What was left of his clothing was bloody and in shreds. But the wound was gone. Closed and scarred as if it had happened years ago.

"Oh. My. God."

"No, it wasn't God. It was that Indian. He came because the doctor couldn't."

"Who came? What happened?"

"You were dying. The doctor at the camp in Snow Valley was gone. The chopper pilot brought this other man back instead." Dennis's eyes lost focus, as if he were seeing it for the first time all over again. "He got out of the chopper and didn't say a thing. He just dropped to his knees beside you, put his hands in the wound and . . . and . . ." He shuddered, then swiped a hand over his face.

"And what?" Major asked.

"Hell, I don't know. You both lit up like a disco ball. I watched, but I still don't believe what I saw."

"Damn it, Dennis! Get over the drama and just spit it out!"

Dennis's pupils dilated as the tone of Major's voice rose.

"He healed you, damn it! With his hands. No surgical instruments. No stitches. No blood transfusions. No friggin' nothing! One minute your guts were strung all over

41

your dick, and the next thing we knew, you'd quit bleeding." He waved at Major's scars. "That's all you've got to show for it. Just be grateful and shut the hell up."

Major didn't know what to think, except the wounds and the pain were gone. Then he heard someone say they were landing.

Before he knew it, they were on the ground in Seattle. His legs were a little shaky, so he'd walked slowly to where he'd left his car, then waited while the others began gathering up the hunting gear and transporting it to their waiting vehicles. Before he thought to question the chopper pilot about the man who'd supposedly healed him, the pilot had refueled and disappeared.

Bourdain felt like he'd been dropped into the twilight zone. His hands were shaking as he continued to feel his belly, running his fingertips along the ridges of scarring.

This wasn't possible. Any time now, he would wake up and realize this was nothing but a dream, but as he glanced at his watch, he flinched. They'd left Seattle on a Thursday. According to his watch, it was Saturday. He'd never had a three-day dream before.

Think. Think. We were hunting elk. Yes. I remember, because I'd just jacked a shell into the chamber. Something rustled in the bushes behind me.

He shuddered.

The bear. That had been real. He couldn't have dreamed anything that painful. He touched his belly. The scars felt real, too.

He swallowed nervously. If this wasn't a dream, then how did he explain away what had happened? He turned around, looking for his friend.

"Hey, Dennis."

Dennis was busy shoving his gear into his SUV. He wasn't religious in any way. Didn't believe in anything he couldn't see with his own eyes. But he'd seen something today that he couldn't explain. He'd seen it, and he'd been so frightened by it that he wanted to forget that he'd ever set foot in Alaska — to forget what he'd seen with his own eyes. To forget he'd ever known a man named Major Bourdain.

"What?" Dennis said at last.

"The man . . . the one you said healed me."

"What about him?"

"Did anyone say his name?"

"The pilot called him Jonah."

"What else?"

Dennis shrugged. "All I can tell you is that he was young . . . early twenties . . . long black hair and tan skin. I figured him for

43

Native American."

After that, Dennis had refused to say anything more.

Major shuddered, then backed away from the bathroom mirror and reached for a clean washcloth. He'd killed a man trying to catch the man he now knew as Jonah Gray Wolf. He'd even had him in his grasp once — long ago. But the animals had interfered, and Jonah had gotten away. There had to be a way to get him back. Gray Wolf had to have a weakness — somewhere. Whatever it took, Major would find it. He would do anything it took to get the healer under his power, because with him, Major Bourdain figured he could live forever.

Two days had passed since Jonah and Chock Barrett parted company in the woods. Jonah had stayed on alert for the past forty-eight hours to assure himself that, at least for the time being, he was once again alone. After that, he'd started moving. He was almost out of food and money. Despite his reluctance to stay in one place for too long, he was going to have to chance it to find himself a job. If he was lucky, he might find a place in which to winter. Being on the road in cold weather was brutal.

He'd done it before, but if he had a choice, he would much rather have a soft bed, a warm fire and a roof over his head when snow began to fall.

It was with that attitude that he walked into a small mountain town called Little Top, West Virginia, population: 2,497.

It was an insignificant, out-of-the-way place that should be safe enough. Now, if he could just find himself a job and a room, he would consider himself lucky.

Shug Marten was filling Ida Mae Coley's 1986 Ford pickup with gas when he saw the stranger coming down the road. Having his gas station at the far edge of town, he had seen plenty of strangers come and go during the past twenty-nine years, but this one seemed different. He studied the man for a bit, watching the set of his shoulders and the length of his stride. The man's clothes were of little consequence — well-worn denim and leather. His boots were covered in dust, as were the lower edges of his jeans. Despite the chill of the day, the man was bareheaded.

Shug eyed the man's brown skin and the length of his straight black hair, and wished he had a little of that hair on the crown of his own head. He'd been bald there for years.

The pump kicked off, and he turned to hang up the nozzle. Ida Mae was inside, waiting to pay. As he started into the station, Mark Ahern, the local mail carrier, honked, then waved at Shug as he came down from the mountain where he'd been delivering the rural mail. It was just after four o'clock. A little late for Mark to be finishing the route; he must have had a heavy load to deliver today, which would have slowed him down.

Shug waved back at Mark, then headed into the station to take Ida Mae's money. Once she'd paid, he walked her back out to her truck. She was lame in one leg and couldn't see so good anymore. If she lived anywhere else but in Little Top, she wouldn't still be driving. But here, everyone knew to get to the side of the road when they met her, and to wait at the stop signs, even if it was their turn to go, because Ida Mae had a tendency to sail on through the intersections.

"You drive safe now, Ida Mae," he said, as he helped her into the truck.

"I drive just fine, thank you," Ida Mae muttered, then fired up the engine and drove away from the pumps without looking to see if the road was clear. Fortunately, it was, and she headed toward Main Street, passing the man who was walking into town.

Jonah barely noted the truck as it passed him. His focus was on the small gas station and the man standing beside the pumps. Either this would be a friendly place or it would not. He hoped it was the former, because this far up the mountains, the towns were few and far between, and he was road-weary to the core.

Shug Marten nodded to the stranger as he approached.

"How you doin'?"

"A little cold," Jonah said, as he paused within a couple of yards of where Shug Marten was standing.

Shug pointed toward the station. "Hot coffee inside," he said.

"I'm a bit short on cash," Jonah said.

Shug didn't hesitate. "It's on me."

Jonah followed the old man into the station, his nose wrinkling slightly at the intermingled odors of gas, grease and old coffee. Still, he wasn't in a position to be choosy.

"Name's Shug Marten," the old man said, as he handed Jonah a disposable cup of hot black coffee.

Jonah took the coffee gratefully. "Jonah,"

he said softly, then lifted the cup to his lips. The coffee was thick and bitter, and it warmed him all the way down.

Shug reached behind the counter, picked up a packet of cupcakes and handed it to Jonah, as well.

"Can't have coffee without somethin' sweet," he said.

Jonah took the cupcakes gratefully and ate them without fanfare. When he was done, he tossed the wrapper into a trash can, then wiped his hands on the legs of his jeans.

"I'm looking for work," he said. "Know of anything around here?"

Shug frowned. "No, I don't, son. It's hard times all around, you know."

Jonah nodded, but before he could answer, the door to the station flew open. He caught a glimpse of a small female wearing a red flannel shirt and jeans as she ran past. Breathless, she grabbed Shug Marten by his arms and began tugging him toward the door.

"Shug! Shug! You've got to help me. Hobo got caught in a trap, and I can't get it off."

Jonah watched the old man pale.

"Damn it, Luce, I'm real sorry, but there ain't no way that monster of yours would let me close enough to help, and you know it."

The woman was frantic. Jonah had heard it in her voice.

"I'll help," he said.

Lucia Maria Andahar jumped. She'd been so desperate to get help that she hadn't realized anyone else was in the room. She turned abruptly, eyeing the tall, dark-haired man with the gold eyes and brown skin.

"I don't know you," she snapped.

"I don't know you, either," he said. "Do you want me to help or not?"

"What's your name?" Luce asked.

"Jonah."

She slapped the outside of her pants' pocket.

"So . . . Jonah . . . I've got a switchblade."

Jonah stifled a smile. "I consider myself forewarned."

Luce frowned. "You mess with me and you're dead."

Jonah felt her turmoil. Fear was warring with the extent of her need. He shook his head. "I will not harm you. I promise."

There was something in the tone of his voice. She hesitated, wanting to believe him. And then there was Hobo. She didn't have a choice. She had to take the chance.

"Follow me," she said, and bolted out the door.

Jonah shifted his backpack to a more

comfortable position and ran out behind her.

She circled the station, and headed straight up the mountain and into the trees. Jonah followed easily, keeping his gaze on the small woman with the long black braid. She wasn't very big, but if her heart was as strong as her backbone, she had to be amazing.

THREE

Luce was so afraid for Hobo that she wouldn't let herself think about the stranger behind her. She'd asked for help. He'd volunteered. All she wanted now was to get back to her dog before he bled to death.

Jonah knew the dog was in danger of dying. The raven flying just above the treetops ahead of them had already told him, but the underbrush through which they were moving made it difficult to run. Still, the young woman ahead of him didn't seem to have any trouble with the slope. They were going straight up the side of a mountain, and she had yet to slow down.

Luce ran with one hand out in front of her, like a running back with the football, stiff-arming the competition, only her opponent was the mountain itself.

Branches slapped at her face as she ducked under and ran past. Brambles caught in her clothing, then tore through the fabric as she pushed them aside. As cool as the day was, she was sweating, and the stitch in her side was so painful that it hurt to breathe, but resting wasn't an option. She'd been listening for the sound of Hobo's cries; the silence frightened her.

It felt like she'd been running forever, but after passing the hollowed-out stump where the summer blackberries grew, she knew they were almost there.

"Hurry!" she shouted.

Jonah felt her panic and increased his stride. Within moments, he was on her heels, then running past her.

Startled that the stranger had chosen to pass her, Luce almost stumbled. What was he doing? He didn't know where to go. But despite her misgivings, she realized he was going in the right direction and moving out of sight.

Before she had time to process that, she began hearing Hobo's anguished cries. That explained his behavior. He must have heard Hobo before she had. That was why he'd raced ahead. The knot of panic in her belly pulled tighter as she struggled to keep up.

But for Jonah, time had no meaning. He felt nothing but the injured animal's pain. The cold was no longer an issue. His hunger and exhaustion were, for the moment, gone.

The closer he got to the dog, the more he realized how serious this situation was. He could hear the sound of running water from the nearby creek, and then the high-pitched yips and howls of an animal in mortal distress.

Seconds later, he pushed through a thicket of buck brush and came upon the dog, lying on its side near the creek bank. The area all around the dog was torn up and bloody where it had struggled to get free. When it saw Jonah, it leaped up, then jerked backward, trying to get away.

Then Jonah spoke. "Easy, boy," he said softly.

Almost immediately, the dog stilled. When he did, Jonah let the pack slide off his back, then dropped to his knees beside him. Blood was everywhere, and he could see signs that the animal had tried to chew off its own leg to get free.

For one brief moment their gazes met. The dog's whine was heartbreaking. Jonah felt his pain.

"I know," Jonah said softly, and without thought, cupped the dog's head with both hands. "I know."

At his touch, the dog shuddered, then licked Jonah's hands and quieted, as if

Jonah's touch had become a welcome anesthetic.

"Hang with me, boy," Jonah said softly. "I'll get you out."

He paused only long enough to get a solid grip on either side of the trap. As he did, he was swamped by emotions he didn't understand. Whoever had set this trap was awash in evil and rage. But there was no time to think about that now. Jonah shook off the feelings and began to pull.

Within seconds, Luce had caught up. Her voice was shaking as she dropped down beside them. She didn't know how to explain why Hobo, who shunned everyone but her, was lying so still. She had fully expected him to fight the stranger every step of the way. Yet here he was, immobile beneath Jonah's touch.

"What can I do to help?"

"Find something to wedge into the trap . . . something big," Jonah said.

Luce didn't hesitate. With the coppery scent of blood in her nose, she jumped to her feet, scrambled around beneath the trees and quickly found a large chunk of a fallen branch.

"Will this do?"

Jonah was strong, but the trap was strong, too. And the teeth that had bitten into the

54

dog's leg were now cutting into him. Ignoring the pain, he caught a glimpse of the branch from the corner of his eye.

"Yes! Come closer and, when I tell you, shove it in the gap."

Luce shifted her stance and bent slightly, until the branch was only inches from the trap.

Jonah took a deep breath and then gave it all he had, pulling with every muscle in his body until the teeth parted from the dog's leg.

"Now!" he cried.

The metal dug into his fingers, shredding flesh and sinew all the way to the bone. The rough bark of the branch that Luce shoved past his fingers added insult to injury, but he held his ground. The moment the branch was in place, he let go of the trap and pulled the dog free.

"I've got him!" Jonah said.

With the branch still in the trap, Luce shoved it aside. Within seconds, the teeth cut through the pulpy wood and snapped shut with a loud, deadly clap. Splinters and bark flew as the branch flopped to the side.

Luce ducked. Then she saw Jonah's wounds.

"Oh my God . . . oh no . . . your fingers . . . you're bleeding," she cried, and reached for his hands.

"No . . . I'm all right," Jonah said, and closed his fingers into fists.

"But the blood . . ."

Luce felt the air shift around them. Somewhere on a nearby ridge, a wolf suddenly howled, which was odd, because they never hunted in the day. Nervously, she looked over her shoulder. They didn't need a confrontation with wild animals with Hobo unable to protect himself.

When she looked back, Jonah was opening his hands. The flesh that had been torn was once again brown and smooth. She was still trying to make sense of that when he leaned down and ran his fingers over Hobo's leg. Huge splinters of bone had pushed through the big dog's flesh, while blood continued to pour from the wounds.

Luce was sick to her stomach. And scared — as scared as she'd been in years. Hobo was all she had left in this world, and she couldn't imagine her life without him.

The dog whined as she laid her hand on his head. The blood showed no sign of coagulating, and his eyes were glassy from shock and pain, yet he lay completely immobile beneath the stranger's touch.

"His leg . . ." Luce whispered.

Jonah glanced up at her.

Breath caught at the back of Luce's throat. The man's eyes were glittering, his nostrils flared. For a fraction of a second she felt as if she were staring into the eyes of a wild animal instead of a man. Then he looked away and everything stopped.

The forest went silent, and the air, which had been chilled and sharp, suddenly felt too thick and heavy to breathe. She saw the man cover the wound with his hands. As he did, the ground on which they were sitting began to tremble. She was still holding Hobo when a heat-filled current hit the palm of her hand, then shot up her arm.

Startled, she gasped.

The moment Jonah heard her, he realized that the energy coming from him was flowing up and into her, too. He lifted his left hand only long enough to give her a quick push.

Startled by the blow, she fell onto her back, held motionless by a force she couldn't see.

Above her, the branches of the nearly leafless trees seemed to be vibrating, and she felt the ground beneath her begin to quake harder. As she watched, an aura of light suddenly enveloped Jonah, then spread to Hobo like water running over an outcropping of rock. Swamped by an overwhelming urge to

57

crawl into that light and lie down beneath his touch, she found, instead, that she couldn't move. She wanted to watch, but she couldn't keep herself awake. She had no idea how much time had passed; when she opened her eyes, Hobo was standing at the edge of the creek drinking water, and Jonah was a few feet downstream, washing the blood from his hands.

"Hobo!" she cried, and jumped to her feet.

The dog turned at the sound of her voice and then licked her face as she knelt beside him. She couldn't believe it!

"What did you do? Oh, my God . . . oh, my God! His leg! It's . . . it's . . ." She rocked back on her heels and stared up at Jonah. "How did you do that?" she cried, as she ran her hands up and down the length of Hobo's leg. The brown-and-white fur was bloody, but the limbs were sound. It didn't make sense.

Jonah stood above her with water dripping from his hands. He'd learned the hard way that trying to explain never worked. He answered, even though he knew she wasn't going to like it.

"I healed him," he said, and wiped his hands on the legs of his pants, before picking up his jacket and putting it back on.

Luce stared at him with an expression of

58

disbelief.

Jonah knew the look, and knew what came with it. He sighed, curious as to how the woman was going to make her mind accept what she'd seen.

Luce heard what he said, but it didn't make any sense. Had she just fallen into some alternate universe?

"No. No. You didn't just swab on antiseptic and set broken bones. You put that leg back together as if it never happened. That's impossible."

The corner of Jonah's mouth twitched as he stifled a smile.

"If it's impossible, then I guess it didn't happen."

Luce frowned. "But —"

"Why question what you saw, when the results are what was needed?"

Luce shuddered. The man's voice was soft, his words persuasive. She'd already been living in fear for the past five months, and trusting a stranger wasn't easy. But now that she'd seen what he'd done, it was disbelief that made her keep her distance. If he could do that, God only knows what else he was capable of.

Before she could answer him, a small brown bird came down out of a tree and landed on his shoulders. The sight was so

59

unexpected that Luce forgot what she'd been going to say. She pointed.

"Uh . . . there's a, uh . . . it's just —"

Jonah turned and looked at the bird, cocked his head sideways, then looked back at Luce.

"He says you have a good heart. He also says you feed him bread crumbs, and that the whole-wheat ones are his favorite."

Luce staggered backward, tripped on the sprung trap and the broken limb, and sat down with a thump.

Jonah rushed over to help her up.

"Are you all right?" he asked, as he offered her a hand.

Luce stared at his fingers, then up at him. His face mirrored concern. The little bird that had lit on his shoulder was gone. Hobo was licking her face in consternation. She wondered if this was how Alice had felt when she'd fallen down the rabbit hole.

"Get back, both of you," Luce muttered, as she rolled over and got up by herself, then dusted the leaves and dirt from the seat of her pants.

The man was still watching her. She couldn't decide if the look in his eyes was friendly or feral. Either way, he gave her the creeps. Then she looked at Hobo. The big brown-and-white mutt was sound and whole, and her world was back on track. She put her hands on her hips and looked back at Jonah.

"What did you say your name was?" she asked.

"Jonah. Gray Wolf. What's your name, little warrior?"

Luce flushed. "Lucia Maria Andahar, but people call me Luce."

She pronounced her name the way someone would say the word *loose,* but Jonah suspected there was nothing loose about her. Everything about her, from the way she held herself to the rigid set of her lips, was coiled tighter than a bedspring.

She fingered the St. Christopher medal hanging from an old chain around her neck without taking her gaze from his face. It was the first time that she'd taken a really good look at him. His features were strong and even. His skin was dark like hers, but she thought he was Native American and not Latino. At the moment, his mouth was slightly curved, as if he were stifling the urge to smile. His eyes, which had seemed frightening earlier, were now a soft amber color, and his expression never wavered. But there was that thing he'd done — making a horrible wound completely disappear.

Then, suddenly, she thought she knew.

"You're an angel . . . aren't you?"

Jonah smiled. "That's a first."

Luce frowned. "That's not an answer."

His voice was soft, but his smile disappeared. "I'm not an angel. I'm not from heaven." He hesitated, then added, "I'm not from anywhere."

"Then how did you do that?" Luce asked.

"I don't know," Jonah said, and then he looked around for his backpack. When he saw it, he picked it up and slung it over his shoulder.

"You're leaving now?" Luce asked.

Jonah paused. "You don't need me anymore."

Something inside Luce protested. Whether it was a premonition or a warning, she knew that if she never saw this man again, it would be a loss from which she would never recover.

She glanced up. This late in the year, evenings were short. The sun was already riding the western sky and sliding down behind the trees under which they were standing.

"It will be dark before you can get back into town."

"I sleep in the dark every night," Jonah said softly.

Luce shuffled nervously, then let out an

audible sigh.

"Look. I don't know why I'm saying this, because every instinct I have is telling me to let you walk away."

Jonah's heart skipped a beat. He knew what she was going to say. He saw into the years and what could be with them. The issue was, should he stay and risk her safety, or leave and risk his heart? He waited. It had to be her call.

When Luce looked into his eyes, she lost focus and fell into what she thought later was a dream. She saw them together, in life and in bed. She saw laughter and tears, and then, out of nowhere, felt danger. She blinked, and the moment was gone.

Jonah was surprised by his own feeling of despair when she stayed silent. He nodded at her once, as if accepting her decision, and turned away.

"Wait!" Luce cried.

Jonah looked back.

"Where are you going?" she asked.

"Nowhere."

"What brought you here?"

"Just looking for a job and a place to winter."

Luce felt panic, but she couldn't stay silent as the inevitability of her words overcame her.

"I might know of something," she said. "But you'll have to wait until tomorrow to check on it. If you're interested, I'm offering my home and a meal, and a warm place to sleep tonight."

It was more than he'd hoped for.

"I'm interested," he said softly.

"Then follow me," she said, and whistled to Hobo, who quickly moved to her side. She turned and began walking higher up the mountain, with the old dog at her side.

Jonah fell in behind them. A few minutes later, they walked out of the trees and into a clearing.

Luce paused, waiting for Jonah to catch up.

"Here we are," she said, pointing. "Home sweet home."

Jonah knew he was staring, but he'd never seen anything quite like it. There was a front door, and a small jutting roof with an accompanying porch that seemed to have been built into the face of the mountain. The path leading up to it was paved with flat pieces of natural rock, and there were small flower beds, now devoid of flowers, on either side of the steps.

"This belongs to you?" he asked.

"Lord no. I don't own anything but the clothes on my back. Even Hobo is his own man. He stays with me because he chooses, not because I own him. This place belongs to Bridie Tuesday, an old woman who lives a bit farther up the mountain. She lets me live here, and in return, I help her out when I can. The rest of the time, I wait tables in the diner down in Little Top."

A gust of chilly wind swept through the clearing, causing Luce to shudder. "Let's get inside and out of this wind."

She moved quickly, and moments later was at the door, then standing aside waiting for Jonah to enter.

His first reaction to the house had been on target. Someone had built a house in a cave. But someone had also taken the trouble to partition off some rooms and lay a floor. The old floors were tongue-in-groove, worn smooth as glass by the passage of time. The only openings that let in natural light were the big windows on either side of the front door. There were candles and oil lamps sitting about the rooms, but when Luce flipped on a switch, he was surprised to see that the place was also wired for electricity.

"Electricity?"

"Even an electric water heater, running water and a propane tank, although the place is mostly heated by the old fireplace."

"This place is amazing," he said.

"It is, isn't it? Bridie lived here with her husband for over thirty years before he built her a new house a bit farther up," Luce said, then tried to get past the awkwardness of having a total stranger in her place by smiling shyly. "Follow me. I'll show you where you can sleep."

She led the way out of the main room to a short passage that led to a pair of doors. She opened the one on the left, switched on another light and then stepped aside.

Jonah stood for a few moments, feeling the confusion of her emotions, but he didn't know what to say to make this any easier. Finally he moved past her and entered the room.

There was an old metal bed against one wall, an aging armoire a few feet from the bed and a small table near the headboard. A handmade, multicolored rag rug was on the floor, and a small stack of books sat on a shelf above the table.

Luce shoved her hands in her pockets, then took them out and clasped them behind her instead, as she stepped just inside the doorway.

"No one ever sleeps here, so the sheets are clean, even if they're not fresh. If you get cold in the night, there's an extra quilt in the armoire. Take your time getting settled. I'm going to start supper."

She had started to leave when Jonah reached for her, then stopped himself and spoke instead.

"Thank you for this."

"I've been where you are . . . on the road, I mean. You helped me. I'm happy to return the favor. The bathroom is next door, if you want to clean up. There are a few extra towels and washcloths in your armoire. Make yourself at home."

Jonah started to say something, then seemed to think better of it and nodded briefly as Luce left. What else was there to say?

He set his backpack on the floor near the armoire, dug out clean clothes, got a towel and washcloth, and headed for the bathroom.

The room was small, but the old claw-footed tub was long and deep. Just the thought of a good long soak had him hurrying to strip off his clothes. Within minutes, he was chest-deep in the tub, with his eyes closed, savoring the warmth and the clean scent of Luce Andahar's soap.

He wondered about her, how she'd come to be in this place and alone in the world, then shifted his focus to the task at hand

and began scrubbing himself clean.

Once he'd finished his bath, he used some of her shampoo. This was all such an unexpected luxury that he was reluctant to get out. But a warm meal was no farther away than the other side of the door, and it was a long time since he'd been invited to someone's table. Hunger won out. Before he could talk himself into staying longer, he opened the drain and then stood up. He was reaching for a towel when Luce knocked on the door.

"Supper will be ready in about five minutes," she called.

"I'll be right there," Jonah answered, and began drying off.

Luce repeated the alphabet on the way back to the stove. It was all she could think of to do to keep her mind off the fact that there was a naked stranger on the other side of her bathroom door.

As Jonah was dressing, he began smelling the aroma of the food she'd cooked. His belly growled, reminding him again of how long it had been since he'd eaten a real meal. He hung his wet towel and washcloth on pegs in the wall, then picked up his dirty clothes and dumped them in his room. He walked into the main room in his sock feet just as Luce was lifting a large pot from the stove.

"Here, let me help," he said, and took the pot and set it on the table. "If this tastes as good as it smells, I'm in heaven."

Luce was surprised at the spurt of pleasure his words gave her. It had been a long time since someone had praised her in any way without trying to get in her pants. Then she frowned. What made her think this man was any different? She'd brought him into her home without knowing a thing about him. Except . . . She glanced at Hobo, who was lying by the fireplace, and remembered what he'd done. A man like him — a man who held the promise of life in his hands — surely wouldn't be a man who also caused harm. It had to be okay.

"It's just vegetable soup," she said, and moved back to the oven to pull out a pan of cornbread.

Jonah's eyes widened. "Did you make all this yourself?"

Luce nodded. "Sit. I'll get the butter and honey."

Jonah sat, then closed his eyes momentarily, letting the warmth and the scents of her home and food envelop him. She'd asked him if he was an angel, but from where he was sitting, she was the one with wings. This place and this food were the closest thing to heaven that he'd known in years.

When he opened his eyes, Luce was filling his bowl with soup. His hands were shaking as he reached for a hot yellow square of the cornbread, and when he took the first bite of the warm bread and butter, he shuddered.

Luce frowned. "Are you okay?" Then she rolled her eyes, a bit embarrassed. "Sorry, that was a stupid question to ask a man who makes miracles."

Jonah swallowed, then looked at her from across the table.

"It's just . . . it's been a long time since . . ." Surprised that he was stuttering, he took a breath to steady his thoughts. "I haven't been inside a home in a very long time."

Luce couldn't help but wonder what had put him on the road alone, as she filled her own bowl. Her curiosity continued as she buttered her cornbread, but she couldn't bring herself to ask.

Hobo glanced up from his place near the fire just long enough to look at the table, then went back to the bone he was chewing. Every now and then he licked at the place on his leg where it had been caught in the trap, even though it was unnecessary. There was no wound. No pain. Just the memory of it, and the man who'd made it go away. For the dog, it was enough.

They ate in relative silence until the first pangs of hunger had been assuaged. Luce was the first to start talking.

"Where are you from?"

An old pain twisted a knot in his belly as he remembered the hunting camp in which he'd grown up.

"Alaska."

Luce's eyes widened. "Really? Is it true that they get six months of darkness and six months of light?"

Jonah smiled. "Pretty much."

"Do you still have family back there?"

Immediately, Jonah's thoughts went to Adam, and what he'd looked like the last time he'd seen him — lying dead in their kitchen in his own blood. "My father . . . he was actually my adopted father . . . was a doctor. A medical doctor. But he's . . . dead now."

Luce heard the word *adopted* and keyed in on that.

"What about your natural parents?"

"I have no idea," Jonah said. He didn't bother to tell her how he'd been told that, for a time, he'd been suckled by a wolf. To stop the questions before they got too personal, he turned the tables. "What about you? How do you come to be here and on your own?"

"I'm not alone. Thanks to you, I still have my Hobo."

Jonah sensed she was dodging the truth and, not for the first time, wondered if she was on the run.

"Where did you grow up?" he asked.

Luce's face lit up. "I grew up in a barrio in L.A. Papa laid tile. *Mi madre* cleaned houses for rich people. I was the youngest of four children. Our life was simple, but it was wonderful."

Jonah felt her sorrow long before she'd finished her tale.

"Every summer after school was out, we would travel from L.A. to Texas to spend time with Mama's family. The summer I was fourteen, we were driving through New Mexico on our way to Texas. We were all asleep, so I only know what I was told, but they say a truck driver fell asleep at the wheel, crossed the center median and hit us head-on. Everyone died but me."

She swallowed around the knot in her throat, then took a quick sip of water.

Jonah sighed. Her sorrow was still as deep and fresh as the day it had happened.

"I'm so sorry," he said softly.

Luce shrugged. "So am I." Then she lifted her chin. "I lived with an aunt and uncle until I was almost sixteen, then left. I haven't seen them since."

"Why? Why cut yourself off from your family?"

A muscle ticced near the corner of her eye.

"Let's just say I got tired of dodging my uncle's affections," she muttered, then looked away.

Jonah flinched. "Again . . . I am sorry."

"You have nothing to apologize for." She stood abruptly. "Enough of the past. I'm going to do the dishes."

"What can I do to help?" Jonah asked.

"You could bring in some wood for the fire. You'll find the woodpile just to the left of the porch."

The conversation had opened up old wounds for both of them, and so they finished the evening in silence, with Hobo following Jonah in and out of the house with every trip he made carrying wood.

It began to rain just after dark. The firewood Jonah had carried in was stacked beside the fireplace. He was bringing in the last armful when the first drops of rain began to fall.

"It's raining," he said, as Luce took a stick of wood from his load and added it to the fire that was already burning.

She looked up at him, saw the raindrops on his face and then the ones glistening in his hair, and had to make herself think past how sexy he was to the conversation at hand.

"Well, shoot," she said, as she grabbed the poker and began stabbing at the logs. "From in here, you can't hear what's happening outside. I was hoping that the rain would pass us by. Now I'll be walking in mud all the way to work tomorrow."

"You have no car?"

She shrugged. "It wouldn't do me any good if I did. I never learned to drive."

Jonah frowned, remembering that she'd told him she waited tables in the diner in town. He put down the last of the wood, then straightened up and looked around.

The room did double duty as a kitchen and living room. The furnishings were old but functional. One thing he took note of was that everything was so clean. He hadn't seen any kind of washer or dryer, and wondered if she had to take her laundry down into town.

"Do you have to do your laundry down in town?" he asked.

"No, thank goodness. There's an old washer and dryer behind that blue curtain on the other side of the kitchen. If you have clothes you'd like to wash, you're welcome to use them."

"I will. Thank you."

Luce sighed. "No, it's Hobo and I who thank you," she said, then, without thinking, laid her hand on the flat of his chest.

There was a moment when all she felt was the thud of his heartbeat against the palm of her hand; then, in the next moment, she thought she'd been struck by lightning.

She lost her breath and, for a moment, even her ability to breathe. Colors spilled, then blended and ran before her eyes, until it felt as if she were drowning. She tried to speak, but her tongue felt stuck to the roof of her mouth. Just as she thought she was losing her mind, a climax rocked her all the way to her toes. Her legs went weak, and her eyes rolled back in her head. If Jonah hadn't grabbed her, she would have hit the floor.

Jonah gasped as the shockwave of her climax rocked him almost as sharply as if it had been his own. Whatever was happening between them was an unknown. He'd been with women, but it had been nothing more than sexual release. He'd never had this

75

happen to him before, but it felt as if he were no longer alone inside his own skin.

Luce was stunned. She couldn't believe what had just happened, and didn't know whether to be embarrassed or ask for more. When she looked up, he was staring down at her with an expression of disbelief.

"What just happened?" she whispered.

Jonah shook his head. "I don't know. . . . I've never —" He took a deep breath and then turned her loose. "Forgive me. I did not do that on purpose."

Luce ran shaky hands through her hair and then smoothed them down the front of her shirt. Her breasts ached, and the skin on her body was so sensitive that it was painful to the touch. She shuddered and took a step back.

"Lord," she muttered, and took yet another step back.

Jonah was rattled. He was never uncertain. He'd always known things and accepted that as part of his persona. But this . . .

He didn't like the frightened look on her face and held up his hands in a gesture of submission.

"Please. You have nothing to fear from me. I would never —" He stopped, wiped a shaky hand across his face, then dropped his hands. "I'm sorry. If you have no further need of help, I will go to my room, heartily grateful not to be sleeping outside in the storm."

He walked away before Luce could stop him. She didn't know for sure how she felt about what had just happened, but whatever this was between them, it was far stronger than the storm.

FOUR

Jonah went to bed feeling confused and unsettled. He'd never had a reaction to a woman like he had with Luce. For him, it went far beyond the physical. He'd never believed in the concept of soul mates, but now he wasn't so sure. And, oddly enough, thinking of the future turned his thoughts to the past.

It wasn't often he let himself think of Snow Valley. Some things were too painful to remember. But tonight, sleep had taken him back to the day the world as he'd known it had come to an end.

If it had been possible to travel back in time, he would never have gotten on the chopper with Harve Dubois and flown in to Wilson Tinglit's hunting camp. But the message from Wilson had been frantic. One of the men he'd been guiding had been attacked by a grizzly, and the doctor, Adam Lawson, had been two hours away, delivering a baby.

If Jonah could have known the hell that would come to him from saving the mauled hunter's life, he would never have gotten on the chopper with Harve. If he allowed himself to wallow in the tragedy, he had to admit that, in saving the hunter, he'd caused his father's death. Still, there had been no way to know what would happen, and Adam would have been the first one to urge him to help. But when he closed his eyes, it was often his fate to relive that terrible time again and again in his dreams.

It always started with the cloud of black flies plastered to the screen on the back door. Then came the blood. The coppery scent of it was thick in the air as he walked into the kitchen. Like a slide show, the image in his mind moved from the flies to his father's body lying on the floor in a pool of congealing blood. Just beyond Adam Lawson's outstretched hand was a single word, written in the same blood that had been flowing through his veins.

RUN.

He could feel the absence of life, and he knew without touching him that his father had been dead for some time and was far beyond anything Jonah could do for him. Before he had time to process the horror of what he was seeing, he heard a sound behind him and turned.

Three masked men in black were coming at him from the living room. He didn't know what had happened, or why they were there, but self-preservation and his father's last message told him what to do.

He bolted toward the door in an all-out sprint, while his heart was breaking and his world was coming down around his ears. Black flies shattered formation and rose en masse into the air as he hit the screen door with the flat of his hand. He leaped from the porch, with the sounds of the killers in close pursuit.

"Get him!" he heard one of them yell.

Jonah heard the shout and sidestepped the gate, then vaulted over the four-foot-high wooden fence surrounding their backyard. His long hair flew out behind him like wings, as he increased his speed. At the same time, he saw the wolves coming out of the trees toward him. He didn't think to wonder how they knew he was in danger. But at the sight, he realized that their arrival might be his only chance to escape.

As he dashed past his neighbors' back door, someone came out and shouted at him.

"Hey, Jonah! What's wrong?"

It was Thomas Klingkit, a man Jonah had

fished with off and on throughout his youth. The only warning he could give him was "Get down!"

He couldn't stop to make sure Thomas had heeded him, but to Jonah's horror, he heard a shot, then a cry of pain.

His heart sank. He knew that his friend had been hit, but he couldn't stop. He couldn't help. All he could do was run.

The wolves were close now. He felt the thunder of their heartbeats in his ears. He knew they would attack his enemies without care for their own safety, but the men were armed, and he didn't know how to stop this.

Then another shot was fired and took the decision away from him. The stab of pain in his shoulder was shocking, as was the immediate lack of motor control. He was in the dirt before he knew he was falling.

Within seconds, the wolves had encircled him. He rolled over on his back, struggling to get to his feet, but they were so close around him that he couldn't move.

Moments later the killers caught up, but now that they had their quarry down, they didn't know what to do with him. Their first instinct was to shoot the wolves, but one of them had already screwed up by shooting at Jonah. If they started shooting wolves, there was every chance that they would kill him, as well, if they hadn't already. Bringing Jonah Gray Wolf in to their boss was worth big money, but he had to be alive.

That point was lost on one trigger-happy gunman when a big wolf snarled at him, then leaped toward him. The wolf was in midair when he shot. Jonah felt the wolf's pain, then the blood spray on his face even before the wolf hit the ground.

He began screaming at them and waving his hands.

"Don't shoot! Don't shoot! Please, don't shoot anymore."

One of the other men knocked trigger-happy's gun arm up before he could fire off another round.

"Damn it, Hicks. You heard Bourdain. Bring him back in pristine condition. What the hell do you think he's gonna say about that hole you already put in his shoulder?"

But Hicks was already panicked. His voice rose an octave as he waved the gun at the tangle of wolves.

"To hell with Bourdain! He's not the one with a damned wolf in his lap!"

The dead wolf lay at Jonah's feet as he struggled to get up. Even as he moved, he could feel the hole in his shoulder closing, the pain ebbing as his body healed itself. Some of the wolves licked at his face and sniffed at his shoulder, while others continued to growl and snarl at the men.

Hicks pointed at Jonah with his gun.

"Call 'em off or I'll start pumping bullets into the whole damn lot of you!"

Jonah tried to stand, but a big gray male moved in front of him. He had heard the panic in the man's voice. He already knew what they were capable of doing. He didn't want more lives on his conscience, but the wolves kept crowding closer until he could feel their breath and the weight of their bodies as they walked on his belly, then on his legs. In the midst of his grief, it was sobering to know they would die to protect him.

"Don't shoot," he begged, as he finally managed to get to his feet. "Please. Just don't shoot again."

Hicks's hands were shaking. "So call off those damned wolves," he ordered.

Jonah's voice was thick with tears. "You killed my father. Why did you do that?"

"He didn't want to cooperate," Hicks said. "Now, if you don't want a lot more of your friends to turn up dead, you'll do what we say."

Jonah felt helpless. "Who are you? What do you want of me?"

"You don't get to ask the questions. Just start walking."

The wolves began to circle Jonah, moving

83

around him in both directions, sniffing at his heels, trying to get between his legs to stop his motion.

He stopped, then looked down at them and held out his hands. Their noses were cold, their tongues warm, as they all touched his hands, acknowledging him as one of their own.

"Thank you, my brothers. Now go home. Go now."

Their anxiety over leaving him was palpable. They whined and snarled and yipped their displeasure.

Hicks's finger tightened perceptibly on the trigger.

"Get rid of them now, or I swear to God I'll shoot!"

Tears were running down Jonah's face. The pain in his heart was sharper than the gunshot had been. He looked up, staring long and hard at the back of the house — the house that had been his home — and thought of the man lying dead on the floor.

Because of Jonah's fear for the others in Snow Valley, his free will had been taken from him. He turned to the wolves.

"Go!" he said sharply.

Without a sound, they left as one, slipping back into the trees and disappearing.

Jonah felt the eyes of the Snow Valley community on him as he began walking toward a bright blue helicopter next to Harve Dubois's old black one.

A neighbor came out of a house with a rifle in his hand, willing to come to Jonah's aid, but when he stepped into sight, Hicks shoved his gun against Jonah's head and screamed at the man.

"Get back in the house, or I'll blow his brains all over the ground."

The man hesitated.

Jonah felt his kidnappers' fears. They'd already killed and would do it again if they had to.

"Go back," he said. "Go back."

The man hesitated.

Hicks fired one shot in the air, then jammed the gun so hard against Jonah's head that he stumbled.

Helpless against such a threat, the man lowered his rifle and stepped back inside. The rest of the population watched from their windows with their children held close. They watched as Jonah was forced into the waiting helicopter. As it lifted off, they ran out of their homes toward Adam's house. When they found the doctor dead, they realized that, by doing nothing, they'd let their only other healer be taken away.

■ ■ ■ ■

Jonah's legs twitched in his sleep as the dream carried him deeper into hell. In the living room, Hobo sensed the man's distress and whined, then got up from his bed by the fireplace and lay down in front of Jonah's door.

In the next room, Luce tossed and turned, unable to find comfort in bed. Finally she got up. Dressed in sweatpants and an old T-shirt, she padded barefoot through the living room. Curious to see if the thunderstorm had passed, she opened the front door and stepped out onto the porch.

Tonight, as sometimes happened after a storm passed, fog had settled over the mountain, muffling all but the nearest sounds. Droplets of moisture clung to her face and bare feet as she walked to the edge of the porch. The storm was over, but the threat she'd been living with for the past five months was still there. She shuddered as she wrapped her arms around herself and peered toward the barely visible trees, wondering if he was out there watching . . . waiting.

Five months of living in constant fear was getting to her. Never knowing if when she came home he would finally be inside waiting for her. Wondering if she had the strength to fight for her life. And it would be a fight to the death for one of them, that she knew for sure. She wasn't the kind of woman who gave up.

It had all started with a note on her door. She'd come home from work to find it hanging from an old nail in one of the porch posts.

I'm watching you.

She'd taken the note to town with her the next day and shown it to the police chief. He'd taken both it and her with a grain of salt, and told her that all she had was an admirer, and unless there was an actual threat to her life, he could do nothing.

Worried, but not defeated, Luce had begun to take more notice of the people around her. But as hard as she tried, she could see nothing different about the people with whom she came in contact. No one seemed more intent on her comings and goings. No one seemed to seek her out when she was alone.

And just when she thought it might be over, another note showed up, then another and another — each one more invasive than the last.

The last one had come only days ago.

Written in red ink, she'd taken it as a concrete threat.

I'm coming for you, and then I'm going to come inside you. I'll make you like it, then I'll make you sorry.

Then had come the trap. The moment she'd found Hobo in it, she'd known why it had been set. He was eliminating her only ally.

And then Jonah had turned up in her life.

Unexpected.

Unfamiliar.

She wasn't sure what his arrival was going to mean in the long run, but right now, she was heartily thankful for his presence. Another winter was almost upon her, and here she was, almost five years after her arrival in Little Top, still living on someone's charity.

Meeting Bridie Tuesday all those years ago had been an accident, but the meeting had turned out to be an answer to her prayer. It meant a lot to Luce not to be homeless. Still, living in this house and waiting tables down in town didn't mean she had added all that much to her life. Except for a stray dog who'd adopted her, she was still alone.

She thought of the stranger who was sleeping in the spare bedroom and wondered if he would still be here at daybreak.

He seemed like the kind of man who never stayed in one place for long. Then she amended the thought. He wasn't like any man she'd ever met. She had no idea what he might do.

She looked along the foggy tree line one more time, and when she saw nothing out of place, hurried back inside, locking the door as she went. The tiny night-lights that she kept plugged into the floorboard outlets glowed just enough for her to see the way as she started to the refrigerator to get herself a drink.

Then he stepped out of the shadows.

"Lucia."

Her heartbeat jerked so hard it felt like a ricochet as she grabbed hold of the back of the old sofa.

"For crying out loud," she muttered. "You scared me into next week."

Still bothered by the dream he had just had, the tone of his voice was less apologetic than it might have been.

"Sorry. I didn't know you were up until I saw you coming inside."

Her heart was thumping erratically as she flipped the light switch. Then, as soon as she had, she wished she'd left them both in the dark.

He was one of the most perfect specimens

of manhood that she'd ever seen. Except for a pair of gym shorts, he was naked. His skin was a smooth coffee-brown all over. His muscles were hard and well defined, although he leaned toward being a bit too thin. His hair was as black as a raven's wing and hung halfway down the length of his back. His long bare legs were braced slightly apart, as if readying for an attack. And his eyes — those strange, beautiful eyes — were fixed on her face. She shivered, remembering the bone-crushing climax she'd had from nothing more than touching him. She couldn't help but wonder if they ever really made love, would she die? She didn't want to be attracted to a man she didn't know — but, God help her, she was.

"Aren't you cold?" she asked.

He knew she was uneasy around him. Hell, he was uneasy around her, too. There was a sexual attraction between them that didn't belong between strangers.

"I've learned not to be," he said softly.

Luce was immediately ashamed of herself. She knew what it was like to be homeless — to live on the road. Ignoring creature discomforts was part of the lifestyle.

"Yes, well . . . don't deny yourself tonight. Remember, there's an extra quilt in your room."

"Yes, I remember," he said softly, but didn't move. "You couldn't sleep, either."

It wasn't a question. Luce's fingers curled into fists. "It stopped raining," she said.

Jonah said nothing about the change in conversation.

Hobo whined.

Luce blinked. She'd completely forgotten about him.

"You want out, boy?" she asked, as she walked back to the front door and opened it.

A cold blast of air circled her feet as the big dog licked her fingers before slipping out.

"He'll be a while, so I'll wait up," Luce said. "Go back to bed."

Jonah turned and went back into his room, but before Luce could breathe easier, he came back wearing a pair of jeans. Still barefoot, he moved to the fireplace and laid a fresh log on the burning embers. Almost instantly, the bark on the log caught fire. Tendrils of smoke curled from it and slipped upward into the chimney as he squatted down before it.

Luce watched the play of muscles across his shoulders and resisted the urge to touch him, just to see if his skin felt as smooth as it looked. Then she remembered what had happened the last time she'd touched him and took a defensive step back instead.

"Aren't you going back to bed?" she asked.

"I had a bad dream."

It wasn't what she'd expected him to say.

"I didn't know angels had bad dreams," she said.

Jonah rocked back on his heels, then braced himself with his hands on his knees, without looking away from the fire.

"I'm no angel."

"You are to me," she said softly.

He hesitated, then sat the rest of the way down in front of the fire as the blaze continued to grow.

"I know," he said softly.

Luce moved to the other side of the fireplace, then sat, too. With at least five feet between them, he surely wouldn't read anything into that except a need to get warm.

The silence lengthened between them. From time to time Luce would glance at him, but only when she sensed he wasn't looking her way. Finally her curiosity got the best of her.

"Jonah?"

He knew what was coming. It was the same question he'd had about himself for as long as he could remember. And there was nothing he could tell her. Still, he knew she was going to ask. Had to ask.

"Yes?"

"Who are you . . . really?"

For a few long moments he stayed silent. When he looked up, Luce thought she saw tears in his eyes; then he blinked, and she decided it had just been her imagination.

"I am Jonah Gray Wolf."

Luce frowned. It wasn't what she'd meant.

"What about your birth parents? Are there others in your family who can do what you do?"

Her question was startling to him. He'd never thought of his unknowns in that respect. Had there been others like him? Were they still around somewhere? And if so, how did he get so lost from them?

"I don't have any parents."

Luce laughed softly. "Everyone has parents, or at least had parents at one time."

"My stepfather, Adam Lawson, was the only parent I knew."

"But there are ways to find birth parents now. Online Web sites where all you have to do is register and —"

"I have nothing to tell."

Luce misunderstood. "All you need is the day you were born, and where. They've

93

located parents with less information than that."

"I don't know any of that."

Luce didn't know why, but she persisted.

"Your stepdad would have had some information . . . like, how you came to him, where you were born, things like that."

Jonah's eyes glittered in the firelight.

"They say when I came to Snow Valley I was less than two years old and holding on to the hair of the she-wolf who'd brought me into camp. My father told me that she licked my face and left me sitting in the dirt."

Luce felt as if she'd been kicked in the gut. She couldn't find the breath to speak, let alone form words that made any sense. She didn't know that her expression had changed from curiosity to shock, then fear.

He looked back into the fire, surprised that he actually cared about what she thought. It wasn't often that he felt defeated, but tonight was one of those times.

A scratch at the front door, then a faint bark, was enough to break the uncomfortable silence.

"That's Hobo," Luce said unnecessarily, then ran to let him in.

Hobo's feet were wet and a little muddy, and there were droplets of moisture from the fog on his fur. He whined a hello to Luce, then, with an apologetic look, left her and walked to the fire. He sniffed once at Jonah's ear, then lay down beside him, snorting softly as he settled in front of the fireplace.

Jonah felt acceptance from the animal as strongly as if it was a physical caress and wondered if he would ever feel that from a human. Most of the time, what he felt from them was a mixture of relief and fear. Relief that he'd healed their loved ones. Fear at how it had happened.

He laid a hand on Hobo's head, feeling the wet fur and the dog's beating heart at the same time as he felt Luce's discomfort. And there was another emotion. One rarely identified. One never acted upon.

The possibility of something happening between him and Luce Andahar was strong. It was up to him as to whether or not it happened, because he knew his power over her was far greater than what she could muster. But all he had to do was remember his father's broken and bloodied body to convince himself that having a relationship of any kind could be life-threatening, if not deadly.

He couldn't afford another death like that on his conscience. Not when he had the power to prevent it. When she came back to the fire, she stopped only a few feet behind him.

"Jonah . . ."

"Go to bed," he said softly.

"But —"

He turned, and the look on his face stopped her heart.

"Go. To. Bed."

The words hit her like blows. She felt the emotion behind them and knew she wasn't ready for what was between them. Might never be ready. Without saying another word, she pivoted sharply and headed for her bedroom, locking the door behind her.

Jonah heard the slight click of the lock and then closed his eyes. If she really knew how useless that lock was, she would never close her eyes again.

Jonah wasn't the only one that night who had nightmares about the past. The failure of Major Bourdain's latest hired gun was weighing heavily on his mind. He'd been trying to find a way to get past Jonah Gray Wolf's power for more than ten years, but so far he had failed miserably. Frustrated, he slept and dreamed of the second time they'd come face to face.

■ ■ ■ ■

The phone rang just as Major was finishing lunch. He heard the ringing and frowned as he swallowed the last bite of his favorite cheesecake. When the butler brought him the phone, his frown deepened. He didn't like being disturbed during meals.

"Yes?"

The terseness of his greeting was lost on his caller as he delivered the news that Major had been waiting to hear.

"We've got him!" Hicks said.

Major smiled. "Where are you?"

"Just getting into the chopper."

"How did it go?"

"We had a bit of a problem, but it's being dealt with."

Bourdain frowned. "What the hell do you mean . . . problem?"

"His father . . . he resisted."

Bourdain's frown deepened. "Resisted how?"

"He's dead."

Bourdain cursed loud and long. "That's exactly what I told you not to do! I told you, don't make waves. Damn it to hell!"

"What's done is done. We'll be there in a few hours."

97

"If you bring down the law on me, I'll deny any part of this."

"Damn it, Bourdain. You're the one who gave the orders."

"I dare you to prove it," Bourdain said. "No money has changed hands. As far as I'm concerned, you're my gardener's brother. If the cops want to know why there's a phone call between your phone and mine, all I have to do is point to him."

"Now you listen here," Hicks began.

"No. You listen," Bourdain said. "Keep your mouth shut and get here as soon as possible, and we'll talk later."

He hung up the phone in disgust, but the emotion soon passed. The ends justified the means, and he would consider the rest as collateral damage. And, looking at the positive, there was no way to connect the hired guns to him, and the chopper they'd flown into Snow Valley on had been painted with fake identification numbers. Once it landed at Bourdain's estate and unloaded the cargo, it would be repainted again, guaranteeing the impossibility of tracing it. Ultimately, the men had done what he sent them to do. He got up quickly, anxious to make sure all was ready for the arrival of his new guest.

He'd had one of the largest bedrooms at the mansion readied for company, adding a minibar and a big-screen TV, as well as all the latest in video equipment. He didn't know that Jonah had never laid hands on a video game, and would not be tempted by television programming or liquor. In Bourdain's world, it was all about who had the best and the most toys. In Jonah's, it had been about family and freedom — the very things that Bourdain had just destroyed.

The carpet in the bedroom was soft and thick, the bed and bed linens luxurious. The burgundy draperies at the twenty-foot windows were of the finest fabric. But it was the lock on the outside of the door and the bars at the windows that ruined the ambiance.

He'd thought of everything — everything except the fact that nature itself was about to revolt at what he had done.

Bourdain was on the verandah at the back of his estate, watching for the arrival of the chopper, when the phone rang again. He stepped back inside the French doors and picked up the receiver.

"Hello."

He could hear men cursing and shouting, and the sounds of heavy impact, then Hicks was screaming in his ear.

"They're everywhere! They're everywhere! Flying into the windows! Flying into the blades! There's blood and feathers all over and —"

Bourdain's heart skipped a beat. What on earth was happening? Were they about to crash?

"Hicks! Hicks! Slow down! I can't understand what —"

"Birds! All kinds of birds . . . they're everywhere! Eagles. Doves. Ducks. Hawks. Little ones. Big ones. They're following us. There's no way to get away from them!"

"What the hell do you mean . . . birds are everywhere?"

"It's this damned Indian's fault. First there were the wolves . . . now it's birds! He won't call 'em off. I told him if he didn't I was going to put a bullet —"

"Hicks! Hicks!"

"What?"

The timbre of Bourdain's voice turned lethal. "You harm that man and I'll kill you myself. Do you hear me?"

Hicks laughed, and it sounded crazy.

"Kill me? Hell! You won't get the chance. This son of a bitch you wanted so bad is going to do it for you."

"Just get him here alive!" Bourdain shouted.

"We're all trying to stay alive!" Hicks shouted back; then he laughed again, and the sound cut through Bourdain's senses like a knife. "Consider this your only warning. You better batten down the hatches at your fancy mansion, because if we manage to get there in one piece, your troubles won't be over. They'll just be beginning."

The dial tone was as startling to Bourdain as what Hicks had said. No one hung up on him. Ever. Yet Hicks had not only done so, he'd seemed to be threatening him, as well.

Bourdain slammed the receiver back onto the cradle. What the hell did the man mean, first wolves, now birds? He stomped outside, scouring the skies for signs of their arrival.

Without waking up, Bourdain rolled over to his other side, then settled back into the dream, picking up several hours after where he'd left off.

Bourdain was in the library reading when he realized it was getting dark. A glance at his watch told him it was too early for sundown. The only other thing it could be was a storm approaching. Frowning, he laid down his book and looked out, expecting to see gathering clouds. But it wasn't clouds. The sky was full of birds.

Suddenly he remembered what Hicks had said about the birds attacking the chopper. His heart skipped a beat. What in hell was going on?

He stepped outside, and the moment he did,

he was assailed by a cacophony of sound. It sounded as if thousands upon thousands of birds were calling to each other from the trees and shrubs surrounding his estate, from the forest beyond, along with those circling in the sky above. The hair rose on the back of his neck as he bolted back inside the house and slammed the door.

But safety was a long way away. He'd loved this room for its massive wall of windows, but now the windows had become its flaw, with their view of the winged horror outside. At that moment the housekeeper came running into the library with a look of terror on her face.

"Mr. Bourdain! There are birds everywhere! It's a sign — an omen from God! Something bad is going to happen, I just know it!"

"Get back to the kitchen and don't come out until I say so!" he shouted.

She didn't have to be told twice. She ran from the room with her hands over her head.

Moments later Bourdain heard the familiar sound of an approaching chopper and ran to the French doors. He had a brief glimpse of the chopper before it was swallowed up by another cloud of birds.

At the same time, his phone began to ring. It was bound to be Hicks. He already knew he didn't want to hear what the man had to say.

"Hicks?"

The man's voice was shaking and hoarse, as if he'd been screaming for hours. "God-damn. . . . Goddamn . . . we're coming in the back way. Unlock the fuckin' doors!"

Bourdain dropped the phone and ran toward the back of the house. By the time he got there, there were three men coming toward the house at a dead run, dragging another between them, while birds dived at them from all directions, pecking at their faces, ripping their clothes with their claws, tearing out chunks of their hair. He could hear them screaming from where he stood.

When they were fifty feet from the door, a massive California condor came out of no-where in a full dive, hit the man next to Hicks with its massive talons and took off his head. A geyser of blood sprayed up into the air a second before the man dropped to the ground. His body was still kicking, but he was undeni-ably dead.

"Sweet Mother of God," Bourdain whispered, and began backing up.

"Open the door! Open the door!" Hicks screamed.

Bourdain stood there long enough to see a huge bird diving toward the windows, then bolted. The sound of shattering glass followed his retreat. Seconds later, he heard the door bang against the wall, then screams and curses followed him as they all ran toward the inner rooms of the mansion.

Windows shattered as they ran past, showering them with broken glass and filling their ears with the infernal shrieks and calls of nature in a rampage.

Bourdain hit the floor just before his face was peppered with glass, then covered his head with his hands.

The other men were in the room with him now, screaming at him, telling him that he had to let the Indian go or they were all going to die.

Birds were diving at him now in wild abandon, flogging him with their wings, nailing him with their talons and beaks. Like the others, he began screaming and cursing. He rolled over, then grabbed a cushion from the sofa and put it over his head.

"Turn him loose! Turn him loose!" he screamed.

"He's already loose. Make him leave!" Hicks screamed back.

Bourdain turned, and then everything seemed to happen in slow motion as he found himself staring into the eyes of the man who'd saved his life.

The birds were everywhere, flying so close together that it seemed as if all the air had gone from the room.

"Get out! Get out!" Bourdain shouted, then dropped the cushion and covered his face as birds clawed at his eyes. "Make them stop! Oh God . . . make them stop!"

The Indian didn't move, didn't speak, and then, to Bourdain's horror, seemed to levitate right off the floor.

The man's long black hair suddenly billowed off his shoulders and flew out behind him as if he'd walked into a strong wind. He lifted his arms over his head and then turned in a circle, speaking words that the other men couldn't hear. Within seconds, the room was empty. Outside, the sky was clear, and the silence that fell over them was now more frightening than the noise that had come before.

The Indian looked at Bourdain.

"You murdered my father."

Bourdain shuddered. "I didn't . . . it wasn't supposed —" He took a deep breath and then started over. "I'm worth millions. I can pay —"

He watched an expression of disbelief spread over the younger man's face.

"You think your money will make my father's death okay?"

"No. That wasn't supposed to happen. I didn't mean for —"

Jonah Gray Wolf pointed a finger in Bourdain's face. "You caused this," he said, then started retracing his steps toward the exit.

"Wait! You can't just —"

The Indian turned, then pointed a finger straight at Bourdain again. The fury in his eyes made Bourdain take a step back, but it wasn't far enough. A visible spike of electricity shot out from the Indian's finger and hit Bourdain in the chest, knocking him off his feet.

Bourdain was still trying to catch his breath when the Indian disappeared. He motioned to Hicks and the other two men, but they ignored his demands and ran in the other direction. They wanted out, and there was no way they wanted that Indian to think they were coming after him as they escaped.

Bourdain cursed helplessly, then lay back on the floor and stared up at the chaos left behind.

His hands were shaking as he touched his chest; then he pushed up his shirt and looked. There was a burn right above his heart. He didn't want to think about how easy it would have been for a hole to burn all the way through him.

"God," he muttered, then crawled under a desk, laid his head on his knees and closed his eyes.

Bourdain gasped and sat up in bed, shaking and covered in sweat. Cursing, he crawled out of bed and staggered to the bathroom.

The digital readout on his clock registered 3:00 a.m.

He wanted this night to be over.

FIVE

The chill cut through Luce's clothing as she opened the door to let Hobo out for his morning run. She noticed that the fog she'd seen last night was already dissipating, and as soon as he cleared the porch, she quickly closed the door.

The fire was burning brightly, but she hadn't been the one to add the wood. She glanced toward Jonah's door. It was slightly ajar, as if he'd left in a hurry without pulling it shut. So it seemed that Jonah had added wood to the fire before taking his leave. She sighed, surprised by the disappointment she felt at knowing he was gone. Once more she was alone and still in fear of the unknown stalker who threatened her life.

Her steps were slow as she moved to the kitchen side of the room and filled the old coffee pot with water, then began measuring coffee into the strainer.

"Got enough for me?"

Luce jumped, accidentally scattering coffee grains on the counter, and she quickly swept them into the sink. She was shocked by the surge of joy that filled her as Jonah came out of his room.

"You're still here!"

Misunderstanding, Jonah frowned. "Is that not okay?"

Luce started to touch him, then remembered what had happened before and clutched her hands together instead.

"Oh . . . no . . . that's great. I'm mean, it's fine. I just thought —" She sighed, then made herself look away from his long legs and broad shoulders. He didn't need to know what she was thinking. For that matter, she didn't need to be thinking it. "I'm going to start over now."

Jonah grinned, unaware that the smile changed his face from interesting to irresistible.

"Then so will I. So . . . Lucia, did you make enough coffee to spare a cup for me?"

Luce's smile slipped. This was the second time he'd called her that. No one had called her Lucia since her mother's death, but the way it came out of his mouth seemed familiar, as if she'd known him for years. She took a deep breath, trying to get past this attraction and back to the daily business of breakfast.

"Yes, there's plenty."

Jonah heard nervousness in her voice, and he'd seen the glances she gave him when she thought he wasn't looking. But discussing their attraction to each other was a bridge he couldn't afford to cross.

"What can I do to help?"

"Nothing," Luce said, as she began breaking eggs into a skillet. "I've got it covered."

"Did you sleep well . . . I mean, after you went back to bed?" Jonah asked.

Luce nodded as she chanced another glance. "How about you?"

He thought about the nightmare. It had been hell, but sleeping indoors during a thunderstorm had been an unexpected luxury.

"Yes. A warm room and a soft bed are luxuries for me. Thank you very much."

Luce shrugged. "After what you did for Hobo, it was the least I could do."

They looked at each other, waiting for the next uncomfortable topic of conversation to be introduced. When neither one of them offered a subject, Luce went back to cooking, and Jonah chose to watch.

Her movements were sure and measured, just like the woman herself. He couldn't imagine how difficult it would be to be female and alone in the world, and he still wondered who was threatening her.

"Lucia . . . ?"

Luce set her jaw and gripped the spatula a little tighter. *The way he says my name . . .* She inhaled softly, then pasted a smile on her face.

"Yes?"

"I've been thinking about that trap."

Luce frowned. "What about it?"

"Do you have any idea who set it?"

She glanced at him, then looked away. She wanted to tell him what had been happening but didn't know how to start.

Suddenly, he knew this wasn't the first incident.

"Who is doing it?" he asked.

"Doing what?"

"Threatening you."

All the color washed away from her face. "How on earth do you do that?" she muttered.

Jonah frowned. "It doesn't matter. What matters is that someone has made you afraid."

"I'm not afraid of anyone. Now give me five more minutes and breakfast will be ready."

Jonah felt the skip in her heartbeat. She hadn't told him anything, but she had ended the conversation, so he didn't push it. What bothered him was why she felt the need to keep what she knew to herself.

He watched her until he ached from wanting her, then turned away. He gave the burning logs in the fireplace a couple of sharp pokes, added a new log, then stepped back and dusted off his hands.

It was strange how awkward this felt — being in someone's home, performing ordinary chores. He'd been on the road for so long that he'd forgotten what it felt like to belong anywhere. With nothing left to do to help, he turned and went outside.

Last night's thunderstorm and ensuing fog had left the air still and chilly. He stepped off the porch and walked a ways out into the yard, testing the ground. It was soft, but not muddy. He shoved his hands in his jeans' pockets, toed a loose rock up from the ground, then turned toward the break in the trees to his left.

The last remnants of morning fog swirled restlessly just above the ground, pushed about by a rising breeze. As he stood, a magnificent buck walked into the clearing, pausing long enough to give Jonah a look.

"Good morning to you, too," he said softly.

Clouds of condensation from the buck's

warm breath formed and held in tiny orbits around his nose. He wore the sixteen-point rack on his head like a crown, with droplets of dew clinging to the tips like so many diamonds. A fitting accoutrement to the king that he was.

Jonah heard the animal's heartbeat, felt the blood pulsing through its veins, and knew the strength of its powerful body.

"Walk safely, brother," he said.

With one giant leap, the buck disappeared. Moments later, Hobo came trotting out of the trees from the other direction.

"Hey, boy," Jonah said, as the big dog's tail began wagging. "You missed that squirrel, didn't you? That's okay. Maybe next time."

Hobo was panting softly as he stopped at Jonah's feet, then licked Jonah's fingers in a gentle greeting. The rough surface of the dog's tongue was raspy and wet against his fingertips as Jonah leaned down and tickled Hobo under the chin.

"You're a good boy," Jonah said.

Hobo whined, then looked up past Jonah's face to a red-tailed hawk that was coming toward them and flying below treetop level. When it lit on Jonah's shoulder, Hobo woofed a greeting.

Jonah felt the impact but had no fear, as

he turned and held out his hand.

"Good morning to you, too," he said.

The hawk fluttered, moving from Jonah's shoulder to light on his outstretched arm. Then the hawk's talons curled into Jonah's arm as it screeched.

The sound cut through Jonah's soul like a knife. It was a warning, and all the warning he was going to get. By the time the hawk lifted off his arm to fly away, Jonah was already on his way to the house. He hit the door running, grabbed his coat from the bedroom and was on his way back out when Luce stopped him.

"Hey! What's the hurry?"

"An old woman has fallen. She needs help."

Luce turned off the burner and shoved the skillet full of eggs to the back of the stove. Her mind was racing, wondering who was hurt and how he'd found out.

"I didn't hear anyone drive up. Who told you?" she asked, as she grabbed her coat.

"It doesn't matter," Jonah said.

Luce frowned. "Wait! If someone drove up here to tell me, then why didn't they help her instead of wasting time coming here? What aren't you saying?"

He sighed. There was no reason for not telling her the truth. She'd already seen what he could do.

"It was a red-tailed hawk who told me. If you're coming with me, you'll have to hurry. The hawk said she's dying."

Luce knew her lips had parted, but for the life of her she couldn't think of a damn thing to say. This man was scary. Maybe scary crazy. Maybe not. But to her credit, she didn't argue.

"I'm coming with you," she said, buttoning up her coat as they hurried out the door.

But when Jonah started up the mountain instead of going down toward Little Top, she panicked. The only person who lived farther up the mountain than she did was Bridie Tuesday, her landlord.

"Wait? Aren't you going the wrong way?"

Jonah glanced back at her. "No. I'm going to have to run now."

Luce's heart sank. It *was* Bridie.

"Go. Go. I'll catch up when I can."

Luce struggled to keep up, but the man's legs were far longer than hers, and the road was slippery from last night's rain. With Hobo at his heels, Jonah quickly disappeared. Luce didn't understand what was happening, but she'd witnessed Jonah's affinity with animals and the magic in his hands. All she could do was pray that, if what he said was true, they wouldn't be too late.

Bridie Tuesday had gotten up with a headache. At the age of eighty, she knew her own body better than any doctor, and she figured all she needed was her breakfast and her usual two cups of black coffee. But the meal hadn't set things to rights like she'd expected. Still, there were chickens to feed and a cow to milk, so her morning malaise would just have to wait.

Knowing that the morning would be not only cold but damp, she bundled up warmly, then picked up the milk bucket as she walked out the back door.

As she'd expected, the fog and the chill hit her squarely in the face, but they had no impact on her intent. Molly needed milking. The chickens needed feeding. Life went on, whether she felt like being a part of it or not.

Within the hour, the old cow had been fed, milked and turned out into the pasture. The chickens had been let out of the pen and were pecking at the feed she'd scattered on the ground. Bridie was at the nests, gathering eggs and thinking about maybe making herself a custard pie today with some of the milk and eggs.

Thinking of custard pies always made her think of her Franklin. Franklin used to say that he only liked two kinds of pies — hot pies and cold pies. Afterward, he would laugh out loud, as if he'd said something original. Bridie always laughed with him, although she'd heard the joke countless times before.

She had loved him something fierce and had wanted to die with him when he'd passed over, only she hadn't been able to figure out how. Doing herself in was against her way of thinking, so she'd wasted a good month or two of her grief being pissed off at Franklin for leaving her behind. Once she'd gotten past the disassociation with life that often comes with powerful grief, she decided to make the best of what she had left. So here she was, ten years later, tending cows and chickens, and still making custard pies to be eaten alone.

She closed the door to the chicken house as she left, then gingerly made her way across the muddy yard to the house. By the time she got there, she was unusually breathless, and her headache was getting worse.

She broke into a sweat as she entered the kitchen, and just as she set down the basket of eggs, she was suddenly sick to her stomach.

"I've just gone and let the house get too hot," she muttered, and turned and walked back out onto the porch, thinking all she needed was some cool air.

The last thing she remembered was seeing Franklin, smiling at her from across the fence.

Almost ten minutes had passed since the hawk had brought Jonah the message. He was running as fast as he could, with Hobo matching him stride for stride, but he was concerned that he would be too late. By the time he came upon the house at the end of the road, he was mud-splattered and winded. This had to be the place, but without sensing life, he couldn't be sure. He looked up. The red-tailed hawk was circling overhead. It must be right. A few yards farther up the narrow driveway, he saw the old woman crumpled on the ground at the foot of the front steps.

He took a deep breath, and with the oxygen came a sense of her life force. It was as weak and faint as the unsteady beat of her heart, but it was still there. He hadn't been too late, after all. He sprinted the rest of the way, then dropped to his knees at her side.

Hobo whined, then licked the old woman's cheek as Jonah ran his hands over her body, searching for the source of weakness and pain.

"Get back," Jonah said sharply, and the dog immediately dropped to his belly, motionless and waiting.

Jonah knew almost instantly that there were no broken bones, but he could hear the gush of blood pouring through a tear in her brain. Her pulse was thready and her heartbeat almost nonexistent. She was so tiny and so old, and he sensed she would gladly pass over, but it wasn't in him to let her die. He needed to get her inside the house and off the cold, wet ground, but her life force was too weak to delay any longer.

Instead, he rolled her over, laying her flat on her back, then took a deep breath. Within seconds, the air around them charged. The hair on Hobo's body stood on end. The dog whined nervously, but couldn't have moved if he'd tried.

Jonah felt the power in him growing. He had never understood it, but he knew how to use it. The only way he could have described it was that, in his mind, he focused on the part of her that had come undone and then put it back the way it was supposed to be. He knew there was blood in her brain. Something had broken in there. Doctors called it an aneurysm. He called it a challenge. With a soft, whispered prayer, he laid his hands on Bridie Tuesday's muddy forehead and closed his eyes.

By the time Luce got to Bridie's house, she was out of breath and grimacing from a serious pain in her side. But when she saw the old woman on the ground and Jonah kneeling at her side, her fear increased.

Moments later, she dropped beside them. Her heart was hammering against her eardrums as she fell to her knees, but this time she knew not to touch. And this time, she wasn't so much shocked by the aura surrounding Jonah and Bridie as she was amazed.

It glowed a white so bright it hurt her eyes, and like before, the pull of the power within the light was so compelling that all she wanted to do was lie down within it. With no way of helping, she lowered her head and began to pray. It seemed a fitting accompaniment to what she was witnessing.

Franklin blew Bridie a kiss and disappeared.

Bridie cried out, "Wait, Franklin, wait!" Then she opened her eyes, somewhat surprised to find herself lying on the ground.

She thought it was silly of her to have chosen to rest outside. She blinked a couple of times to clear her vision, only to realize there was a man hovering over her.

"Franklin?"

Jonah brushed at the mud on her forehead, then shook his head. He'd seen what she'd seen just before she woke up. He'd felt the love that she had shared with the man and knew a sense of regret. His father's murder was all the proof he needed that that kind of love was something he would never be able to have and keep his woman safe.

"I'm not Franklin," he said softly. "Franklin is gone."

Before she could ask him what business he had on her place, he picked her up. She found herself staring into his eyes, then forgot what she'd been going to say. When he carried her into the house, she didn't argue. It seemed like the sensible thing to do. Then she saw Luce following them in and felt easier seeing a familiar face.

"Well, hello, little girl. I didn't know I was going to have company."

Luce was too close to tears to manage more than a smile. When Jonah paused, Luce pointed down the hall.

"Her bedroom is the first door on the left. I'll help her clean up."

Bridie's clothes were wet and muddy, as were her hands. She could only imagine what the rest of her looked like, and she swiped shakily at her face, muttering to herself when her fingers came away muddy, too.

"Well, for goodness sake. What have I gone and done to myself?"

"You fell off the porch," Jonah said, as Luce led the way to Bridie's bedroom. "I'm going to sit you down on the side of your bed. Lucia will help you get cleaned up, okay?"

Bridie stared at the stranger long and hard as he put her down. When Jonah would have backed away, she suddenly grabbed his wrist.

Jonah felt the questions surging through her mind, read her confusion as well as her curiosity, and smiled.

"Yes, ma'am, I am a strange one at that," he said.

Bridie's eyes widened. "I didn't say that." Her grip tightened. "I was thinking it, but I hadn't said it."

Jonah knelt so that he wasn't towering over her. "You're shivering. You need to get out of those wet clothes."

Still, she wouldn't turn him loose. "What am I thinking now?" she asked.

Jonah hesitated; then his expression grew shuttered.

"Knowing where I come from won't tell you anything about who I am."

Bridie's eyes narrowed as her gaze slid to Luce. "What happened to me, girl? And don't lie. I don't like being babied."

Luce didn't know what to say. "You'll have to ask Jonah."

Bridie's focus shifted from Luce to the tall, dark-haired man beside her.

"Well? I'm waiting, mister."

Jonah touched her head.

"Do you remember having a pain in your head?"

Bridie ran her fingers along her forehead. She'd completely forgotten that.

"I woke up with a headache this morning. Did my chores, then I think . . . I believe I . . . uh, went outside and . . ." She frowned. "I can't remember after that."

"The red-tailed hawk that flies over your barn saw you fall. He came and told me you needed help. So I came . . . and I fixed you."

No one spoke.

No one moved.

Bridie sat, watching the man's steady gaze. Franklin had always said that you could tell a lot about a man by the look in his eyes. This man didn't flinch or look away.

"You fixed me?"

He nodded.

"How?"

He held out his hands.

Bridie stared at them, then back up at him. "Exactly what about me was broke?"

"Does it matter?" Jonah asked.

"It does to me, mister."

"Something burst inside your head. You were dying."

Bridie started to shake. She'd lived all the way to eighty years old and was now being asked to believe something she'd only heard about in old wives' tales.

"You're claiming you laid hands on me and I was healed?"

Luce sighed. "It's true, Bridie. I saw him do it."

"I just fainted, that's all," Bridie said.

Jonah shrugged, then stood up and stepped back.

"It doesn't matter what you believe. You are well now." He glanced at Luce. "I'll wait in the other room while you help her change."

He walked out before anyone could argue.

Bridie glared as Luce began undoing her clothes.

"I can do that myself," she said.

"Yes, ma'am," Luce said.

Bridie undressed, then went into the

bathroom and washed the mud from her face and hands.

"My hair's a mess," she muttered, as she swiped at the muddy streaks with a wet washcloth.

Luce followed her into the bathroom. "Let me help," she said, then took the washcloth and began cleaning the bits of mud and grass from the side of Bridie's head.

Bridie sat, letting Luce work, while her mind ran wild.

"Where did you come by this man?" she asked.

"I met him down in town."

An expression of disgust spread across Bridie's face. "And you just brought him up to your home for a little fun? I thought better of you, girl."

Anger slid through Luce hard and fast.

"And I thought you knew me better than that," she snapped, and handed Bridie the washcloth. "You're clean. Do the rest yourself."

Bridie sighed. She suspected she needed to apologize as Luce strode toward the door.

"Wait now. Talk to me, Luce."

Luce paused, then turned around.

"I can't say that I actually saw the red-tailed hawk come tell him anything, because I was in the house making breakfast. But I know he went outside for a bit, and when he came back, he was running. He went straight up the road to your house like he'd lived here all his life. I didn't show him the way. When I got to your house, he was beside you, and you were on the ground."

"I remember having a real bad headache," Bridie said, then added, more to herself than to Luce, "I remember seeing Franklin, too."

Luce snorted. "Now you're asking me to believe that you saw a man who's been dead for ten years, but you aren't willing to believe what you already know in your heart to be true?"

Bridie ducked her head and began putting on clean clothes. The silence lengthened between them. Finally Bridie tried another tack.

"So, you brought him home with you last night?"

"Not exactly," Luce said. "Someone set a trap down by the creek near your old house. Yesterday afternoon, Hobo got his leg caught in it, and I couldn't get it off. I ran down to the station to get help. Jonah was there. He came back with me."

Then Luce shivered and suddenly sat down in a chair beside the door. "Oh, Bridie . . . I've never seen anything like it.

Hobo's foot was almost separated from his leg. Blood was everywhere. Jonah tore up his own hands getting the trap off, and I thought —" A sob tore up her throat. "I thought Hobo was going to die and the stranger had wounded himself something awful just helping me."

Bridie frowned. "I saw his hands. There wasn't anything wrong with them."

"Exactly," Luce said. "One minute they were shredded and bloody, and then they weren't. And when he put his hands on Hobo, a light enveloped them that was so bright I couldn't see. When it was over, Hobo was sound and walking around as if nothing had happened. I asked him if he was an angel. I'm still leaning toward that theory, because if he's not, then I have to believe what I've seen, and I find that almost impossible."

Bridie's eyes widened. "If what you've said is true, then I reckon you've gone and found yourself a healer."

"A what?"

"A healer. My granny used to talk about such people, but I always thought she was just telling stories."

"Bridie . . ."

"What, honey?"

"How do they get that way?"

"Who, the healers?"

Luce nodded.

"Well, I'm not sure, but Granny said that they were people who'd been touched by God."

"So . . . then, are you saying he's like . . . like a real angel, after all?"

Bridie shrugged. "Can't say I'd go that far . . . but I reckon he's as close to one as you'll ever find on God's earth."

Luce sighed. "I saw a bird fly down and land on his shoulder as if he was a big tree. He talked to it like I'm talking to you."

"Animals know more about people than people do. So . . . I don't exactly know who you've gone and brought home with you, girl . . . but if all you say is true, I'm guessing he won't do you any harm. Now come on into the living room and introduce me proper to your angel. I've got a little apologizing to do."

"He's looking for work," Luce said.

Bridie smirked. "Are you trying to make me feel guilty now?"

Luce shrugged. "Just telling you what he said."

Bride sighed. "Well, then, let's just see what happens."

Six

Jonah was on his knees by Bridie's dining table when they walked into the room. He looked up, a little startled at being caught. Without saying anything, he opened his hand. Moments later, a tiny wood mouse scampered off his palm and ran back beneath the sideboard.

"Oh, Lordy . . . there's that mouse! I've been trying to catch it for a solid week. Why on earth did you let it go?" Bridie shrieked.

Jonah stood, looking a little shamefaced, but willing to stand his ground.

"He's sorry you're bothered, but he only came to the house after the snake moved in beneath the hay in the barn where he'd been living."

Bridie's mouth dropped open. She sputtered through a couple of breaths, then plopped down on one of the dining-room chairs.

"Well, I never," she muttered, then looked

up at Jonah. "There's a snake under the hay?"

Jonah shrugged. "It's what he said."

Bridie glared at Jonah, then down toward her sideboard, picturing the little gray varmint hiding below.

"So . . . what'll it take to get him out?"

Jonah smiled, thinking how funny it was that this old woman was willing to believe he could bargain with a mouse, but not that he was able to heal her.

"I think maybe if you promised to sprinkle some extra chicken feed through the cracks in the floor of the chicken house, Brother Mouse would consider making a move."

Bridie snorted. "Brother Mouse, indeed. Well, then, if that's what it takes, tell him it's a deal. But . . . the first time I see a mouse back in this house, the deal is off."

Jonah walked past the dining room to the front door.

"Hey! I thought you were going to tell . . . Mr. Mouse . . . or Brother Mouse or whatever that rodent's name is, to move to the chicken house."

"He heard you," Jonah said softly, and opened the door.

To Luce's delight and Bridie's disbelief, the tiny gray mouse poked its head out from under the sideboard. It paused a moment,

130

its whiskers twitching as it seemed to judge the distance from the sideboard to the open door.

"Oh, Lordy!" Bridie shrieked, unable to maintain her composure.

At the shriek, the little mouse made a break for the door, scampering across the floor so fast that they could hear his nails scratching against the old wooden floor.

As the mouse neared the door, Jonah squatted briefly and held out his hand. The mouse ran right into Jonah's palm.

Jonah knew the courage it took for the mouse to come out from hiding. For such a small animal, it had a very brave heart. The least he could do was give the little fellow a ride to the chicken house.

"I'll be back in a few minutes," he said, and walked out with the mouse in his hand.

Bridie glanced up at Luce. "Where do you reckon he's going with that varmint?"

Luce walked to the door, then out on the porch, watching this strange man as he walked toward Bridie's chicken house.

"It appears that he's taking the mouse to the chicken house himself."

"And this is the man you want me to hire?" Bridie muttered.

Luce turned to her, then smiled and shrugged. "At least you know you'll have the best cared for critters on the mountain." A twinkle came and went in Bridie's eyes, but Luce knew her old friend was sold.

"We'll see," Bridie said, waiting for Jonah to come back.

A few minutes later, Jonah returned. He got as far as the front door and stopped. "Am I still welcome here?"

"Luce said you're looking for work," Bridie said.

Jonah glanced at Luce, saw the flush on her cheeks, then shifted his focus back to Bridie.

"Yes, ma'am. I need a job. It's getting too late in the year to stay on the road."

Bridie frowned. "Don't you have any family?"

"No."

"Not anywhere?"

"No."

"Are you on the run from the law?"

"No, ma'am."

"Are you lying to me?"

"I don't lie."

Bridie crossed her arms over her chest. "Can you milk a cow?"

Jonah resisted the urge to grin. "Yes."

"I can't pay you much, but you can board here for the winter if you don't get in my way."

"There's also the extra room where I'm staying," Luce said, and then sighed. Why didn't she just come right out and ask him to stay? She didn't want to be alone.

Jonah stared from one woman to the other. Obviously the decision was his to make. He knew that it would be easier to stay with Bridie, since the job would be here.

But then there was Luce. She was afraid. He didn't know why, but he knew she felt hunted, and he could certainly empathize with that.

"I'll take the job and gladly," Jonah told Bridie. "But if you don't mind, I think I'll stay with Lucia."

Bridie nodded. It wasn't a surprise. If she'd been Jonah, she would have chosen the younger woman, too.

"Fine with me. I reckon I can manage a hundred dollars a week. If that's not enough, you'll have to look elsewhere."

"It's fine," Jonah said.

Bridie stifled a grin. She would have paid fifty dollars more if he'd negotiated.

"Molly needs to be milked no later than eight in the morning. I'll see you tomorrow."

"Yes, ma'am," he said.

"Do you have a driver's license?" she asked.

Jonah nodded.

"Franklin's old pickup truck is in the shed. If you'll take Luce to work every morning before you come up here, I'll let you use it."

"I can get myself to work just fine," Luce said.

Bridie rolled her eyes. "If you'd had a driver's license, I would already have given it to you to use, and you know it."

Luce stood her ground, but there was no way to argue with the truth. She'd never learned to drive because she'd run away from home before she'd had a chance to get her license.

Jonah stood quietly, watching the two women fuss and feeling the love that was between them. It felt good, even though it was a vicarious experience. His father had loved him like this once. He shoved a shaky hand through his hair, then looked away, gazing out into the yard and the forest beyond.

The sky was gray. The clouds were few and stringy as the wind pushed them along. If he squinted his eyes as he looked into the tree-lined hills and the mountains around them, he could almost believe he was back in Alaska. But if he had been, they would already be in the season of darkness, and

134

everything would be covered in snow.

"Jonah?"

When he turned around, his face was expressionless.

"Yes?"

Something was wrong, but right now, Luce didn't have time to figure it out.

"I need to get back to the cabin and get dressed for work. Here are the keys to Bridie's truck."

She laid the keys in his hand, then turned around and hugged the old woman.

"You are a dear, and I'm very, very glad you're all right now."

Bridie returned the hug with a smile. "All things considered, I guess I'm up to giving this old world another try." She gave Jonah a stern look. "Since you supposedly saved my life this morning, don't mess up the good deed by being late to work tomorrow morning."

"I'll be back later," he said.

"Oh . . . there's no need. You can start fresh tomorrow."

But Jonah wouldn't budge. "There are some things that need to be done before it snows tonight."

Bridie snorted beneath her breath. "It's not gonna snow tonight."

"It will snow," Jonah said.

Bridie frowned. "What makes you think it's gonna snow?"

"I just know," Jonah said, ignoring the looks of disbelief both women were giving him. "You need chicken feed, and the sack of sweet feed that you give your cow when you milk her is almost empty."

"Well, I'll say," Bridie sputtered. "You sure saw a lot for the short time you've been here."

"I didn't see it. The owl who roosts in your barn —"

"Stop right there!" Bridie said. "I don't want to know another blasted thing about how you get your information. Someone has to have some measure of sanity around here, and it looks like it's gonna be left up to me. When you take Luce to work, stop in at Middleton's Feed Store. Tell them you're working for me and to load up my regular order in the truck. They'll mail me the bill at the end of the month."

"Yes, ma'am."

"One more thing, Jonah."

"Yes, ma'am?"

"What's your full name?"

Jonah hesitated. The less that was known about him, the harder it was for Bourdain to find him. Still, it wasn't in him to lie.

"My name is Jonah Gray Wolf."

Bridie held out her hand.

"My Franklin always said that when you make a deal with a man, you should shake on it."

Jonah extended his hand, and when they shook on it, Bridie nodded in satisfaction.

"I look forward to knowing you," she said.

Jonah blinked; then a slow smile spread across his face.

"And I, you," he said softly. "I'll be back in a couple of hours."

"I'm making custard pie today."

"I only like two kinds of pie," Jonah said.

Bridie's heart skipped a beat. She was almost afraid to ask.

"What kinds of pie might that be?" she said.

"Hot pies and cold pies," Jonah said. Then, just before he turned and walked away, he winked at her.

Bridie was still shaking as her unexpected visitors took their leave. Her heart was hammering so hard against her eardrums that she thought it would burst. This was the most remarkable morning she'd ever had, and the day was just getting started.

She lifted her hands and smoothed down the hair on her head, then looked up at the sky.

"Okay, Franklin . . . if that was your way

of telling me I did the right thing, you could have warned me. Hearing your words come out of his mouth was a low blow."

She stood on the porch, watching until the taillights of Franklin's old truck had disappeared, and then she went inside. There were pie crusts to be made.

Jonah was just finishing the fried egg sandwich Luce had made for him when they passed the city-limit sign for Little Top. Bridie's old truck pulled a little to the left, and Jonah guessed the tires needed to be rotated, but other than that, it ran smoothly.

"The sandwich was good," he said, as he gave Luce a quick glance. "Thank you."

Luce nodded. "No sense wasting good food," she said, referring to the skillet of eggs she'd set aside when they'd gone up to Bridie's house.

Jonah ventured another look. Luce was fussing with her clothes as he pulled up to the curb in front of Harold's Eats.

Jonah checked the time. It was only a little after seven-thirty in the morning, but it felt like they'd been up for hours.

"What time do you get off work?" he asked.

"The diner only serves breakfast and lunch. I usually get off around three."

"I'll be back," he said.

Luce nodded and started to get out of the truck, then stopped and made herself look at him.

"Thank you."

"For what?" Jonah asked.

Luce sighed. "For staying with me instead of Bridie."

"Why do you think I did that?" he asked.

She hesitated to answer; then her shoulders slumped. "You know . . . don't you?" she said.

"I know you're afraid of something . . . or someone."

"Yes."

"Why won't you talk about it?"

She shrugged. "I don't know who's doing it."

"Besides the trap, what else has he done?"

"Notes . . . lots of notes with ugly and threatening messages."

"Did you tell the police?"

She rolled her eyes. "For all the good it did. Since I haven't been attacked, there's nothing they can do."

"And you don't have any suspicions at all?"

Luce shook her head. "None."

"You realize that my presence could

escalate what's happening, rather than deter it?"

"Maybe that will be for the good. I just want it to be over."

"Since we're being honest with each other, there's something you need to know about me, too," Jonah said.

Luce rolled her eyes. "Besides being an angel who converses with animals, what else could there possibly be?"

"There's a million-dollar bounty on me."

Luce gasped. "By the law?"

"No. Just a man . . . a man who's been after me for years."

"A million dollars! Why?"

"I saved his life once. Now I guess he wants to live forever and thinks I can make that happen."

"That's some thanks for your trouble," Luce said.

"It's only fair that you know, and if it makes you uncomfortable, I can still go stay with Bridie."

Luce felt the blood rush from her face. "No. Stay with me . . . please," she said, hating the panic in her voice.

There was nothing in life he would rather do than stay with her — forever. But for Jonah, wanting and having were two different things.

"It's your call," he said.

The tension in Luce's body eased. That was all she needed to hear.

"Then it's settled. I'll see you this afternoon."

Jonah was watching her expression closely, memorizing everything there was to know, knowing there would come a day when memories would be all he had left of her.

"Yes. Have a good day, Lucia."

There was a smile on her face as she got out of the truck. For the first time in a long time, she felt good — and even better, she felt safe.

He'd been standing at the counter in the drugstore, waiting for a prescription to be filled, when he'd turned around and seen Bridie Tuesday's old truck pull up to the diner. When he saw Luce Andahar get out and go inside, a knot formed in his gut. He'd wanted her the day she'd shown up in town, and he'd wanted her every day since. It was a sin to want a woman like that, and since he was already married, it was an even bigger sin.

But he couldn't get her out of his mind. He'd prayed on his knees until they'd ached to be delivered from the insanity of such lust. He'd closed his eyes when he made love to his wife and pretended she was Luce. He bought things for his wife with Luce in mind. The unholy desire had eaten at him for the past five years until his thoughts about Luce were no longer rational. He'd though that when he married his wife, this lust for other women would end. And for a while, it had. Then Luce came to town, and everything he'd tried so hard to forget had returned. He'd fought the desire until he could fight no more.

One night a few months ago, he'd had a dream. When he woke, he was convinced it had been a sign from God. In the dream, he'd finally had her. He'd used her over and over until the very sight of her naked body had been abhorrent to him. And in the dream, he'd been delivered from the lust and cleansed by God Himself for the deed, just like so many times before.

By the time he woke up, the plan was already in his head. He would have Lucia Andahar — and then, of course, he would have to kill her. He couldn't possibly leave her behind to tell what he'd done, but the lust would be gone.

And so he'd begun what he thought of as courtship by leaving her a note. It didn't matter that it had been more warning than promise. Over the ensuing weeks, he'd become empowered by the "chase," and the notes had turned into sick promises of what he was going to do.

Then, a few days ago, his mother-in-law had taken ill. He'd put his wife on a plane to Dallas, then driven home, convinced he'd been given a sign. It was time to make his move.

It was after six in the evening when he got back to Little Top, fielded all the questions and well-wishes from friends and neighbors regarding his mother-in-law's poor health, while waiting in feverish anticipation of nightfall.

Sometime after midnight, he'd driven up to the old Tuesday place and parked a few yards down from the house. He'd reached for the duffel bag containing surgical gloves, condoms and the knife he intended to use when he was through. Just as he'd reached for the door handle, a huge dog came out of nowhere.

"Shit!" he'd gasped, and let go of the handle.

The dog was barking ferociously. If this kept up, there was no way he could get to Luce without being seen. Frustrated, he'd started the car and quickly driven away.

He'd known she had a dog, but he had forgotten to take its presence into consideration. Frustrated by this unexpected roadblock to deliverance, he'd begun making plans as to how to get rid of it.

On his way to work, he'd seen Luce enter the diner, then watched her dog meander down the block into the little park across the street from the library. Once the dog curled up and went to sleep beside a large pine, he'd known his chance had arrived.

During his workday, he'd stopped long enough to set a trap down at the creek below her house. All animals went to the creek to drink. Most wild animals would shy away from man's scent on the trap, but a tame dog would only be curious and willing to eat the meat he'd used for bait. He'd driven away, confident that he'd taken care of the problem.

Then, last night, he'd gone up the mountain, expecting to find the dog dead, or at least incapacitated, only to find the trap sprung and empty. He'd debated about setting it again, then changed his mind. Tonight he would bring his pistol. Just a pull of the trigger and that would be the end of the dog — then the woman was his. The sooner he had her, the sooner this madness would end. So he'd gone home.

Now this.

He wasn't sure what to make of it. Curios-

144

ity got the better of him, and he quickly walked to the front of the store just as the truck backed up and started down the street.

He tried to see who was driving, but all he could see was an indistinct figure of a man before the truck moved out of his sight. He glanced across the street. It was Bridie Tuesday's truck, all right, but that had not been old Bridie behind the wheel.

"I'll be back for that prescription later," he called out, and headed for the diner, knowing he was going to be late for work, but it didn't matter.

Luce had been almost an hour late. By the time she walked in, the diner was filling up fast. Harold was ready to fuss until she quickly explained that Bridie had taken a fall and she'd been tending to her. It seemed an easier explanation than trying to convince her boss that she'd watched a man bring Bridie back from the brink of death with nothing more than a laying on of hands.

Harold easily accepted her excuse, and so Luce's day began. By the time she'd turned in her first two orders, the place was filled with regulars, with more coming in as fast as others were going out.

Harold slid a pair of plates onto the pickup window as Luce hurried up.

"Hey, Harold . . . what's going on in town this morning? This is double our usual clientele."

Harold slid a plate of eggs and hash browns toward her, then finished it off with a side of hot biscuits and gravy.

"Other than the first of the month, I haven't a clue. Here . . . this is Junior Coker's order. You take it on, and I'll have Mike and Stu's up by the time you get back."

Luce nodded, thankful he wasn't angry that she'd been late. She couldn't afford to lose this job. It was all there was in this small mountain town, and the only thing she knew how to do well. She carried the order to Junior, then grabbed the coffeepot and went through the room, refilling cups and laughing at the usual teasing she got from the regulars as she went.

"Hey, Luce . . . top mine off, will you?"

Luce smiled at Walter Ferris, the local banker, who was waving his cup in the air, while she was emptying the pot in the pastor's cup.

"Would you bring me an order of sausage and eggs over easy?" Mark Ahern asked, as he slid into the empty chair beside Walter. "Tell Harold to put a rush on it. New phone

146

books are out, and they've been added to the regular mail delivery. Today's gonna slow me down something awful."

"Coming up," Luce said, and headed for the kitchen as Ferris clapped Ahern on the back and began talking to him about football.

Pastor Wagner eyed the sway of the long braid hanging down her back, then reached for the jelly.

Across the room, Hank Collins sat in his chair against the wall, watching the little waitress as she dashed about the room. But when she started his way, he quickly turned his attention back to his biscuits and gravy, too shy to say what was on his mind.

Sherman Truesdale grabbed Luce's wrist as she moved past his table. "Hey, girlie . . . when are you gonna let me take you out?"

"As soon as Gertie says you can," Luce fired back.

Everyone laughed, including Sherman. His wife, Gertie, wasn't about to let that happen.

The bell over the door jingled, announcing the arrival of more customers. Luce turned to see who was coming in but was sidetracked by Harold calling her name. By the time she gathered up the next order and delivered it to the table, her curiosity was forgotten.

The rush of breakfast customers finally ended, and except for a couple of old-timers who were lingering at their table over their third cups of coffee, the place was empty.

"Thank goodness," Luce said, as she moved past Harold to the storeroom to get some fresh packs of napkins.

The napkin dispensers needed refilling, as did a good portion of the ketchup bottles. She'd never understood putting ketchup on breakfast food, although her Latino roots showed through with her liberal use of salsa on her scrambled eggs, which, now that she thought about it, was pretty close to the same thing.

Now that business had slowed down, she had time to think of Jonah. In the long run, she wasn't sure what his presence was going to mean to her personally, but she knew she would be forever blessed for having met him.

She glanced at the clock. It was almost ten o'clock. Only five more hours before she would see him again.

SEVEN

Jonah found Middleton's Feed Store with no problem, parked at the loading dock and walked in the side door. A couple of old men wearing flannel shirts, overalls and gimme caps from a popular implement company were sitting around a freshly blackened potbellied stove, taking advantage of the warmth emanating from it as they argued the pros and cons of the current political environment.

The man behind the counter looked up as Jonah entered. As soon as he realized it was a stranger coming in the store, he straightened up to give him the once-over.

Jonah passed the old men and went straight to the clerk. Just as he was about to introduce himself, an old gray-striped tomcat leaped up on the counter.

"Well, hello, boy," Jonah said softly, and gave the cat a scratch under the chin.

The cat began to purr so loudly it made

everybody smile.

"I'm Paul Binger," the man said. "That there's Tiger. He don't like just everyone, but it's obvious you passed inspection."

"Acceptance is a good thing," Jonah said, then reached across the cat and offered his hand. "I'm Jonah. Mrs. Tuesday hired me to work for her this winter. She sent me down here, said for you to load up her regular order and send her the bill."

Paul eyed Jonah closer. "Well, now . . . I can't say that I've ever known Miz Bridie to hire help before."

Jonah shrugged. "Age changes things," he said, then hooked a thumb toward the truck. "How much chicken feed and sweet feed does she usually buy at a time?"

"A couple of sacks of each," Paul said.

Jonah shook his head. "I think you'd better double that. It's going to snow tonight, and I don't want her to run out before I can get back."

One of the old men at the stove laughed out loud and slapped the other on the shoulder.

"See! I ain't the only one who's predictin' snow."

Jonah glanced toward the stove, smiling slightly as the two old fellows resumed arguing, this time about the weather.

Paul looked out the window, then frowned. "It don't look much like snow to me."

"It will snow," Jonah said.

Paul shrugged. "I'll load you up with whatever you want."

Jonah gave the old cat a last scratch between the ears. "Show me where it is and I'll load the sacks," he said.

"I won't argue none with that," Paul said, as they started into the storeroom. "My back ain't what it used to be."

Jonah followed the clerk into the back, loaded the sacks onto a dolly and wheeled them to the loading dock, before putting them in the back of Bridie's truck.

A pair of pigeons roosting under the eaves of the roof cooed a hello. Jonah saw them, but thought better of saying anything. The less notice people took of him, the better off he would be. He signed the ticket Paul produced, then drove away. As he passed the diner, he thought of Lucia. It appeared most of the tables were full, which meant she would be busy. It occurred to him that the man who was stalking her could very easily be inside, watching her work. With a town this small, it was possible — even likely. Just the thought of her in danger made him sick to his stomach. If he ever got his hands on the man who was stalking her . . .

Frustrated, he shook off the thought and turned his attention to the winding road that led up the mountain to Bridie's home. By the time he got back, unloaded the sacks, chopped some firewood for Bridie's fireplace and fixed a gate out by the barn, it would be time for the noon meal.

He was coming from the shop building a few hours later when he saw Bridie step out on the back porch and wave a tea towel at him. He took it to mean that dinner was ready and headed for the house. Something told him that working for this old woman was going to be a gift in so many ways.

A few minutes later he was sitting down to her home-cooked meal, complete with two custard pies she had cooling on the sideboard. From the looks of the overflowing dishes, it appeared that Bridie had gone all out. There was a heaping platter of crusty-fried chicken, a blue-willow bowl filled with mashed potatoes and a matching gravy boat filled with chicken gravy, as well as an old yellow bowl with brown beans and another with coleslaw. A bread basket was near Jonah's elbow. The scent of hot biscuits coming from under the cover made his belly growl.

He thought about how close Bridie Tuesday had been to death that morning, and now here she was, pink-cheeked from the heat of the kitchen, with a sparkle in her eyes. It was obvious she'd overdone herself. He would have to make sure she understood that this wasn't expected.

"This looks wonderful, ma'am," he said, as he stood beside his chair.

"Sit, sit," Bridie said, as she carried a pitcher of iced tea to the table.

Jonah took the pitcher out of her hands, filled the glasses she had set at their places, then pulled out her chair.

"After you, ma'am."

Taken aback, Bridie fidgeted as she let Jonah seat her.

"Thank you, kindly," she said, and then laid her napkin in her lap. As soon as Jonah sat, she said the blessing, then eyed him curiously as she pushed bowls of food in his direction. "You been talking to any more of my critters?"

He grinned. "Do you really want to know?"

She frowned, irked that he'd called her bluff. "I see you've been busy this morning."

Jonah began filling his plate as he answered. "Yes, ma'am. I did what I could see needed doing. If you have special things for me to do, just let me know."

"First off . . . call me Bridie. Ma'am makes me feel old."

Jonah grinned. She *was* old, and they both knew it.

"Okay . . . Bridie, and just so you know, I'm not used to having such fine food. Don't wear yourself out trying to fix so much. A sandwich would be fine."

Bridie smoothed her hair self-consciously, then picked up her fork. "I like to cook, especially when I have someone to cook for, so eat."

Jonah did as she suggested, rolling his eyes in appreciation as the first bites went down.

"This is so good," he said. "I don't remember when I've had food any better."

Bridie beamed. "Franklin always liked my cooking."

Jonah ate while Bridie began telling a story about Franklin. It was obvious she was lonely. He understood the emotion, but she was letting her food get cold without eating. No wonder she was so frail.

He took a biscuit from the basket, slathered it with butter, and then put it on her plate.

Bridie stopped in midsentence, stunned by what he'd done.

154

"You should eat," Jonah said.

Bridie was speechless. It had been so long since anyone had cared what happened to her. Except for Luce, of course, but she didn't see her all that much. She picked up the biscuit and took a bite, then blinked through tears as she chewed.

Jonah saw the tears and quickly changed the subject. "Brother Mouse thanks you for the new home."

Bridie snorted lightly, then grinned. "Is that so?"

Jonah nodded, and took another bite of chicken, then poured gravy over his mashed potatoes. Without asking, he did the same for Bridie.

She took a quick drink of her tea, then bent to her plate. Without saying anything else, they began to eat. It wasn't until the meal was over that Bridie spoke again.

"Have you saved some room for my pie?"

Jonah looked up at her, then winked. "What do you think?"

Bridie giggled, and in that moment Jonah saw her as she'd been — a slender young girl with curly blond hair, blue eyes and a ready smile. No wonder Franklin had been taken with her.

Bridie got up, retrieved one of the pies and dessert plates from the sideboard, then carried them to the table. Her hand was trembling by the time she picked up the knife to cut the pie, but she persevered.

"It's wonderful," Jonah said, when he took the first bite.

Bridie beamed. "That's what Franklin always said."

"Sounds like your Franklin was a pretty smart fellow."

Bridie's smile slipped. "I miss him something awful."

Jonah hesitated, then laid a hand on her arm, feeling the tiny bones beneath.

"I know what that's like," he said gently. "My father's been dead for more than ten years. He was all the family I had."

Bridie couldn't quit staring at this man who was sitting at her table. The warm brown skin, high cheekbones, the strong chin and slight hook to his nose marked his Native American heritage. But his eyes were different — even strange. She couldn't remember ever seeing anyone with eyes that color. In the light, they looked . . . gold? That couldn't be right. She shook off the notion and refocused her attention. He was eating and talking to her with such ease that it felt as if she'd known him for years.

"Aren't you going to have some pie?" Jonah asked.

Bridie blinked, then looked down at her plate. She hadn't touched her piece.

"Oh. Yes, I suppose I could hold a few bites more."

Again they ate in mutual silence. It wasn't until they were finished and Jonah was helping her clear the table that Bridie introduced another subject.

"I think the world of Luce."

Jonah paused. He'd been expecting this.

"She thinks the world of you, too," he said.

Bridie paused, fixing him with a pointed stare.

"I'd like to think you're not the kind of man who will hurt her in any way."

"No, ma'am."

She pursed her lips, trying not to sound judgmental about two consenting adults.

"Living under the same roof makes messing around pretty handy," she said, and then blushed.

"She's afraid," Jonah said.

It was the last thing Bridie had expected to hear.

"What do you mean . . . she's afraid? Afraid of what?"

"Someone is stalking her . . . leaving threatening notes. Whoever it is set a trap down at the creek to get rid of her dog so she would be all alone."

Bridie's eyes widened in disbelief. "Good Lord! You two are total strangers to each other, and yet she told you all that?"

He hesitated, then sighed. "Not exactly. I just know it. The rest she admitted."

Bridie sighed. "Like you know what the owl says, and the mouse says, and the hawk that told you I'd taken a fall?"

"I know this is a lot to take in," he said.

"Do you know who's messing with her?"

"Not yet . . . but if I ever come in contact with him in some way, I'll know then."

"Poor little thing," Bridie muttered. "And she didn't say a word to me."

"She's a very strong woman," Jonah said. "I don't think she likes the feeling of not being in control."

"Just take good care of her," Bridie said.

"I intend to," Jonah said. "Now . . . it's going to snow tonight, so what can I do to help you get ready for that?"

"Snow? Oh, I don't think it will snow this early in the season."

Jonah shook his head firmly. "It will snow . . . and Molly is drying up."

Bridie laughed out loud. "I've been noticing her milk production slacking off. It's all right. I'm getting too old to mess with such things. I just hated to give up my old ways."

"I'll bring in some wood for your fireplace.

What else would you like done?"

"When do you go get Luce?"

"She said around three. I'll take her home, then come back here and do evening chores . . . if that's all right."

Bridie smiled. "That sounds fine by me. I made an extra pie, so you could take one home."

Jonah felt the jolt of the word *home* as if he'd been slapped. He hadn't had a home in a very long time. And he reminded himself, as long as Major Bourdain persisted in his quest to find him and control his powers, he couldn't have one.

"That extra pie will be much appreciated. So . . . I'll bring in some wood for your fireplace before I leave to go get her."

"You finish your pie," Bridie said. "I'll be right back." She left the room as Jonah took his last two bites.

She came back moments later with a handful of bills.

"Here," she said, handing him the money. "I thought you might be needing an advance on your first week's pay."

"Thank you," Jonah said, and surprised Bridie by enfolding her in his arms. "I won't let you down."

Within moments of being gathered into his embrace, Bridie was filled with such a sense of peace. It was stronger than anything she could remember. She sighed as the emotion engulfed her.

Even after he'd left the house, she could still recall that warmth, and that feeling of believing anything was possible. It was then that she finally let herself believe that Luce might be right about him, after all. If the man who called himself Jonah Gray Wolf wasn't a real angel, he was surely blessed beyond normal men.

Luce saw Jonah walking into the diner just as she was taking off her apron.

"Harold . . . my ride is here. See you tomorrow, okay?"

"It will snow tonight," Jonah announced.

At seventy-one, Harold's mind still worked fine, even though he weighed about a hundred pounds too much. But when he looked up at the man coming through the door, he didn't know what to comment about first. The fact that a stranger, and an Indian at that, had come to take his little Lucia home, or that the Indian was claiming it was going to snow.

"Uh . . . wait, I —"

Luce could see the surprise in Harold's eyes and decided the best way to deal with what was bound to become gossip was to introduce them herself.

"Harold, this is Jonah. Bridie hired him to help her out this winter. Jonah . . . this is my boss, Harold Carter."

"It is my pleasure, sir," Jonah said softly, and shook Harold's hand.

Within a heartbeat of the handshake, whatever fears Harold might have had about the stranger were gone. All he could feel was a sense of peace.

"Well, now . . . it's fine to meet you, too," Harold said, and then remembered the comment Jonah had made about the weather. "I heard the weather forecast at noon, and they didn't say anything about snow."

Jonah shrugged. "It will snow."

Harold grinned at the notion and then patted Luce on the shoulder.

"Well now, missy, if it does come a good snow, you might as well take the day off. Won't be anyone out and about in that kind of weather, and if they do come in, I can handle whatever customers we might have."

The idea of getting to sleep in was wonderful, but Luce didn't want to leave Harold in a jam.

"Are you sure? I don't mind —"

"No, no," Harold said, still laughing. "But remember . . . only if it snows."

Luce waved goodbye, then tried not to notice when Jonah put a hand in the middle of her back on the way to the truck.

"Is Bridie still okay?" she asked.

Jonah smiled slowly. "She made us a custard pie."

"Oh, yum," Luce said.

"Yum is right. I've already had a big piece out of the one she made for us at noon, and I'm looking forward to another tonight."

Luce shivered. The thought of them spending time together made her anxious. Would something more come of the sexual tension that flowed between them, or was she going to have to settle for that toe-curling climax she'd already had? She sighed as she crawled up into the seat.

"Tired?" Jonah asked, as he paused before closing the door.

"Yes, I guess that's it," Luce said, finding it easier to claim exhaustion than to admit she was turned on, then changed the subject. "Do you have to go back to Bridie's this evening?"

"Yes."

"Do we have time to stop by the supermarket before you drop me off?"

"We'll make time," he said.

Luce grinned. "If it's going to snow, I need to pick up a few things."

"It will snow," Jonah said. "Which way to the grocery store?"

He didn't like to refer to himself as a stalker, but that was what he'd felt like as he watched Luce serving breakfast. He'd stayed in the diner, visiting with first one customer and then another, until he'd had to leave to start his day, then spent the day trying to lose himself in work. But, by the end of the day, he was in a foul humor. It wasn't until he walked into his own home, savoring the familiar smells and comforting touches that his wife added to the rooms to make their house a home, that he began feeling better.

The phone was ringing as he tossed his keys on the hall table. He ran to answer. "Hello."

"Hello, dear, it's me. I thought I'd call and see if you're managing all right on your own."

He leaned against the wall, smiling slightly as he heard the concern in his wife's voice.

"I'm fine. How's your mother?"

She began to explain what was happening with her mother's treatment, but for the life of him, he couldn't make himself care. His thoughts had slipped to Luce Andahar again. Would this be the night he had her? Could he get rid of the dog without alerting her to his presence? He didn't know, but he was damn sure going to try.

"Dear? Dear? What do you think?"

He flinched. He had no idea what his wife had been talking about, but he quickly covered up for his inattention.

"Oh . . . you know what? I think I'll leave the decision up to you. You're in a better position to choose than I am."

"Oh, thank you . . . you are such a sweetheart. So I'll go ahead and stay with Mother for another week, and then reassess the situation."

He resisted the urge to cheer. "That seems the sensible thing to me, as well. Take care, give her my love, and stay in touch."

"Absolutely," his wife said. "I love you."

He closed his eyes, picturing Luce's face as he answered, "I love you, too," while wishing it wasn't true. He didn't want this torture in his life. Sometimes he thought he was going crazy. He knew this fixation wasn't normal, but he couldn't quit thinking about her. Couldn't stop imagining how red her blood would be against her warm brown skin. He wondered if it tasted salty, like her tears, then knew he would find out soon enough.

He went to the office, pulled a blue notepad from the desk drawer and began writing her another note. Just a brief mention of the things they would be doing together — when the time was right.

Bourdain was hosting a luncheon for some of his business partners. They had just been seated and were waiting for the first course to be served when one of his guests, a man named Karl Kaiser, began to fidget.

Bourdain noticed that the man's color had turned ashen and that there was sweat across his forehead, although the house was not overly warm.

"Karl? Are you okay?" Bourdain asked.

Before Karl could answer, he grabbed his chest, then slumped forward, going face-down on the plate.

"My God!" someone shouted as Bourdain jumped up and ran for the phone.

Within moments, he'd contacted 911, while another couple of men had lowered Kaiser to the floor and were performing CPR while waiting for help to arrive. But it was obvious to Bourdain that they would be too late.

Karl Kaiser had come for lunch, but he was going to leave in a body bag.

Bourdain was sick to his stomach as he sat with his head down and his hands clasped between his knees. He knew firsthand how quickly life could take a nasty turn. In the distance, he could hear the siren from the approaching ambulance — for all the good it was going to do Karl.

He closed his eyes, and as he did, he thought of Gray Wolf. If he'd been here, Karl wouldn't be dead, and the consortium they'd been going to form wouldn't have just ground to a halt.

In the middle of his dilemma, the doorbell rang.

He heard the maid letting the EMTs into the house. He stood, then took a deep breath, readying himself to face the next few hours. One thing was for sure, watching Karl Kaiser die had just reinforced his intention to catch that Indian healer. Once he had a chance to talk to him, he was certain he could make the man see things his way. The Indian could name his price and live in luxury forever. All he had to do was stay with Bourdain.

Go where he went.

Eat where he ate.

Sleep within the sound of his voice.

Whatever it took to keep Bourdain alive.

Hours later, after the police and the coroner had finally left, taking Kaiser's body with them, Bourdain was still trying to figure out a new angle to get Gray Wolf. Upping the bounty certainly wasn't the answer, and over the past ten years, he'd sent some of the world's toughest mercenaries on the hunt. To a man, they'd all failed. Even if they managed to get to Gray Wolf, no one had been able to escape past the animals who were willing to die to protect him. He didn't understand it, but he wanted the power that Indian possessed, and it was going to be his some day. He just had to find a way.

Then it hit him. D. J. Caufield. He should have thought of that crazy hunter before now. He clapped his hands together, then laughed out loud. By God, he was going to make this happen, after all.

EIGHT

Hobo was asleep in front of the fireplace, just out of range of any popping embers, leaning against the generous stack of firewood that Jonah had carried in earlier before going back up the mountain to do Bridie's evening chores.

Luce had stood on the porch and watched Jonah leave a few minutes earlier, then couldn't help but give the tree line a nervous glance. As she did, she realized that she'd forgotten to get the mail from the mailbox at the end of the drive.

Irked, she stepped off the porch and started down the drive, dodging the muddy ruts by staying on the grass along the edge. Within a few yards of the mailbox, she saw a dark blue Jeep top the rise below. There were only two houses this far up the mountain, hers and Bridie's, so she couldn't imagine who it might be; then she realized it was just Mark Ahern, the mailman. Her first thought was that he was running late on his route. Then he pulled up at the mailbox and waved.

"Hello, Luce . . . don't see much of you outside the diner."

Luce grinned. "By the time I get through at Harold's, I don't do much of anything when I get home except get off my feet."

Mark nodded. "I can empathize. The last thing I want to do after I finish the route is go for a drive."

Luce laughed out loud.

Mark thought how pretty she was when she smiled, then remembered what he'd been doing. "I'd better keep moving," he said, and patted the box beside him in the seat. "Got to deliver Mrs. Tuesday's order. Looks like she's been catalogue shopping again."

Luce saw a JCPenney mailing label on the large package. She knew Bridie was fond of mail-order catalogues.

"So here's your mail," Mark said, as he handed Luce a couple of magazines.

"Thanks," she said, and then stood back as he spun out a little before the tires caught traction.

He drove away as Luce went back to the cabin. Once inside, she laid her mail aside and put up the groceries they'd purchased, then went to her room. The first thing she liked to do after coming home from work was to get out of her work clothes and take a shower. By the end of her shift, she always smelled like cooking grease and cigarette smoke.

It was just after four-thirty when she got to the kitchen to begin making supper. As she began prepping the food, she remembered what evening meals had been like when she was a child — before her parents were killed, before she realized there was no such thing as happily ever after.

She and her sister would be underfoot in the kitchen, listening to their parents talk about their respective workdays, and sneaking bites of food. A favorite had been the handmade tortillas. It wasn't until she was older that she realized her mother knew all along they were snitching, but at the time, they'd thought it a great sport to outwit her.

She remembered the way her father's dark eyes would twinkle as she and her sister escaped with the warm, soft tortillas. Even after they were outside on the front stoop, wolfing down their prize, they could still hear the sound of his laughter.

She drew a slow, shaky breath, her throat aching with unshed tears.

God. She missed them so much.

She shook off the sadness as she took an onion from the vegetable bin. It wasn't the first time she'd wondered why she had been spared when the rest of her family had died in the wreck. It wouldn't be the last.

She peeled the onion and some potatoes, then cut them into bite-size chunks before opening a can of tomatoes, and dicing some celery and carrots to go in her stew. As she worked, she let herself fantasize about what it would be like to have someone special in her life. Someone who would always be there for her the way her father had been there for her mother — for all the family.

Immediately, her thoughts jumped to Jonah, although she felt foolish, daydreaming about someone she'd met only yesterday. She reached for the package of stew meat, poured some oil into the old cast-iron pot heating on the stove, then dumped in the meat to let it brown. She added some salt and pepper, then, as an afterthought, a big dash of hot sauce in honor of her Latino roots. As soon as the meat had browned, she added the prepped vegetables, the can of tomatoes and a couple of cans of beef broth, and covered the pot.

Soon the small cabin was filled with the scent of stew bubbling on the back of the stove. With an eye on the clock, she decided to mix up cornbread batter, then put it in the oven to bake. Thanks to Bridie, there would be custard pie for dessert. To Luce, this was as close to a feast as she could muster.

Hobo whined in his sleep, his legs kicking slightly as he lay beside the fire. Luce grinned and wondered if he was dreaming about trying to catch that squirrel that lived in the big oak down by the creek. She'd seen him chase it from time to time, but so far without any success.

Without thinking, her gaze automatically went to Hobo's leg; then she quickly shifted her focus to something else. Rational thinking had no place in what she'd seen since Jonah Gray Wolf had walked into their lives.

She had no idea how much time had passed when she crossed the room to lay another log on the fire, but it seemed much darker outside than it should have been. Curious, she moved toward the windows at the front of the house. Gathering clouds were bringing on an early night. With a quick glance back at the stove to make sure nothing was burning, she stepped outside for a better look at the sky and was met with a chilling blast of air. It felt as if the temperature had dropped a good ten degrees since she'd come home. Jonah had predicted snow, and if this kept up, it could certainly happen.

Shivering, she started to go back in the house when she caught a flash of movement from the corner of her eye. Curious, she moved toward the edge of the porch, squinting slightly as she stared into the darkening shadows of the forest. Often at this time of evening she would see deer on their way to the creek, and once in a while a raccoon, although when Hobo was outside, they always steered clear.

She stared into the shadows until her eyes began to smart from the chill wind, but nothing else moved. She finally decided she'd been imagining things and turned to go back inside. Just as she opened the door, Hobo charged out of the house, nearly knocking her down as he bounded from the porch. Barking ferociously, he headed toward the trees.

Luce frowned as she watched him go. He was running right toward the place where she'd been looking. Maybe she'd seen something there, after all. Still, it was too late in the evening for him to go hunting. He would be out all night if he took off after some animal.

"Hobo! Hobo! Come back here!"

But her calls were futile. The dog was gone.

He'd been asleep inside the cabin. She couldn't imagine what had alerted him from in there, but she could hear him baying at his prey. She listened for a few moments longer before she realized what she was hearing. That wasn't the sound he made when he was hunting. He was on the attack.

Her eyes widened as she stared into the tree line.

The stalker? Was it him? Was that who Hobo was chasing?

Panic filled her as she ran into the cabin, quickly locking the door behind her. As she did, the timer on the stove went off, startling her anew. With shaky hands, she took the cornbread out of the oven and took the stew off the burner, then grabbed a knife. If she was going to be attacked, she wasn't going down without a fight.

She ran through the cabin, turning off lights as she went, then, as an afterthought, she flipped on the porch light. Within a few minutes it would be completely dark outside, but if this was the night her stalker finally made his move, at least she would see him coming.

She gripped the knife a little tighter and

was about to pull up a chair to the window when she saw headlights coming down the mountain.

Thank God.

It had to be Jonah.

Jonah was tired, but it was a good tired. He'd made sure Bridie had plenty of wood inside, and reassured her that, no matter the weather in the morning, he would be up to deal with her livestock, so she should keep herself indoors.

She'd readily agreed, then waved him off before retreating to her nice warm home to enjoy her purchases. The mail-order package contained her new winter coat, a couple of dresses and a pair of new rubber boots for outside work, although when she'd ordered the boots, she hadn't known she was going to hire someone to take over those chores. Still, a person could always use boots, especially in a mountain winter, and she dug through the package with delight as Jonah made his way down the mountain.

He'd been thinking of Lucia, fantasizing about how it would be to have a permanent home and have her to go home to. His heart already knew what she could mean to him. The longer he stayed with her, the more difficult it was going to be to leave. But he didn't see any way around it. As long as Major Bourdain lived, anyone Jonah cared for would be in danger.

It was with that thought in mind that he pulled in to the yard. It didn't occur to him that something could be wrong until he realized that, while the porch light was on, there were no lights on inside the cabin.

His nerves were on edge as he opened the truck door and got out. Within seconds, he felt the negative energy of fear and knew something was wrong.

"Lucia! Lucia!"

His heart was pounding as he cleared the steps. Then she opened the door, and all he could think was *thank God.* He took one look at her face, saw the knife in her hand and knew he'd been right.

"What?" he asked, as he touched her face, then her arm, assuring himself she was still in one piece.

"I think someone was watching the cabin."

Jonah felt the shock and the fear in her body as vividly as if they were within himself.

"Did you see him?"

"I saw something, but it was getting so dark . . . then, when I started back inside, Hobo came flying out, barking and growling like crazy. I tried to call him back, but he disappeared. I locked myself inside, then you came."

"Get back inside, and lock the door. Don't open it to anyone but me."

Luce grabbed his arm. "It's getting dark. You could get lost out —"

"I don't get lost — ever," he said.

Her fingers curled into his wrist. "I'm scared."

"I'll be back," Jonah said, then impulsively bent down and kissed her.

Hard. Fast.

There was a sudden burst of air all around them, like the wings of a thousand birds, then that heart-stopping, mind-shattering force of energy beginning to center between her legs. On the brink of another climax, Jonah turned her loose, pushed her inside the cabin and shut the door in her face.

"Lock it!" he yelled.

She turned the lock, then sank to the floor. The knife fell from her fingers as she sat in the darkness, remembering the feel of Jonah's lips on her mouth. In that brief moment when they'd been connected, he'd shown her something within herself that she'd never known was there.

Passion. So much passion.

She was shaking now, but not from fear.

Please God, bring him back to me. I don't want to leave this earth without spending at least one night in Jonah Gray Wolf's arms.

Jonah ran without looking back, knowing that what he'd done had crossed a line he'd sworn not to cross. But he hadn't been able to leave her afraid and alone. The only thing he could think of to do was give her something else to think about besides fear.

And he had. Maybe more than he'd meant to. But it was done, and he would never regret letting his true feelings for her show.

Within moments of entering the trees, he stopped to get his bearings, and as he did, he felt the presence of evil. The skin crawled on the back of his neck as he heard Lucia's dog let out a howl.

Hobo had run something — or someone — to ground.

He turned in the direction of the dog's persistent baying and started to run, dodging branches and leaping over roots, using every preternatural sense he had to navigate the darkening land.

Luce's stalker was, literally, up a tree and cursing himself for his carelessness. In the long run, he'd been unable to outrun the dog and was still a good half mile from his vehicle. Once up the tree, he'd pulled his handgun, intent on getting rid of the dog before someone followed it to him.

But when he'd gone up the tree, he hadn't counted on darkness. It caught him before he could see where to aim. All he had to go by was the sound of the dog's movements below. Scared and cursing Luce, her dog and his own sick desire for the woman, he began firing in desperation.

The first two shots went wild, but he could tell that they had frightened the dog. He shot again and heard the dog yelp.

"Good," he muttered, believing that he'd either hit it or scared it away.

As a stray, Hobo had been shot at before, and he was deathly afraid of the sound of gunfire. When the third shot came, it ripped a burning path across his shoulder. With a sharp yelp of fear and pain, he turned tail and ran.

The moment the stalker heard the dog running, he jumped out of the tree, firing one more shot into the air just to make sure the dog kept going. A few minutes later, he came upon the car, jumped in, and took off in a flurry of flying gravel and dirt.

It wasn't until he was driving into the outskirts of Little Top that he began to breathe easy. Once at his house, he hit the garage-door opener and drove straight inside. He slammed on the brakes just before he hit the wall, then pushed the button to lower the door.

Only after he was out of the car and walking into the kitchen did he begin to think of how close he'd come to getting caught. He pulled off his clothes and tossed them in the laundry bin, then walked naked into the bathroom. He turned on the light, braced himself on the sink and stared at himself in the mirror, then leaned over the toilet and threw up.

When Jonah heard the shots, then the frantic yelp of a dog in distress, he increased his speed, ignoring the slap of branches against his face and the brambles tearing at his clothes.

A buck, startled by all the unwarranted noise in the forest, jumped out of a thicket across Jonah's path before dashing away. Jonah stumbled to keep from running headlong into the animal, then felt the deer's panic and inhaled the musky scent of its body as it bounded out of sight. By the time he regained his footing, the sounds of gunshots had faded. Hobo was no longer baying. He didn't want to think of the consequences and kept on running.

Just when he thought he'd taken a wrong turn, he ran up on the dog lying near the path and licking at his side.

Hugely relieved to find the dog still alive, Jonah stopped and dropped to his knees.

"Hey, boy. What have you gone and done to yourself this time?" he said, as he ran his fingers along the big dog's body.

The dog whined, then licked Jonah's fingers. Moments later, Jonah felt a sticky trail along the bone of Hobo's shoulder and guessed that one of the shots had nicked him. Without hesitation, he laid both hands on the wound.

An eerie silence came over the forest as, once again, the healing light enveloped both man and dog. An owl watched from a nearby tree branch, while a fox on its way to the creek walked up beside Jonah, sniffed at his heels, then quietly slipped away into the darkness.

Moments later, Jonah rocked back, then stood up. Hobo stood, licked Jonah's boots, then the tips of his fingers.

Jonah touched Hobo's head. "Go home," he said.

Hobo turned without hesitation and loped up the mountain to the cabin. But Jonah wasn't through. As long as there was a trail to follow, he was going to take it.

He watched until the dog disappeared, then lifted his head. He closed his eyes, letting all his senses go free until, once again, he could smell the man's fear. With that scent for a guide, he began to track the stalker with every animal instinct he possessed.

It wasn't until he came upon a small clearing attached to a single-lane road that he realized he'd lost it. Even though darkness had completely enveloped the forest, he could still see everything, including the tire tracks where the man had driven away. Frustrated, he had no other option but to return to the cabin. He thought of Luce, waiting and afraid, and hastened his steps. As he did, he felt the first flakes of snow against his face.

By the time he reached the clearing in front of Luce's cabin, the snow was falling heavily, masking all but the closest sounds. Jonah had seen glimpses of the porch light Luce had left burning, and now that he'd cleared the trees, it touched him to think she'd kept it on as a beacon for him to find his way home.

As he started across the yard, he was suddenly aware of the chill in the air and the dampness of his clothing, and lengthened his stride. Just before he reached the steps, the door swung inward. Luce paused, silhouetted in the doorway, then ran forward and threw herself into his arms.

He caught her in midstep and lifted her off her feet as he pulled her close against him.

"I was so scared for you," she said, as she buried her face against the curve of his neck.

"I was afraid for *you,*" he said. "I wanted to catch him . . . but I was too late."

"It doesn't matter. Nothing matters but that you and Hobo are back. You're back, and you're safe," Luce said, then wiggled out of his arms. "And you're freezing. Come inside . . . hurry. You need to get out of those wet clothes before you get sick."

He followed her inside, then locked the door after it was shut. Hobo was lying beside the fire, none the worse for wear. Luce was already at the fireplace, adding a couple of large logs to the fire.

Within a few moments the bark on the logs had caught fire, and the warmth of the blaze was welcome. As soon as the heat began to seep through his clothes, exhaustion hit.

"That fire feels so good," he said, then began to undress, suddenly anxious to get out of his wet clothes. "These are coming off," he warned.

"Oh. Sure," Luce mumbled, and thought to move away to give him some privacy, but found herself mesmerized by the process.

Piece by piece, he stripped off the clothes, revealing a body toned to perfection. She watched with her lips slightly parted, remembering now and then that she needed to breathe. When he was standing before the fire wearing nothing but his briefs, she shuddered, then closed her eyes and turned away, only to look back when he began to move.

She watched as he scattered the clothes about on the floor in front of the fire to dry. When he turned around, he caught the hungry look in her eyes and groaned.

"Luce . . . I —"

"I kept some stew and cornbread warm for you," she said.

He took a slow shaky breath, then nodded. "Give me a couple of minutes to get some dry clothes," he said, and reluctantly left the warmth of the fire to go to his room.

Luce's hands were shaking as she began dipping some stew into a bowl. Then she took the cornbread out of the warming oven, poured hot coffee into a thick crockery mug, and carried it all to the table. By the time she had his place set, he was back.

"This looks and smells wonderful," he said

as he sat.

"Thank you," she said.

"No, as always, it is I who thanks you."

He began to eat while keeping an eye on Luce's nervous movements. She was uneasy — but he also felt her desire. She wanted him, but she was afraid. And while part of him hated the fact that she felt uneasy around him, he could hardly blame her. He had no previous experience with women that even came close to what happened when they were together. How could he expect her to trust him when he couldn't even trust himself?

Luce couldn't sit still. Every time she looked at him, she kept remembering how he'd looked, silhouetted against the firelight. His long, muscular arms and legs, the wide shoulders and flat belly, and the plain white of the briefs against his smooth brown skin.

When he'd dressed in dry clothes, he'd also pulled his hair into a ponytail at the nape of his neck, giving her full access to his face. She knew it wasn't politically correct to think of a man as beautiful, but it was the only frame of reference that came to mind.

Jonah caught her looking at him and smiled, then winked, as he took another bite of stew.

Luce flushed, then smiled back. "So sue me for staring," she said. "Besides, after that striptease, you can hardly blame me."

"I warned you first," he said.

"Which only made me look harder," she countered.

He laughed out loud, then shook his head. "An honest woman. What is a man to do?"

The smile slipped off her face. "I'm toying with the notion that he could do just about whatever he wanted to do."

Jonah's heart skipped a beat.

"What if he wanted to . . . do it with you?"

Luce was standing on the edge of her future. She knew that if she told him no, that would be the end of it. But she didn't want to tell him no — about anything — and the knowledge that she held so much power was scary.

"Then I would tell him to go for it."

Jonah laid down his spoon and took a deep breath.

"You remember what I told you . . . about the bounty on my head and the people always looking for me?"

Luce nodded.

"It's one of the reasons why I've never let myself become involved with anyone. I've never invested emotion in loving because it could get the person I love killed."

He watched as Luce's nostrils flared slightly; then her dark eyes narrowed.

"All the people I loved are already dead, Jonah Gray Wolf, and I had nothing to do with it. It wasn't me who caused their deaths, but it doesn't change a thing. Nothing ventured. Nothing gained. I don't understand it, but I don't want to lose whatever this is between us."

Then she shoved a shaky hand through her hair in frustration. "Look at it this way. I've been living with fear for months. Your presence may be what's keeping me alive." Then her chin quivered slightly. "And I'm so tired of being alone."

Jonah knew what she meant. Loneliness was such a part of his life that he'd begun taking the emotion for granted. But here was Lucia, willing to risk everything for a chance at love.

He reached across the table, then turned his hand palm up, waiting for her to take it.

Luce didn't hesitate.

She laid her hand in his, and when their fingers threaded, then clasped, she knew this was right.

She stood.

Jonah followed.

Together, they walked across the floor, then paused in front of the bedroom doors.

"In my room," Luce said.

"Why?" Jonah asked.

"Because when you're gone, I want to remember you here . . . in my room . . . in my bed . . . in me."

Jonah's blood surged so fast through his body that he lost his breath. With a muttered oath, he picked her up in his arms and carried her into her room, shutting the door behind them. She was trembling as he laid her down, but he knew it wasn't from fear. She wanted him as much as he wanted her.

Without wasted motion, he stripped. Then, without a word, he removed her clothes, leaving her lush, curvy body bare to the world.

"Ah . . . Lucia," he whispered.

She held out her hand.

He crawled into bed beside her, then wrapped her in his arms.

NINE

When Jonah took Luce in his arms, she lost her sense of self. Within moments of his embrace, their heartbeats synchronized. Luce felt the shift within her body and would have panicked at the thought of someone with this kind of power, but she couldn't think past the feel of his mouth on the side of her neck and the growing ache in the pit of her stomach.

Jonah didn't know how to reconcile the overwhelming urge to lose himself in this woman with his normal reticence. For a man who never let on what he was thinking, he could hide nothing from Lucia.

With every sweep of his lips against her skin, with every breath that he took, he was imprinting her as his own — branding her essence into his soul. For the rest of his life, in the dark, in a storm, blind and lost in a land in which he'd never been, he would still be able to find her.

For Luce, thought had ceased. He was a force of nature. A man whose touch she couldn't resist. From the silky feel of his skin, warm to the touch without an ounce of extra flesh, to the long, dark fall of his hair brushing across her face, she couldn't get enough.

When she felt his teeth graze the flesh below her ear and his hand slip between her legs, she grabbed a fistful of his hair and held on. A brief image of a wolf with amber eyes flashed through her mind, coupled with what sounded like a howl, and then the sense of running through air, but it all disappeared, and when she looked up, it was Jonah she saw above her. His voice was soft and coaxing, but the glitter in his eyes betrayed the depth of his passion.

When he leaned down, she held her breath as his mouth brushed across her lips, then her cheek, and then he whispered against her ear. "Lucia . . . Lucia . . . let me in."

She exhaled softly, then closed her eyes as she moved to make way. When she did, he slid between her legs. It wasn't until she felt him inside her body that she finally knew why she'd been born.

From the moment of their joining, he felt a bonding that had never happened before. He began to move, rocking back and forth, lost in her heat, caught by the pull of her muscles surrounding him, until he slowly lost his mind. Minute after minute, they rode the feeling, taking from it what they needed to survive. Then, suddenly, her fingers were digging into his forearms, and when he heard the stuttered gasps of her impending climax, he shattered.

Swept into the explosion of pleasure, Luce moaned as her bones melted and her mind went blank.

Jonah quickly followed her, riding surge after surge that left him weak and shaking, until, with a groan, he collapsed on top of her.

Almost instantly, he realized she was too small to bear the full measure of his weight and quickly pushed himself up. Braced on both elbows, he looked down at this woman who'd captured his heart.

Her eyes were closed, her lashes wet with tears. She was breathing through slightly parted lips as aftershocks from her climax continued to ricochet through her body.

"Lucia?"

She opened her eyes, then touched his face, as if to assure herself this was real. "Am I still breathing?"

He rolled off her, then laid the palm of his hand in the valley between her breasts until

191

he could feel the pounding rhythm of her heartbeat.

"Yes."

Luce moaned, then sighed and reached for his hand, threading her fingers through his. "Jonah?"

"Yes, Lucia?"

"That was magic."

He brought her hand to his lips as he rose up on one elbow, then traced the shape of her mouth with his fingertip.

"Yes," he said softly, then leaned over and kissed the path his finger had taken. "Umm . . . Lucia."

"Yes?"

"This shouldn't have happened."

Luce's eyes widened in shock, which quickly morphed into pain. "Then get out of my bed," she said.

"Don't," Jonah said, and rolled over on top of her, then grabbed her wrists and pinned her down so that she couldn't move. "It shouldn't have happened . . . but it did . . . and I will never regret it."

Luce was blinking back tears. "Then why did you say that?"

He leaned down until their foreheads were touching, then let go of her wrists and cupped the sides of her face.

"Because it's the truth. Loving you gives

Bourdain leverage over me. If he ever finds out you exist, he will use you to get to me. I have put your life in danger."

A tear slid from the corner of Luce's eye, then down onto the pillow.

"Oh. Well. My life is already in danger. I came with a stalker, remember?"

He thought back to the wild chase through the woods a short while ago. "I remember all too well." Then he traced her tear with the tip of his tongue, tasting the saltiness.

Luce groaned. "I won't tell anyone about us if you don't," she said.

Jonah shook his head. "We won't have to. They'll be able to tell by the look on my face."

Luce looked up; then her heart skipped a beat. He might be right about that after all. The look on his face was fierce. "What are you thinking?"

His eyes narrowed. His nostrils flared. "A wolf mates for life. You belong to me now."

Luce's lips went slack. "Uh . . . I . . ."

"Yeah. I'm as surprised by this as you are, but we've known each other almost forty-eight hours. It's not like I didn't give you time to get to know me."

Luce grinned. His humor was as unexpected as the love in her heart, and he was right. She'd been alone for such a long time.

She'd had almost two whole days to get used to his presence. For a man as special as Jonah Gray Wolf, it was more than enough.

"Come here, you," she said softly, then wrapped her arms around his neck and kissed him hard and long until she heard him groan. Just when he was of a mind to die in her arms all over again, she scooted out from under him.

"You didn't get to eat dessert. I'm going to go cut Bridie's custard pie."

"You're my dessert," Jonah said, and reached for her, but she kept on moving. "I'm going to let Hobo out while you get dressed."

Jonah swung his legs off the side of the bed as he sat up, then paused, admiring her curvy body as she moved across the room.

"Okay, Lucia, you're calling the shots, but you might want to put something on, too, or you're going to freeze those pretty nipples."

She made a face at him, but she knew he was right. She grabbed a pair of sweatpants and pulled them on, then yanked a sweatshirt over her head on her way out of the room.

He heard her calling the dog, then her high-pitched squeal as she opened the door to a blast of cold air. Still smiling, he went into his room, put on a clean pair of pants, then followed her into the living room, where she was about to put more wood on the fire.

He kissed the back of her neck, then took the log from her hands.

"Let me do this. You're supposed to be cutting pie."

Luce grinned as she relinquished the wood, but she didn't move. Instead, she watched the play of muscles across Jonah's back as he squatted down to feed the fire with new fuel. Impulsively, she reached out and tunneled her hand into the length of his hair. Sometime during their lovemaking, it had come undone. It was thick and still slightly damp — and like silk beneath her palm.

He rocked back on his heels and looked up at her. "What?"

"Nothing . . . I just . . . just . . . I wanted to touch you."

Tenderness was an unknown in Jonah's world. His voice grew husky with emotion.

"Then I thank you, my Lucia, because it's been a very long time since anyone has cared enough to want to do that for me."

"It's going to be okay," she said.

Jonah stood up, then tilted her chin with

the tip of his finger.

"Is it, now?"

She nodded.

He wrapped his arms around her, holding her cheek against his chest until all she could hear was his heartbeat and the sound of his voice, promising that he would never leave her — that she would never be alone again.

D. J. Caufield liked the finer things in life, so when the call came from Major Bourdain about bringing in a man for a million-dollar bounty, Caufield grinned. For Caufield, the love of the chase was the biggest part of the kick. Anticipating the bounty yet to be claimed, Caufield decided to take a risk, picked up the phone and placed an order for a Hummer. The Hummer was a sure thing, because Caufield never failed.

The next day, FedEx delivered a file from Bourdain pertaining to the prey, a man named Jonah Gray Wolf. Caufield scanned it while eating breakfast. It soon became clear that this man wasn't a normal bounty, but Caufield was intrigued. The part about animals coming to Gray Wolf's aid was a bit far-fetched, but a million dollars was enough incentive to get past the crazy twist of character Bourdain was claiming the guy had.

According to the last entry in the file, Gray Wolf had most recently been seen in the mountains of West Virginia, and from the morning's weather report, it was snowing there.

Caufield grimaced. Winter sucked. But a million dollars would warm up some really cold feet.

Hobo was scratching at Luce's door to be let out when she finally opened her eyes. Jonah was still asleep in the bed beside her. She didn't know whether to be horrified by her behavior or count herself blessed among women that this man had walked into her life. When he rolled from his back to his side and reached for her in his sleep, she sighed. It was definitely the latter.

"I've got to go let Hobo out," she whispered, and kissed the tip of his nose as she crawled out of bed.

Within seconds, Jonah was wide-awake and reaching for his pants as he glanced at the clock. It was five minutes to seven.

"I'll do it. I've got to go to Bridie's, and besides, you're supposed to get to sleep in this morning, remember?"

"Only if it snowed enough," Luce reminded him.

Jonah arched an eyebrow. "You're still doubting me?"

"I just want to see it," she said, and made her escape while Jonah was getting dressed.

She opened the door for Hobo, who bounced past her and into the snow like a child who'd been let out to play. She smiled as she watched him leaping from bush to tree, biting at the snow and barking his excitement at the new arrival.

The snow had piled up past the bottom porch step, leaving the yard covered in a pristine blanket of white that Hobo was quickly destroying. Luce watched for a moment, then closed the door and went to stir up the fire.

Hot coals still glowed beneath the ash. All it took was a few digs with the poker, some kindling, then a chunk of dry wood, and she soon had the fire blazing. Once she was satisfied with that, she turned to the kitchen to make coffee. Even if she crawled back into bed later, she wanted a cup of hot coffee in her belly first.

The coffee was already brewing when Jonah came out of his room. His jeans were old but clean, and he was wearing a T-shirt underneath a red-and-black flannel shirt. She'd left his boots warming by the fire, and he smiled his thanks as he sat down to put them on.

"If you have some laundry you need done, leave it in the middle of your floor before you leave, and I'll do it with mine."

Jonah stood up, stomping his feet slightly to set his feet comfortably inside the boots, then eyed Luce's bare feet.

"Don't you have any house shoes?"

She shrugged. "No. I usually just wear a pair of heavy socks."

He frowned, then realized he was smelling coffee.

"Can I take a cup of that with me?" he asked.

"Yes, of course, but I was going to make you some breakfast."

"I'll take one of those sweet rolls we bought yesterday. That will be enough."

Luce dug the prewrapped honey bun out of the pantry, poured him a cup of coffee in her biggest cup, and carried them to the door where he was waiting.

"I didn't want to track dirt across the floor," he said, pointing to the boots he'd forgotten to clean when he'd stripped by the fire last night.

Luce smiled as she went on tiptoe to kiss him.

"Hobo tracks it for you," she said, as she

handed him the roll and coffee. "Give Bridie my love."

He frowned, then set down the coffee and roll, and took her in his arms.

"I'll tell her you said hello," he said gruffly. "The love is mine."

Then he kissed her.

And, like before, Luce felt the world around her shifting. When his mouth centered on her lips, the face of a wolf slid past her senses. Then suddenly he picked her up, her feet dangling against his legs as he turned her around and sandwiched her between the wall and his body.

Luce locked her legs around his waist and slid her arms around his neck as he tore his mouth from her lips. She moaned, wanting to regain that connection with him. But then all thought left her as he laid his cheek against her cheek and whispered in her ear.

It was a promise of things to come that Lucia Maria Andahar had never thought of, let alone become a willing participant in. It was enough to make her crazy. Then he nipped the lobe of her ear ever so gently with his teeth and pressed his lips hard against the pulse throbbing down the side of her neck.

Luce began to moan as the unexpected climax shattered her from her head to her toes. While she was still trembling from the force of his touch, he carried her back to bed, laid her gently in the same spot where she'd been sleeping earlier and pulled up the covers.

"Sleep," he said softly.

She closed her eyes and willingly obeyed.

Jonah stood for a moment, watching the flutter of her dark eyelashes against her cheeks, then gritted his teeth and went outside. He whistled once.

Hobo came running.

"Inside," he said, holding the door open for the dog to go in. "Don't let anyone hurt her," he added, then turned the lock on the doorknob before pulling it shut.

He trudged through the snow to the side of the yard, where Bridie's old truck was parked beneath the shed. It started more easily than he had expected, and soon he was driving up the road to tend to the needs of the other woman in his life.

He was dreaming about his wife, but when he started to make love to her, she turned into Luce Andahar, at which point he woke up in a sweat, certain he was about to be found out. When he realized he'd been dreaming and remembered that his wife was still at her mother's, he rolled over on his back and wiped his face with shaking hands.

"Damn. I say . . . damn it all to hell," he muttered, then glanced at the clock, cursed beneath his breath again and got out of bed.

It wasn't until he got to the bathroom and happened to glance out the window that he saw the snow. He hated winter. For that matter, he hated West Virginia, too. He'd been trying to get his wife to move to Miami for years, but she was afraid of hurricanes and afraid of getting too far away from her mother.

He sighed, then focused on peeing. If he was lucky, his mother-in-law would kick the bucket this time around. Then maybe he would be able to talk his wife into the move. They didn't have to live on the coast. They could settle inland. He just wanted to live in a place where the grass was always green and most of the days were sunny. Besides, it was far easier to have an extra girlfriend in a heavily populated area. Then, when they went missing, it was sometimes days, even weeks, before anyone noticed. Not like here. When Luce failed to show up for work, it wouldn't be long before she would be classified as missing. Finding her body would be another thing altogether.

Still, he had to be careful here. He often wondered why he'd ever stayed in this place.

Why he'd fooled around and married Sue instead of doing to her what he usually did to his women. Maybe it was because she reminded him of his mother. Maybe it was because, in their marriage, she was in charge. But that was where her control ended. When he was on the road, he was the king of everything.

Later, as he shaved to get ready for work, he thought about dropping by Harold's for breakfast. He could watch Luce's tits bounce as she brought him his food. It would be a damn good way to start the day.

But when he backed out of the garage to drive to work, he found out that it wasn't as simple getting around as he'd thought. The city manager was obviously not up, or he would have ordered the few city employees out to plow and sand the streets.

Cursing ineptitude, the weather and his wife, he slowly made his way to the diner to eat.

Harold was sitting in the back booth, finishing his own breakfast, when the bell over the door jingled. He looked up, swallowed his last bite of toast and waved the customer in.

"Hey there! I didn't think I was gonna be cooking breakfast for anyone but myself this morning. Sit. Sit. I'll be right there with the coffee."

"Where's Luce?"

"I told her to stay home. No need her coming in to work when I doubt there'll be a dozen customers all day."

"Oh."

"So . . . what'll you have?" Harold asked, as he poured coffee.

"Got any biscuits and gravy?"

"Oh, sure, sure. Got plenty. How about some hash browns to go with them?"

"Whatever," he said, as he added cream and sugar to his coffee. But he was pissed off again. First the snow. Now he wouldn't see Luce.

"Say, heard Sue's mother took a bad turn. How's she doing?" Harold asked.

"Not good. Not good at all. The wife is staying with her for the rest of the week."

"So you're batchin' it, are you?"

He nodded, acknowledging Harold's reference to being on bachelor status while his wife was gone. If only.

"I'm gonna make some chili and corn-bread for later. If you're still at work around noon, come on back. It'll be better than opening up a can of soup on your own," Harold said.

"Yeah . . . thanks . . . I'll probably do that,"

he said, and then opened up his paper and pretended to read, hoping Harold would take the hint and shut the hell up.

Truth was, he didn't know what he was going to do later, but he just might be tempted to take a drive up the mountain. If Luce Andahar was snowed in, she might be ready for a little company. God knows he was more than ready for her.

The lights were on inside Bridie's house when Jonah drove into the yard. Instead of parking at the house like he usually did, he drove down to the barn. When he was finished there, he was going to stop by the woodpile on his way back and bring a big load of firewood inside.

He saw Bridie at the kitchen window and honked as he drove by. She waved. He waved back and kept on driving.

Old Molly was waiting inside the barn. She lowed softly as he walked in.

"Good morning to you, too," he said, and rubbed behind her left ear before turning her in to the stanchion.

He quickly filled a bucket with feed, poured it into the trough, then grabbed a milk bucket and a stool, and sat down beside her.

The warmth of her udders felt good

against his cold fingers as he began to coax the milk from her teats. Within a few moments, she let it flow, and soon the scent of fresh warm milk mingled with the aroma of the hay and sweet feed that Molly was eating.

Milking a cow was one of those mindless tasks that took no skill other than patience, but Jonah liked the solitude of the barn and the sounds of the morning that came from the inhabitants who lived there.

The big black snake that was wintering beneath the hay was sleeping soundly. The barn owl was roosting on the highest rafters, pretending to sleep. But Jonah knew it was keeping one eye on him, making sure there were no surprises.

Just outside the aisle of the barn, a small red fox was making the rounds, hoping to find a mouse, or maybe an egg or two for breakfast before retreating to its den.

Jonah knew that Brother Mouse, who was now living under the floor of the chicken house, was well aware of the fox, which was good. He'd taken a liking to the little gray mouse and would hate to learn that he had become food for the wily fox.

By the time he finished milking, Molly was through eating and was standing patiently, chewing her cud and waiting to be turned out. But Jonah had other plans for her today.

"It's too cold, and the snow is too deep for you, old girl. I'm going to leave some extra hay in here for you, and turn you out in the corral. If you want to come back inside the barn, you can. If you want to freeze the tips of your ears, then you'll be free to do that, too."

Molly turned her head and looked back at him, then mooed softly.

Jonah grinned.

"It was just a joke, okay?"

He set the milk bucket inside the truck, then went back to the barn, cut the baling wire on a couple of square bundles of hay, then separated a half dozen blocks from one bale and carried them to the trough where Molly had been eating earlier.

"So . . . here's a morning snack and enough for lunch. I'll be back later. You stay out of trouble, old girl."

Molly butted him gently.

He smiled. "Yes, thank you, I will, too," he said, and headed out to the corral, where he broke the ice on the watering trough, then headed for the truck and drove to the woodpile.

Within a few minutes, he'd loaded the better part of a rick of wood into the back of the truck bed, then crawled back inside.

Even though he was wearing gloves, his hands were cold, as were his feet. It made him remember the long Alaskan winters and the years he'd had with his father. They'd both been cheated out of so much. Adam's life had been cut short, and Jonah had lost the only home he'd ever known. Still, he was grateful for the years they'd had.

Then he thought of Lucia. Being away from her was like a physical ache. He'd never had this kind of feeling for a woman before. It was frightening to know that such a small woman could have such a profound influence on his life. It was even more frightening to think of what Bourdain would do with her if he ever found out.

But loving Lucia had turned something around inside Jonah that was giving him a different outlook on life. He could never leave her. Would never leave her. But, at the same time, he would never ask her to live a life on the run with him.

Because of her — because of this love that he'd found — Jonah had come to a momentous decision. The next time one of Bourdain's hired guns found him — and they *would* find him, of that he was sure — he was going to dig in and fight back. No more running. No more looking over his shoulder.

He would end it now, like he should have the first time.

TEN

Jonah's demeanor was calm, but Bridie could tell something was different. She couldn't put her finger on what it was, but something was off. She was straining the milk while he unloaded the wood onto the back porch. When she finished, she called him inside to warm up, then sat him down with a hot cup of coffee and some fresh gingersnaps that she'd just taken out of the oven.

"These are delicious, thank you," Jonah said, as he reached for a third cookie.

Bridie beamed. She loved to cook. Having someone around to eat her cooking was even better.

"You're welcome. Now tell me. What's wrong?"

Jonah didn't bother to pretend he didn't know what she was talking about, and he'd been raised in a culture that revered the wisdom of their elders. Besides that, he

210

knew she cared about Lucia.

"I think Lucia's stalker was at the cabin yesterday evening. I drove up in the middle of her panic. Hobo was in the woods, chasing something . . . or someone. I made her lock herself in and went after the dog."

Bridie frowned. She didn't like to think there could be someone that evil on the mountain.

"Maybe it was a deer . . . or a big cat. There are some around, you know. Maybe that's what her dog got at."

"It wasn't a deer, and it wasn't a cat . . . unless one of them can drive. It was a man. I trailed him all the way to where he'd parked, but he was already gone."

Bridie couldn't quit playing devil's advocate, because if his suspicions were right, that meant something bad was afoot.

"Maybe it was just a hunter."

"Then why did he run? Why not just stop and acknowledge his presence? Besides, whoever it was shot her dog after it treed him. It wasn't a mortal wound, but it was painful. I healed it before we went home, though. She'd already witnessed him nearly losing his leg. I didn't want her worrying about Hobo, even though I think the stalker is definitely trying to get rid of the dog. That would leave her open for whatever he has in mind."

Bridie frowned. "But there's you. You're at the house with her."

"Not many people know that, and I never got close enough to him last night for him to know I was trailing him. It was all between him and the dog."

Bridie leaned back, watching Jonah's face, knowing in her heart that he was telling the truth as he saw it, but she had yet to witness his supposed healing firsthand and was still inclined to harbor a bit of doubt.

She reached for the cookie jar and took a gingersnap for herself, then studied the shape of it for a moment before commenting. "So, you gonna tell the sheriff about this?"

"I suggested it, but Lucia said she went once and he pretty much blew her off. She isn't willing to do it again."

Bridie frowned. "Then what are you gonna do to make sure nothing happens to my girl?"

A muscle jerked at the side of Jonah's jaw as he cupped his hands around his coffee cup and stared her square in the eyes.

"I'm going hunting. When I find him, I might turn him over to the sheriff . . . or I might make him wish he'd never been born.

I haven't decided yet."

Bridie frowned. "I thought you didn't see him."

"I didn't."

"Then how are you gonna go about picking someone out of all the people who live in and around Little Top?"

"I'll know him."

Bridie snorted lightly. "That don't make a lick of sense. All you're gonna do is get yourself in trouble, then I'll be left up here to milk old Molly by myself again."

Jonah could tell she was worried for him, not for herself. He laid his hand over hers.

Bridie felt a sudden burst of energy, as if she'd just been shocked by a little jolt of electricity. She gasped and would have pulled back her hand, but he was still holding on.

"I will not let you down, and I will know the man who was at the cabin."

"Then tell me how," Bridie asked.

"I can smell him."

Bridie grinned. "Now I know you're putting me on. Man can't track by scent."

Jonah moved his hand, then rocked back in his chair and emptied his coffee cup. "Those cookies were really good, as was the coffee. I'm going to go feed your chickens and gather the eggs. Do you have a special egg basket you'd like for me to use?"

Bridie frowned. "Are you changing the subject on me?"

Jonah stood. "Franklin used to use Old Spice on his face after he shaved, didn't he?"

Bridie's mouth dropped. "How did you know that?"

"The scent is still in the wood in your floor."

Bridie's eyes widened. "But he's been gone for ten years, and I've mopped these floors many a time since."

"I can smell beeswax and lemon oil in this house, as well as mothballs and some kind of liniment compound. Your bath powder has a gardenia scent, and there's something else . . . something faint that's stronger in the living room than it is in here." Jonah closed his eyes, concentrating on the scent. "Ah, yes . . . roses. I smell roses."

Bridie gasped. Over the years, she'd made a habit of tucking sachets of flower petals beneath the cushions of her sofa. The last ones she'd made had been from the rose-bushes just off the back porch. There was no way he could have known. No way he would have found them. No one knew she did that. Not even Franklin had known that little secret. It had been hers alone — until now.

214

She glared at him, then pointed toward the door.

"The egg basket is hanging over there by my coat and scarf. Watch that old red hen when you gather eggs. She's bad to peck."

"Yes, ma'am," Jonah said.

Bridie watched him leave, then closed her eyes and took a deep breath. All she could smell was coffee and cookies. Then she shook her head as she carried their cups to the sink.

Whatever Jonah Gray Wolf was, he was doing a good job for her and looking out for Luce, which was all that mattered.

By the morning of the next day, the snow was beginning to melt. All the while Luce was getting ready for work, Jonah prowled the inside of the cabin like a caged animal. He'd slept fitfully during the night, getting up and down to stoke the fire before looking out the windows to make sure they were still alone. After that, he would crawl back into bed with Luce. Each time, he would pull her close, then rest his chin on the crown of her head and fall back asleep with the scent of their lovemaking still around them.

But now it was morning, and he was going to have to relinquish her care and safety to a man named Harold, who ran a diner down in Little Top.

He poured himself a second cup of coffee as Luce came out of her room, then sat down on the sofa to put on her tennis shoes. With all the walking she did during the day, she needed a comfortable pair of shoes.

And luckily for her, Harold didn't have a uniform policy, so she was free to wear whatever she chose. This morning she was wearing blue jeans and a red sweater, and had her long, wavy hair pulled back in a ponytail. He felt a surge of satisfaction knowing that he'd put that small love bite on the side of her neck, wondered if she'd seen it, then decided not to mention it. But there was something else he did need to mention. His conversation yesterday with Bridie had started him thinking, and now he couldn't get it out of his head.

"I think you should show the sheriff all the notes from the stalker."

Luce frowned. "I already showed him."

"You showed him one."

Luce stood and faced Jonah with her hands on her hips.

"So I show him the rest, then what? I've never seen anyone. No one has tried to break in to the house. I can't prove that he was the one who set the trap that hurt

Hobo. What the hell do I say?"

"That someone's frightening you."

Luce slapped the sides of her legs, then threw up her hands.

"Why? Why, Jonah? Why is that going to change anything?"

"It might help explain why, when I find him, I'm turning him over in little pieces."

Luce flinched. She was almost afraid to ask.

"But we can't find him, because we don't have any idea what he looks like."

"I can find him. I *will* find him. If he's anywhere in town today when I come back to get you, I will find him."

"Oh, for Pete's sake. How?"

"I can smell him."

Luce stared. She heard what he was saying, but it didn't seem possible. Then she reminded herself that this was Jonah. She'd witnessed his powers with her own eyes. Finding someone by his or her scent didn't seem like such a big deal after that.

"Oh. Well." Then she grinned. "What about me? Could you track me?"

He crossed the room and took her in his arms.

"In the dark, with my eyes closed," he said.

Her smile widened. "What do I smell like?"

He picked her up, then swung her off her feet as he kissed her soundly.

"You didn't answer," Luce said, when he finally turned her loose. "What do I smell like?"

"You smell like me," he growled.

Luce's heart skipped a beat. After the past two nights, it was no wonder.

"I need to go to work now," she said.

Jonah didn't budge. "You need to take the notes with you. Please."

Luce rolled her eyes. "Fine. I'll take them. I'll show the sheriff . . . for all the good it will do."

"It's for *my* good. It's part of my alibi when I take the bastard apart, remember?"

"I remember," Luce said. "But I don't know how you're going to convince the sheriff that the man you drag into his office is the right man because of his smell."

"I won't have to. The man will confess."

Luce suddenly shuddered as she realized how serious Jonah was. He really *was* going hunting for her stalker. She didn't know how that made her feel, other than to worry about his safety.

"You won't do anything foolish, will you?" she asked.

Jonah's chin jutted mutinously. "He's the one who's been foolish. I'm just going to

218

make him sorry."

"Fine. I'm going to get the notes."

She went back into her bedroom and came out with a large manila envelope. Jonah was already holding her coat for her. She put it on, then grabbed her purse.

Jonah got his coat and the truck keys, then opened the door for her, before following her out to the porch.

"Wait here," he said. "I'll drive up to the house so you don't have to walk in the mud."

"I could get used to being treated like this," she said.

Jonah paused on his way down the steps and looked back at her. Her dark eyes were sparkling, and the breeze was tugging at the curls around the edge of her face. She looked so happy, and he was so afraid that his presence in her life was going to destroy her and everything they were trying to build.

"I'll see what I can do about that, too," he said softly, then headed for the shed.

A short while later, he was pulling up to the curb at Harold's diner.

"Have a good day," Luce said. "Tell Bridie I said hello."

"I will do that," Jonah said.

Luce opened the door and was about to get out when Jonah said her name again.

"Lucia . . ."

She was smiling as she looked back.

"Yes?"

"Love you."

Luce froze; then her eyes filled with tears. He *would* wait to tell her when she was standing in the street in front of God and everybody.

"Oh, Jonah . . . I love you, too."

He nodded once, as if satisfied that he'd gotten that off his mind.

"See you at three."

Still rattled by his revelation, Luce could only stammer, "Uh, yes . . . at three."

"Don't forget to show the messages to the sheriff."

"I won't," she promised.

Jonah waited until she got inside the diner, then headed up the mountain to do Bridie's chores. He'd learned over the years to say what was on his mind, because sometimes, tomorrows never came. Telling Lucia he loved her had been in his heart since their first kiss. It had been time to say it aloud.

Luce was still floating on the joy of Jonah's claim as she sailed through the diner to the back room, put the envelope on a shelf above her coat, which she hung on a peg, and went straight to work.

Shug Marten came in on his way to open

the gas station, waved her down, ordered his breakfast to go, and then proceeded to question her in detail about her dog.

"Say, Luce . . . I hope you understand why I didn't go with you to get your dog out'a that trap, but he just don't like me one bit."

"I know," Luce said. "It's all right. Jonah got him out."

Shug frowned. "That the Indian's name who went with you?"

"Yes."

"Was your dog hurt very bad?" Shug asked.

Luce didn't know how to answer without going into detail, but she figured the less said, the better.

"Yes, but Jonah fixed that, too," she said, and quickly changed the subject. "You still take cream and sugar in your coffee?"

"Yep," Shug said. "So . . . I saw you caught a ride to work."

She tossed some powdered creamer and sugar packets into his sack.

"Um . . . yes, I did. Glad not to have to walk through all that snow and slush. Hang on, Shug. Harold has your order. I'll be right back."

She came back, slipped the to-go box in the bag and totaled up the order. "That will be six dollars and fifty-four cents."

Shug counted out the money and picked up his sack, but still lingered, eyeing Luce closely. "Was that Miz Bridie's old truck I saw you riding in?"

"Yes."

"Who was driving?"

Luce laughed nervously. "My gosh, Shug. Are you writing my biography or something?"

Shug had the grace to blush. "Oh. Well. I didn't mean to pry none."

Luce grinned. "Yes, you did, but that's all right. I've really got to get back to work, though."

"You still didn't tell me who was driving," Shug said.

Luce sighed. "It was Jonah. Bridie hired him to work for her this winter."

Shug nodded. "So . . . he gives you a ride to work now?"

"Shug! For goodness' sakes," Luce said. "Your food is getting cold."

Shug grinned, shrugged and finally left.

Luce breathed a sigh of relief when he was gone and quickly returned to the other customers.

In an ordinary week, she usually served the same people every day. And it was very likely that in doing so, she'd been serving her stalker his food, cleaning up his dirty dishes, even taking his tips. She paused to look about the room, studying each and every face, trying to imagine one of these familiar people being evil enough to put her through such hell.

She didn't see the evil in any of them, but that didn't mean it wasn't there.

"Hey, Luce. Order up!" Harold called.

She headed for the kitchen, and the day passed.

It was sometime after two before Luce had a minute to herself. Without going into details, she told Harold she needed to run an errand, took the envelope of notes and headed up the street to the sheriff's office.

Tom Mize had been the sheriff in Little Top for almost ten years. The worst things he'd ever had to deal with were car wrecks. Every so often one of the Bateman boys would take a brother's car or boat without asking, which always caused a stir. Once one of them had even taken his brother's wife. But those situations usually worked themselves out — even the wife. Eventually they'd both dumped her and sent her packing.

This afternoon he was at his desk, writing up a report about an alien abduction of one of Ida Mae Coley's tomcats, despite his best efforts to convince her that it was most likely holed up somewhere, waiting for the snow to melt.

He had to admit that there had been a rash of disappearing pets in and around town, but he figured it was some varmint from off the mountain coming down to do a little in-town shopping of its own.

As he finished the report, he absently reached toward his shirt pocket. When he realized it was flat and that there was a reason his usual package of cigarettes wasn't in there, he sighed. He'd been trying to quit smoking for almost a week, and in a fit of need, had sent the deputy on desk duty to the supermarket to buy him a snack. He was expecting a cold Pepsi and a package of Ding Dongs at any moment, and he needed it bad. When he heard the door open, he looked up, anticipating the food that would get him past the need to smoke.

Only it wasn't the deputy who walked in; it was Luce Andahar. When he saw the envelope she was carrying and the look on her face, his frown deepened. This looked like work, which was something he didn't much like.

As Luce entered the office, the knot in her belly tightened just enough to make her heart skip a beat. She didn't know why she was so nervous around lawmen, but figured it had something to do with their connection to her life. It was a police uniform that she first remembered seeing after the wreck that had killed her family. And it had been the police who'd been on her case for running away from her uncle's home, until she'd reached the age of consent. Now this. How could she explain the gut-wrenching fear of knowing someone was watching her every move?

Tom Mize eyed her expression, then ventured a quick sweep of her body before giving her his full attention.

"Miss Andahar . . . how can I help you?"

She walked up to his desk, turned the manila envelope upside down and let all the notes spill out onto his desk.

"Here, now!" Mize said, as he grabbed at them to keep them from sliding everywhere. "What's this all about?"

"Do you remember a few months ago when I came to you with a threatening letter that I'd received from an unknown stalker?"

Mize frowned. "I wouldn't call a note from a secret admirer a threatening letter."

Luce pointed to the pile of folded notes. "And I don't call those love notes."

Mize frowned. "Are you claiming these

are more of the same?"

She nodded.

"Have a seat," he said shortly, then sat down and began unfolding the pieces of paper. By the time he'd gone through more than a dozen, he was frowning. When he finally opened the last, his face was flushed and there was an angry glint in his eyes.

"God almighty, woman. Why did you wait so long to tell me something like this was going on?"

"You didn't believe me the first time," she said. "I had no reason to assume you would change your mind."

His flush deepened. "Then I apologize if I've given you the impression that your safety was not important."

Luce began to relax. Jonah had been right after all to encourage her to bring these in.

"Do you have any idea who's doing this?" he asked.

"No. I've tried to pay attention to everyone I serve at the diner . . . but no one treats me any different than usual."

"And you've never seen anyone around your place?"

She hesitated, then scooted forward to the edge of her chair.

"Last night, just as it was getting dark, I thought I saw someone at the edge of the woods. But whoever it was either hid or left. When I started back into the house, my dog came running out, baying like crazy, and took off into the woods right in the same place where I thought I'd seen someone."

"What happened?" Mize asked.

"Jonah came home before I could think what to do and went into the woods after my dog, hoping to get a look at whoever it was. He found where Hobo had treed the man, then he found where the man's car had been parked, but the man was long gone."

Mize frowned. "Who's Jonah?"

"Jonah Gray Wolf. He's a friend . . . no, more than a friend. He's working for Mrs. Tuesday and staying with me."

Tom Mize looked startled. In all the years he'd known Luce Andahar, she'd never dated a local, never had a boyfriend of any sort.

He leaned forward. "When did this Jonah come to town? Have you ever considered the fact that he might be your stalker . . . that he's wormed his way into your affections by pretending to be your protector?"

"He came to town two or three days ago, and I've been getting notes for months. Besides . . . it's not him. If you knew him, you wouldn't even think that."

"Two or three days and he's already in your bed?"

Anger shot through her so fast that she stood before she thought.

"Who's in my bed is none of your damn business," she said. "You can find the man who's doing this to me or not. Either way, you and I have nothing left to talk about."

She stormed out of the office, slamming the door shut behind her.

Moments later, Mize's deputy, Earl Farley, came back carrying a small brown bag. He set it on the sheriff's desk, then pointed toward the door.

"Was that Luce Andahar I saw flying out of here?"

Mize sighed, then nodded. "Yeah, it was her." He swept the notes back into the manila envelope, then set it aside as he dug into the bag, pulled out the package of Ding Dongs and peeled it open. He sighed with bliss as the chocolate rolled across his tongue, momentarily stifling the need for a cigarette.

"She sure is pretty, isn't she?" Earl said.

Mize didn't bother to comment. He was too busy working on his second Ding Dong, then opening his bottle of pop.

Luce's face was still red when she got back

to the diner. Harold looked up, noticed the flush on her cheeks and waved her in.

"That cold air sure put some color in your face, girl. Come on over here and I'll make you a cup of hot chocolate."

"I'm fine," she said, as she stomped to the back room to hang up her coat.

A few minutes later, Jonah walked in.

"Hey, how you doing?" Harold called, as Jonah entered the diner. He'd already been informed of Luce's new travel arrangements and thought it a fine idea. He didn't want to lose the best waitress he'd ever had, and anything to keep her from having to walk to work every morning was good.

"I'm fine," Jonah said, as he turned to look for Luce. Then he took one look at her face and grabbed her by the shoulders.

"What happened?"

She was still so angry her voice was shaking. "I took the notes to the sheriff, like you wanted."

Jonah frowned. "What did he say?"

"At first he was all business, then, when I told him you'd chased after the man last night, he just zoned out. Once he found out about you being with me, all he wanted to know was how you got in my bed so fast."

Jonah flinched as if he'd been slapped; then his eyes suddenly glittered as a muscle jerked at the side of his jaw.

"Where is his office?"

"Down the street to the right, second building on the west corner."

"Wait here."

Luce was beginning to realize what she'd stirred up by telling him what had happened. She didn't want Jonah in trouble, and certainly didn't want to be the cause of it happening. She grabbed his arm.

"Wait, Jonah. Just let it go."

He grabbed her shoulders. "Damn it, Lucia. I said, wait here." Then he sighed regretfully, and added in a softer voice, "Please."

Without waiting for an answer, he was out the door and back in the pickup before Luce could think.

"What was that all about?" Harold asked.

"It's a long story," she said, and then sat down at the counter with her chin in her hands. "If you're still offering . . . I'm up for that hot chocolate now."

As always, Harold was the kind of man to live and let live. If she didn't want to talk about it, it was fine with him.

"Coming right up," he said, and headed to the kitchen.

Tom Mize was downing the last of his Pepsi

when the front door flew open, hitting the wall with a thump. Startled by the sudden appearance of the stranger standing in the doorway, he instinctively reached for his gun.

"Who the hell are you?" he asked.

Jonah walked to the desk, then stared Mize straight in the face.

"My name is Jonah Gray Wolf. I understand you have some concerns regarding Lucia Andahar's personal life."

Suddenly the Ding Dong that Mize had eaten was hanging at the back of his throat. Either it hadn't gone down just right, or it was on its way back up.

The deputy, Earl Farley, had heard the commotion and was now standing in the doorway to the back room where the jail cells were located, gawking at the dark-haired stranger.

Mize tried to hold his ground, but there was something in the big Indian's eyes that made him take a step back. "I don't allow anyone to come into my office and threaten me," he blustered.

Jonah took another step forward, then spoke, his voice so soft that Mize had to strain to hear it. "And I don't allow anyone — not even a pissant with a badge — to belittle my woman."

Mize felt sick. He'd never been afraid of another man in his life, but he was afraid now. "You can't —" The Indian pointed a finger at him, and the rest of his words stuck in his throat. He was thinking them, but they wouldn't come out. His fear grew. Was he having a stroke? What the hell was happening to him?

"No. *You* can't," Jonah said. "And if I find out that you've said one more denigrating, belittling thing about Lucia, you will be sorry. Do. You. Understand?"

Mize nodded.

"Are you going to take what's happening to her seriously, or do I have to take matters into my own hands?"

Mize tried to answer, but the words still wouldn't come out. A quick sheen of sweat broke out on his face as panic for his own health pushed past his fear of this man. Weakly, he dropped into his chair and put his head in his hands.

"Look at me," Jonah said.

Mize's head came up of its own volition, as if it were no longer attached to his body. Panic spread. He felt like a marionette, and Jonah Gray Wolf was pulling the strings.

"I'm not angry yet. I'm just pissed. Don't make me angry," Jonah said, then turned his back on the pair and, like Luce, slammed the door on his way out.

The moment Jonah left the building, Mize's faculties returned.

"Jesus . . . oh, Jesus. . . . Earl, see if Dr. Bigelow is in. I think I'm having a stroke."

Earl scrambled for the phone, while Tom Mize leaned back in his chair and closed his eyes.

At least now he knew what must have happened to Luce Andahar. She'd been witched by the man, just like he had. It was the only explanation.

D. J. Caufield was in West Virginia, holed up in a hotel in Charleston, waiting for the weather to clear. It would be at least a day's drive from here to where Jonah Gray Wolf had last been seen, and for now, the weather wasn't conducive to road travel.

Room service had just delivered a T-bone, cooked to a perfect medium rare, a baked potato with ranch dressing on the side, and a serving of steamed vegetables. D.J. had no intention of eating the vegetables, but they gave the plate an attractive appearance. Best of all, there was a piece of pecan pie waiting to become dessert. All in all, D.J. figured if one had to be delayed somewhere, this was as good a place as any.

The first bite was tasty. The second bite

even better. A raunchy porno flick was turned down low on the television. Watching was better than listening, anyway. It wasn't like porn films were known for their dialogue.

The night wore on. Around midnight, D.J. called it quits and crawled into bed. No need to rush all over the state like a bat out of hell. Patience was a virtue. From all the info in Gray Wolf's file, Bourdain had been after him for years. Another day or so couldn't matter.

ELEVEN

Jonah walked back into the diner as if nothing had happened, smiled at Harold, then put his arm around Luce, who had been nervously nursing her cup of hot chocolate.

"That looks good," he said.

She pushed it aside. "Is everything okay?"

He set the cup back in front of her, then brushed a curl from the corner of her eye.

"Everything is fine, honey. Finish your hot chocolate and then we'll head home, okay?"

Harold liked seeing someone be kind to Luce. She was such a solitary person, he'd thought she would never get herself a man friend. He did think they might have rushed things a bit, but Harold wasn't one to judge, and they both seemed happy. He hoped it lasted, for both their sakes.

"How's Miz Bridie doing?" Harold asked.

Jonah smiled. "She's fine. If she keeps cooking for me like she has been, I'm going to get too big for my clothes."

Harold grinned. "She's a corker, that's for sure. Don't see much of her since her Franklin passed. She comes into town now and then, but nothing like she used to."

Jonah frowned. "Really?"

"Yeah, she's become a real stranger."

"Where did she like to go when she came into town?"

"Oh, she and Ida Mae Coley used to buddy up and eat lunch together, and if I'm remembering right, Bridie is . . . was quite a reader. She had herself a library card and everything. Course, she might not see so good to read anymore. That might be one of the reasons why she quit coming down to the library and all. That and the fact that she doesn't drive anymore."

"How does she get her groceries?" Jonah asked, suddenly aware that he'd been oblivious to a lot of things concerning Bridie.

"I think she calls down to the supermarket with her list, and one of the boys who sacks up groceries usually drives her order up to her."

"She has no other family in the area . . . no children?" Jonah asked.

Harold shook his head. "Nope. Her and Franklin never had any kids, and Bridie's people were from Charleston. To my knowledge, they don't visit."

Jonah listened intently, absorbing Harold's comments, and decided that he might need to have a little conversation with his boss lady, but not this evening, when he went back to do evening chores. He would wait until tomorrow when she was rested and he'd had time to think things through. Still, it saddened him to think that she'd become stranded in her house because of her age and having no one to help make things easier.

Luce was listening to the conversation without taking part, but she already knew Jonah well enough to know that he was thinking of a way to make life better for Bridie. He was such a good man — and such a beautiful one. She smiled to herself. After that, she had to quit thinking about what that healing touch of his did to her, or she was likely to make herself blush.

Luce finished her hot chocolate; then, while Jonah and Harold were still talking about Bridie, she went to the back room to get her coat. She put it on as she was walking back, then slung her purse over her shoulder. Without thinking, she stuffed her hands in her pockets. As she did, she felt paper beneath her fingers. She hadn't noticed it earlier when she'd gone to the sheriff's office, then remembered that she'd been carrying that manila envelope and hadn't checked her pockets for anything.

Thinking it was probably an old grocery list, she pulled it out and started to throw it away, then recognized the blue paper and froze. Her hands were shaking, and her heart was pounding so hard she felt sick. She stood for a moment, staring down at the paper before she got the guts to unfolded it.

My hands are on your breasts and my dick is down your throat. How do you like it, bitch?

"Oh, Jesus . . . oh, Jonah . . ."

Luce went to her knees.

Harold jumped toward her, but Jonah was faster. He had her up and in his arms as she started to shake.

"He was here. In the diner. Sometime today, he was here. I fed the bastard. I poured his coffee. I cleaned up after his mess while he laughed in my face, and I didn't know it. I didn't know it!"

Harold was puzzled. His expression clearly said he had no idea what she meant, but Jonah did.

"Where was it?" he asked.

"In my pocket." Then Luce started to cry. "In my pocket!" she yelled, and slapped the note into Jonah's hands.

"What's going on?" Harold asked as Jonah

opened the note.

"I've been getting threatening notes from some stalker for months. Before, he'd left them at my house while I was here at work." Then she slapped a table with the flat of her hand, enraged by the continuing threats. "Now he puts this in my coat, knowing I'll find it, and that I'll know he's had his hand in my pocket. He's laughing at me! The bastard is laughing at me!"

Harold was horrified. "I'll call the sheriff."

Jonah's words were short and clipped. "We've already talked to the sheriff. I'll handle this myself." He pointed to Harold. "Take care of her until I get back."

"I live over the diner," Harold said. "There are outside stairs on the west side of the building. Come for her there."

"Wait!" Luce cried, as Jonah started out the door with the note in his hand.

Jonah stopped. "Lucia . . ."

"Please, Jonah, don't —"

"Trust me," he said.

Her voice broke as she struggled to speak through her tears. "I'm afraid for you."

"Be afraid for *him*," he said, and walked out the door.

Harold locked the door behind Jonah, then put his arm around Luce's shoulders as he guided her up the stairs in the back room that led to his apartment above.

"My goodness, girl . . . I'm so sorry you've been going through this on your own. Why didn't you tell me? Didn't you know I'd'a done all I could to help you?"

Luce didn't have a good answer. She'd spent so much of her adult life coping with problems by herself that it had never occurred to her to ask for help.

"I told Sheriff Mize when it started," she said.

"Well, now," Harold muttered, as he ushered her into the apartment, helped her off with her coat, then sat her down in an overstuffed chair covered with a patchwork afghan crocheted in colors of blue. The room smelled slightly of cigar smoke and the lemon drops that Harold favored, but it was clean, and she was safe. It was Jonah who had her worried.

"What did Mize say when you talked to him?" Harold asked.

"He called it a note from a secret admirer."

Harold cursed, then reached for the phone. "I'm calling Mize."

"I'm not talking to that son of a bitch," Luce said.

Harold frowned. "Is he the reason you were upset earlier?"

240

"Yes."

"Well, now . . . we'll just have to see about that," Harold said. "He got voted into office. If he doesn't know the meaning of respect, he can find himself voted out the same way."

He dialed the number to the sheriff's office, while Luce leaned back and closed her eyes.

"Hello, Earl. It's Harold Carter. I need to talk to Sheriff Mize." There was a moment of silence as he listened. "What's he doing over at Doc Bigelow's? A stroke? You don't say? Well, then, since you're in charge, you need to come on over to the diner. Use the back stairs. Yeah. What? Oh . . . Luce Andahar just found another note from her stalker. It was in her coat pocket. She was getting ready to go home. I don't know. That's why I'm calling you. Come over here and ask her yourself."

Luce could hear the faint sound of Earl Farley's voice coming through the receiver, but she couldn't have cared less. Whatever happened, it would be Jonah who would make it all right, just like he did everything else. And if he could track a person by scent as well as he healed them, then the sorry bastard who'd been leaving her notes was in trouble.

■ ■ ■ ■

Jonah clutched the note in his fist as he walked out onto the sidewalk. The stalker's scent was mingled with Luce's, which made him even angrier.

Bastard.

Without hesitation, he started down the sidewalk. His nostrils flared as he began to sort through the scents of Little Top. There was a small beauty shop on one corner and a bank on the other. He could smell diesel fuel, gasoline fumes, hair spray and some kind of animal feces. They weren't pleasant odors, but that was what was there.

He lifted the note to his nose, inhaling slowly to refresh his memory, then put it in his pocket. There would be a thread of this scent somewhere. All he had to do was find it.

Cold wind whipped through his hair, lifting it off his shoulders as he reached the end of the block. After checking for traffic, he crossed the street. His long, jeans-clad legs made short work of the distance as he strode up on the curb, then paused. Something teased at the back of his senses, and he turned slowly until it localized.

It was faint, but it was what he was searching for. The only problem was, this scent could only tell Jonah where the stalker had been, not where he was now. Still, it was a beginning, and he started to follow it step by step, moving with it as if it were a visible path.

Jonah followed it down the entire length of the block, and at each business, the scent was there, but why? What could possibly cause a man to need to visit a bank, a beauty shop, a barber shop, a lawyer's office and a plumber — and all in one day? When he crossed at another intersection, still moving north, the scent was fainter. He stopped, turned around and faced the way he'd come, trying to make sense of things. It was like the man was playing games, doubling back and forth on himself, trying to throw someone off his trail.

Another cold gust of wind blew down the front of Jonah's shirt. He buttoned his coat, then crossed the town square, still on track — still confused.

Ignoring the stares of people driving by, as well as the few he passed on foot, he continued to walk from one end of the little town to the other. And nearly everywhere he went, the scent was with him. If he hadn't known better, he might have thought he was trailing an animal that was meandering through a forest and marking every tree.

It was nearing dusk. He knew Luce was probably worried out of her mind, but he couldn't help it. This game with the stalker would end now. He'd crossed a line when he'd physically touched her personal belongings, putting his hand in her pocket, knowing that when she found his note, it would almost be like they were holding hands.

A car passed him as he started into the residential part of town. He felt the driver's gaze centered on his face. While he knew he was a stranger to most of them, he didn't have time to reassure the residents of Little Top that he meant them no harm.

Lights were coming on in one house after another as he moved from street to street. Twice he lost the scent, and once he actually thought he'd lost it for good, then found it again just as frustration started to kick in.

When he realized how strong it was here, his heart began to race. He was near. He could feel it.

When he turned east into a cul-de-sac, the scent was so strong that he almost gagged. There were only five houses on the cul-de-sac, with lights on in three of them.

A kid on a bike rode past him, while another across the street rode a skateboard up and down his sloped driveway like a pro.

Through one window, he could see a woman talking on the phone, and through another, an old man was sitting alone at the kitchen table, eating his supper with a book propped open in front of him.

He started toward the first house, then stopped when he heard the sound of an approaching vehicle. Out of habit, he turned toward the sound. It took him a few moments to recognize the car as the same one the mailman drove, right down to the American flag decal on the windshield. Then he recognized the face of the man he'd seen on the road delivering mail — the same one who'd delivered a package to Bridie. He started to nod a hello when the ground beneath his feet seemed to shift.

The scent was so strong he could taste it.

He stared at the car as it drove past, then all of a sudden, it hit him.

The mailman. It was the mailman.

Son of a bitch.

That was why the scent was everywhere. Who else but a mailman would have reason to visit every place in town?

When he realized that the mailman was turning up the driveway of a dark house in the middle of the cul-de-sac, he started running.

Mark Ahern was more than a little surprised by the sight of the Indian in his neighborhood. He'd seen him at Bridie Tuesday's house, and now he was here. But why?

He glanced up in the rearview mirror as he passed by, and when he saw the expression on the big man's face change to one of rage as the man suddenly gave chase, he panicked. He didn't know how it had happened, but something told him that the man *knew.*

He stomped the accelerator at the same time as he hit the garage-door opener. The door was barely up when he sailed inside. The brakes squealed as he slid to a stop on the concrete. The front bumper hit the wall with a thud as the garage door began to descend. He was fumbling with the door handle and scrambling to get out, when all of a sudden the man was in the garage.

Jonah grabbed him by the collar and was dragging him out of his car when Mark Ahern began to scream for help.

"Help! Somebody! Anybody! Help me! Help me!"

Then the garage door hit the floor with a soft thump, closing them in together. Mark was swinging at his attacker and kicking with both feet, but had yet to connect with a blow. Then suddenly the man's breath was hot against the back of Mark's neck as he found himself slammed facedown on the hood of his own car.

"Let me go," Mark said. "My neighbors will have heard me. They're probably calling the sheriff right now."

"Let's both call him," Jonah said, as he yanked the man up, then shoved him back down again, this time faceup against the car. "Let's tell him all about the nasty little game you've been playing with Lucia Andahar."

Mark groaned inwardly. He'd been right. The man knew! But how?

Jonah saw the shock on the mailman's face. He knew he had the right man. Now it was time to make him sorry.

He grabbed Ahern and slammed him face-first against the wall of the garage.

Blood splattered as the blow broke Ahern's nose.

"Oh, God . . . my nose . . . my nose," Ahern moaned.

"Next time it'll be your neck," Jonah said.

Ahern began to cry. "You're crazy! I don't know what you're talking about," he said, and tried to get away, but something was wrong with his arms. They moved, but not where he wanted them to go. They were flopping at the ends of his shoulders like the arms of a rag doll. Panicked, he tried to scream, but nothing came out of his mouth.

Jonah moved closer until there were only inches separating their faces.

Mark saw his own reflection in those strange, gold-colored eyes and found himself unable to look away. He was totally helpless — at the mercy of a stranger who he was sure was going to kill him. It was ironic that, at that moment, he realized he was in the same position as his other victims had been before he'd finished with them. It was not a comforting thought.

"I said . . . talk," Jonah said.

Mark opened his mouth. "I didn't hurt her."

Jonah grabbed him by the collar with both hands and flung him across the hood of his car, then circled it and dragged him up to his feet.

"Yes, you did, you son of a bitch, in every way that counts. And you know it. You tortured her with words. What was next? The real thing, or are you the kind of coward who can't get it up and has to be satisfied with just talking about it?"

Mark didn't want to tell him, but he couldn't seem to stop himself. When the words began to spill out of his mouth, he was horrified. All the years he'd gotten away with murder because he wasn't the kind of man who had to brag, and now he was talking louder and faster than Pastor Wagner on Sunday morning. The only explanation was that he was losing his fucking mind. That was it. He'd gone crazy and just hadn't known it.

"I picked her because she was alone. Because she didn't have anyone to protect her. I always pick them like that. Those are the best kind. They scream the loudest and bleed the longest."

Rage swept through Jonah like wildfire in a drought-stricken land, burning hot, burning wild, burning out of control.

He grabbed Ahern by the arm and dragged him into the house.

"Where is the proof? Show me! The blue paper! The red and black ink pens! Where are your little keepsakes? And don't tell me you don't have any, because I can see them in your head."

Ahern wanted to run, but his legs would function only to follow the Indian as he dragged him from room to room in his house.

Ahern felt his shoulder separate as Jonah yanked him hard. "Tell me now, or I swear to God I'll kill you where you stand," Jonah muttered.

Screaming in pain, Ahern could only point to the library. And once Jonah dragged him in there, he found himself digging out the blue pad and his pens from a drawer, and showing them to Jonah. Then he took a key out of his pocket and held it in the air.

"What's this for?" Jonah asked.

Ahern pointed to a large ornate trunk against the opposite wall.

"Open it," Jonah ordered.

Ahern staggered to the trunk, dropped to his knees and jammed the key into the lock. It turned with a click. He fell backward as Jonah looked inside.

The scent of death was everywhere, on everything. Jonah didn't touch anything inside, but he knew within seconds that the trinkets and scarves, the purses and wallets, were all trophies from this man's other victims. He felt their fear; he knew that they'd died horrible and violent deaths.

Ahern was rolling on the floor, squalling and begging for mercy as Jonah backed away from the trunk, then pointed at him.

"Get up."

Ahern stood, but when he tried to run, all he managed to do was wet himself.

"You're coming with me," Jonah said, and grabbed him by the arm.

Ahern tried to say no. He tried to pull

free. He tried everything he could think of to get away, but the only things that worked were his feet and legs, and they were moving at someone else's whim.

Jonah eyed the pad of blue paper and the pens Ahern had pulled out of his desk, then decided to leave them where they lay. Those were things for the sheriff to deal with. He headed for the door, taking Ahern with him. Moments later, they were outside, going down the sidewalk, then across the street, moving back toward town.

The kid on the skateboard stopped to stare. Something was wrong with Mr. Ahern. Blood was running out of his nose, and it looked like he'd peed his pants. Startled, he ran into the house to tell his dad, who looked out the window, then quickly called the sheriff.

Tom Mize was in his patrol car on the way back from Doc Bigelow's office, relieved to know he had not suffered a stroke or a heart attack after all, when he got the call from Earl that an Indian had assaulted Mark Ahern and was dragging him down the street.

He didn't know what the hell was going on, but just the thought of facing that man again made him sick to his stomach.

"I need assistance," Mize told Earl. "Get yourself into a patrol car ASAP."

"But, Sheriff, there won't be anybody to man the dispatch if I —"

"Move it, Earl! Now!"

Deputy Earl Farley keyed off the mike and grabbed his coat. He was on the way out the door when he realized that Harold Carter was waiting for him to come talk to Luce Andahar about her stalker. Well, she would just have to wait. He checked his handgun, making sure it was riding safe in the holster, then headed for his patrol car. He'd never shot at anything but paper targets and critters with fur or feathers, and he hoped this wasn't the day that all changed.

Ahern was only vaguely aware that people were coming out of their houses. Some even began following, calling out to know what was happening, but Jonah didn't answer and Ahern couldn't, so the crowd kept their distance.

Someone called Shug Marten to share the gossip, and he dropped his half-eaten sandwich and grabbed the phone to call Harold Carter.

Harold was heating up some soup for himself and Luce when the phone rang.

"Hey Luce, get that, would you?"

She picked up the receiver. "Carter residence."

Shug was surprised to hear a woman's voice at Harold's place, then realized it was Luce.

"Luce, is that you?"

"Yes . . . Shug?"

"Yeah, it's me. Something big is happening. I just got a call saying your Indian friend beat the hell out of Mark Ahern and is dragging him toward town. I just thought —"

Luce dropped the phone and grabbed her coat.

Harold caught her on the way out the door.

"Whoa, there . . . where's the fire?"

"That was Shug. He said that Jonah is heading toward Main Street with Mark Ahern, who's beat all to hell." She shuddered. "That means Mark is the man who's been stalking me." Then she covered her face with her hands. "Why? Why would he do something so ugly? I thought he was a good person."

Harold patted her shoulder. "I don't know what's happening, but what say we both go find out? Let me get my coat."

Moments later they were down the stairs and hurrying out onto the sidewalk. A couple of cars drove past, and the barber shouted a hello to Harold as he locked up his business for the night.

Harold waved without looking to see who it was, then pointed down the street to their right.

"Down there! I see people running."

They started down the street together, but within moments, the crowd parted and Luce got a glimpse of a tall, dark-haired man dragging another man by the arm.

Jonah.

She began to run.

She ran past the beauty shop and the bank, and then started to cross the intersection just as Earl Farley came flying around the corner in a patrol car.

"Oh, Lord," Luce muttered, and jumped back in fright.

Jonah was oblivious to the crowd and their cries of alarm. When one man roared up in a four-wheel truck and jumped out with a rifle in his hand, Jonah never missed a step.

"Stop right there!" the man yelled, and then lifted the rifle to his shoulder. "I'll shoot you where you stand if you don't turn him loose."

Jonah turned and looked at him. Without raising his voice, he fixed the man with a steady stare.

"Get in your truck and go home. Now."

The man turned pale. His hands began to shake, and despite every instinct he had to shoot the stranger who'd beat up their mailman, he put down his rifle, got in his truck and drove away.

All that did for the crowd was add to the mystery of what was going on. By the time Jonah got to Main Street, at least forty people were behind him, shouting and talking and calling out to Ahern in concern.

He felt their fear and distress, but he also knew they wouldn't act. Then he heard an approaching siren. Finally he could turn Ahern over to the authorities.

At that moment Tom Mize came flying out of an alley in his patrol car, running hot, with lights and siren blasting. At the same time, Earl Farley, in the other patrol car, turned the corner by the bank.

Jonah sighed, then braced himself for the impact he saw coming. Damn it all to hell, this was going to make turning the stalker over to the sheriff even more difficult than it already would have been.

Earl screamed out in shock as Sheriff Mize shot out of the alley right in front of him.

Mize caught a glimpse of movement from the corner of his eye, and turned to look just as Earl hit the brakes and turned left.

Cursing the world and everyone in it, Mize hit the brakes and turned right. Both cars began to spin out. The ensuing crash was like something out of a Hollywood movie.

Mize sailed past Earl on the first spin, as Earl's car began to slide, leaving wide streaks of black on the concrete. The scent of burning rubber filled the air. Then, somehow, they managed to miss each other on the first spin. Just when the onlookers were about to breathe a sigh of relief, the separate vehicles slid sideways, and again, collision was imminent.

Still cursing, Mize did the only thing he could think of and jammed his car into Park. The roar and clank that followed from the engine was the sound of every gear in the box shearing off to the hub. His car shuddered and jerked as Earl's car sailed on past, coming to a stop up on the curb only a few inches from the plate-glass windows of the jewelry store.

The crowd was silent, waiting to see what happened next.

Both sheriff and deputy sat for a moment, then, in unison, got out of their cars, and turned and looked at each other.

Jonah took that moment to drag Mark Ahern out into the street, then dump him at Mize's feet.

Sheriff Mize looked at Ahern, then at Gray Wolf. He could still remember the helpless feeling of being unable to speak or move, and was almost afraid to open his mouth. Still, with so many witnesses, he felt safe in giving it a try.

"What have you done?" he asked.

"Talk," Jonah said, pointing to Ahern.

Mark rolled over onto his back, then opened his mouth.

"I'm the one who's been stalking Luce Andahar. I've been leaving her notes for months. I set a trap and tried to kill her dog so she wouldn't have any protection. It didn't work. Then I left a note in her coat pocket when I was at the diner this morning."

He covered his face with his hands, unable to believe what had just come out of his mouth.

To a man, the crowd was silent, stunned by what they were hearing.

Then Jonah looked up and saw Luce. She was coming toward him. Her steps were staggering, and her face was pale. He could tell she was in shock. He couldn't blame her. The damned mailman. Who would have guessed?

She walked into his arms and hid her face against his chest as he held her close.

"You did it," she whispered, and then looked up at him. "Is it over . . . really over?"

"It will be if Sheriff Mize can find the time to arrest the bastard," Jonah muttered.

Mize was staring at Ahern as if he'd never seen him before.

"Is this true, Mark? Why would you do such a thing?"

Ahern started to hedge, then Jonah kicked the sole of his shoe and said, "Don't lie."

Ahern's nose was so swollen he could barely see, and his mind was in a panic, trying to find a way to shut up. But like before, he began spilling his guts without reserve.

"I've been doing it for years. It's what I do. Luce was only one of many. I pick out the ones who are alone. They're the easiest."

Mize felt like he was going to throw up.

"What are you saying? That you've been stalking and torturing women for years?"

Ahern nodded.

Jonah held Luce a little tighter as he glared at Ahern, who quickly shut up.

"Mize . . . before you search his house, you might want to get a warrant, just so everything is proper. Because besides the notepad and pens on his desk, which match the notes he was leaving for Lucia, there's a trunk in his office with trophies from his

258

other kills."

Luce gasped as her legs went weak. *Kills?*

Tom Mize swayed as if Jonah had punched him. "Kills? He kills them?"

"Said he'd been doing it for years. He keeps mementos of his victims in that trunk. You may be solving a lot of cold cases with this arrest, so do it right."

Then Jonah squatted down in front of Ahern. "Don't lie. Don't leave out a thing, or I'll know it, and I'll make you sorry."

Ahern glared. "You can't —"

"I can, and I will," Jonah said, then leaned closer to Ahern until his lips were against his ear. "And they'll never find your body. Do you understand what I'm saying to you?"

Something slid through Ahern's mind — something darker and more frightening than the thoughts that already lived in him — and he knew, without understanding how, that the Indian could do what he said.

He blinked. When he looked again, the Indian was gone.

Jonah moved past the crowd without looking at any of them. His focus was on Lucia. She was trembling and crying, and it was making him sick. He couldn't stand it any longer.

He picked her up in his arms and cradled

her against his chest, carrying her as he would have a child. She shuddered on a sob, then laid her head in the crook of his neck and closed her eyes.

Shock rippled through every facet of her body. She couldn't quit thinking of all the times she'd served that man food, laughed with him, been alone with him as he'd stop to visit when he delivered her mail. It was nothing short of a miracle that she was still alive.

"You're going to be all right," Jonah said softly, as he carried her toward Bridie's old truck.

Harold had fallen into step behind them without talking, but once they reached the diner, he called out to Jonah.

"She left her purse upstairs. Hang on a minute and I'll go get it."

Jonah eased Lucia into the truck seat, then laid his hand against her cheek.

She could feel the warmth of his hand and hear the deep timbre of his voice close to her face, but she couldn't seem to keep her eyes open.

Jonah kissed the side of her face, then whispered softly, "It's over, Lucia. You have nothing left to fear. You are strong. You are safe. Rest. We'll be home soon."

Lucia sighed as his voice swept through

her, wiping her mind clean of everything except peace.

She remembered leaning back; then, within seconds, she was asleep.

Jonah stepped forward and took the purse from Harold at the bottom of the stairs and had started toward the truck when Harold called him back.

"I just want to shake your hand, son," Harold said gruffly. "You did a fine thing, taking care of her like you did. I don't rightly understand how it all happened, but I'm sure grateful she doesn't have to live in any more fear."

"So am I," Jonah said, as he shook the man's hand. "We'll see you tomorrow," he added.

Harold cleared his throat nervously. "Listen . . . if she isn't up to —"

"She'll be fine," Jonah said. "You'll see."

And then they drove away.

He carried Lucia into the cabin, then laid her on her bed.

Hobo whined anxiously as he followed Jonah into the bedroom.

"She'll be fine," he said gently. "But if you feel like staying with her, I know she'd like that."

Hobo sniffed at her hand hanging off the side of the mattress, licked the ends of her fingers, then lay down on the rag rug beside her bed and put his chin on his paws.

"I'll leave the door open," Jonah said. "Let me know when you want to go out."

Hobo blinked.

It was enough. Jonah got the message.

Outside, night was upon them. For the first time in months, all was well in Lucia's world.

And Jonah's was about to come undone.

TWELVE

D. J. Caufield had been in West Virginia for several days, flashing Gray Wolf's picture around in small towns along the way, but with no success. Disgusted and cold, D.J. finally stopped for lunch at a little café in a small town just inside the Monongahela National Forest. Local programming was showing on the television hanging over the counter while D.J. was chowing down on a BLT, when they began flashing a news bulletin. Caufield listened absently as the journalist began his report from a town called Little Top, where a serial killer had been jailed days earlier. According to the reporter, the man who'd committed the murders, Mark William Ahern, would not be moved from where he was now incarcerated until jurisdiction for his crimes could be determined. And also, according to the reporter, the FBI would be taking over the case, since there were many deaths and they crossed several state lines.

None of this story was of much interest to Caufield, until the name Jonah Gray Wolf was mentioned as the person who'd brought him in. At that point, the sandwich was forgotten.

Caufield pulled out a map and began looking to see how far Little Top, West Virginia, was from this current location. At best guess, it was about a half-day's drive. The town had better have a decent motel, because that was going to be the first order of business. It was too damned cold for stakeouts.

Luce felt like the weight of the world was gone from her shoulders. She went through the days with a permanent smile on her face. All the regulars at Harold's diner had their say about what she'd endured, then added their own choices for meting out justice to Mark Ahern.

Luce kept reminding them that it was only thanks to Jonah that she was still alive, unlike the earlier victims, who'd been reduced to nothing but trophies in Mark Ahern's steamer trunk.

But Jonah's heart was heavy, although he did a good job hiding his concerns. He hadn't known that a national news crew had descended on Little Top until he'd gone to pick Luce up from work the day after Ahern's arrest. But the moment he'd seen them and learned that Sheriff Mize was giving out interviews right and left about how he'd come to be in possession of a serial killer, his heart had almost stopped.

It was no longer a case of *whether* Bourdain found him again so much as *when* the next hunter would arrive. He wanted to grab Lucia and run, but he'd already made up his mind not to drag her into the kind of life he was forced to live. And yet, leaving her behind was equally impossible, even though everyone in town knew about them, which not only meant Lucia's life was in danger again, but that he'd been the one to put it there.

The small mountain town was still full of news crews, and would be until Ahern was moved to another location for incarceration until trial. There were many — too many — unfamiliar faces, which kept Jonah on constant alert. He had no way of knowing who was legitimate and who might be hunting bounty. He was sick to his stomach about the mess he'd put her in. Even worse, he didn't know how to tell her.

But there was one thing he *had* done right in the past few days. He'd brought Bridie into town to spend the day with her old friend, Ida Mae. Bridie was over the moon with excitement, already dressed and waiting for her ride when Jonah arrived to do chores.

Jonah saw the light on in the kitchen and stopped at the back of the house to check on Bridie before he went to do chores.

She met him at the door, pink-cheeked, her eyes sparkling. "Good morning, Jonah. Have you had your breakfast?"

"Yes, ma'am. I have." He eyed the clothes she was wearing and realized she was already ready to go.

"Have you talked to Ida Mae?"

Bridie nodded. "Oh, yes. We talked on the phone last night for almost an hour. She's been piecing a quilt for a Christmas present for one of her granddaughters, and I told her I'd help her set the batting. That's quite a job for one person, you know . . . trying to get the backing and the quilt top in proper perspective with the batting in between."

Jonah smiled. "I hope you're not planning on working all day?"

"Oh, no . . . we're going to go to Harold's for lunch. Land sakes, it's been ages since we've done that. And Ida Mae says she'll

266

run me by the library before the day is over. I can't remember the last time I checked out something to read. They've probably got all kinds of new books since I was there."

"That's good," Jonah said. "Remember, Luce or I can always return them for you, and whenever you want to check out some more, or go into town for another lunch with Ida Mae, all you have to do is say so."

Bridie patted Jonah on the cheek as if he were a child.

"You're a good boy, Jonah. I don't know what set you to thinking about me this way, but I'm sure glad you did. Ever since I quit driving, I've just turned myself into a hermit. Franklin would have had a fit at the way I've been acting."

"It's all in the past," Jonah said. "You've given me the use of your truck while I'm working for you. The least I can do is act as chauffeur now and then."

"Can we go now?" she asked.

Jonah glanced at the clock. "It's not quite eight o'clock. Do you think Ida Mae will be up this early?"

Bridie grabbed her coat from the back of the kitchen chair and began putting it on as she reached for her purse.

"Oh, yes. Ida Mae is an early riser, just like me. We can have coffee and catch up on some gossip before we get to the quilt."

"Then that's what we'll do," Jonah said.

He promptly loaded her up and took her right into town and dropped her off at Ida Mae's house, which was on the edge of town. As soon as Ida Mae opened the door to let Bridie in, she turned and waved him away.

He was still smiling as he drove back through town. The light turned red just as he reached the intersection. As he was waiting for it to change, he saw Deputy Farley standing outside the sheriff's office, and from what he could tell, it appeared that Farley was being interviewed.

To his dismay, the moment Earl saw him sitting at the light, he waved, then pointed the news crew in his direction. He saw the cameras swing toward him just as the light changed, so he accelerated through the intersection and headed up the mountain as fast as the law would allow.

All morning, as he went through his chores, he kept watching the road, making sure no one had followed him. He wasn't in the mood to talk about Mark Ahern or his part in the man's capture.

He finished the chores before tending to a task Bridie had mentioned on their way into town. She had three big pumpkins and a half dozen gourds of all shapes and sizes sitting out on her front porch. Her plan was to add a couple of square bales of hay to use as part of a harvest display.

Tomorrow was Halloween, and even though no one trick-or-treated this far away from town, she still liked to observe the occasion. And, she had claimed, the decor went right into Thanksgiving without changing a thing.

Observing holidays was a luxury Jonah had never had. Yet here he was, unloading hay and stacking her pumpkins. When he finished, he dug through the old toolshed until he found some lumber and a hammer and nails, and loaded up the truck. There were panels in the corral fence that were broken, and one that had rotted through. And so he worked, stopping only to eat the lunch that he'd brought for himself.

It was nearing time to go get Lucia when he heard an odd sound in the distance. Sounds carried in the mountains, and it was difficult to tell exactly what he was hearing or how far away it might be. He had begun dusting the hay from his clothes as he paused to listen, and he heard what sounded like the squeal of brakes and then a terrible noise of shattering tree trunks and crushing metal. He didn't know what had happened, but he knew it wasn't good. He jumped in the truck and headed down the mountain as fast as he dared.

He sailed past Luce's cabin without a glance. The closer he got to town, the more anxious he became. He could feel the oppression of pain and fear, and in his mind, he was hearing screams and cries for help. When he topped the next hill and started down, his chest tightened. There was a path of broken trees a few hundred feet ahead that led past the ditch, then into the sloping forest and down the side of the mountain.

When he got closer, he could see rising smoke from somewhere down below. As he slid to a stop and jumped out, the smell of diesel fuel and the scent of burning rubber was thick in the air. Then he heard voices screaming and crying for help, and he ran to the verge, where the trees had been mowed down.

Through the trees and the smoke, he could barely see the rear end of a vehicle, but what he saw stopped his heart. The back door of a yellow school bus was hanging ajar. From where he was standing, he could see one child hanging headfirst out of the back of the bus, while another had been thrown free and was lying near a wheel. He had no way of knowing if the bus had run over the child before it had come to a stop, or if either one of the two was still alive.

Just as he started to go down, a car came around the curve. He stopped, ran back up to the road and waved them down.

The man and woman inside leaned forward as Jonah spoke.

"Do you have a cell phone?"

"Uh . . . yeah, but what —"

"Call the ambulance. Call the sheriff. Tell them to get all available medical help up here. The school bus went off the side of the mountain."

The woman suddenly screamed and jumped out of the car before anyone could stop her.

"My child! She's on that bus! Oh, dear God, she's on that bus!" Jonah grabbed her by the shoulders. There was no time to waste on protocol as he yelled at the man, "Make those calls! Now!"

The man's face was colorless and his hands were shaking as he tried to punch in the correct numbers. When Jonah was satisfied that help was on the way, he turned to the woman.

"Stay here. I'll find your daughter."

"I'm going down!" she screamed. "She's my child. You can't stop me. She's mine!"

She wrenched out of Jonah's grasp before he could argue, and down she went, stumbling and falling, then rolling before she could get back to her feet.

Jonah leaped over the side of the mountain and went down behind her, slipping as he ran but managing to stay upright. He passed the woman and kept on going, past shattered tree trunks, jumping over a backpack full of schoolbooks, dodging someone's Power Rangers lunch box, trying not to think of the children who owned them, or if they were still alive. He just needed to get there.

The inside of the bus was in chaos. Children were crying, some calling for their mothers, others only moaning. There was a little boy named Travis, who was caught between two seats that had been crushed together. He was crying for his mama in between screaming from the pain.

Suddenly he felt hands on his face and heard a man's deep voice pushing through the panic, ironing out the pain.

"What's your name, son?" Jonah asked.

"Travis . . . my name is Travis."

"Okay, Travis, I've got you now. Don't cry. Everything's going to be all right," Jonah said, and with a surge of adrenaline, pulled the seats far enough apart to get the boy out.

Jonah ran his hands over the boy's body like a scanner, searching for internal injuries and blood loss. When he determined that the child was not in immediate danger, he picked him up and moved to the open doorway at the back of the bus just as the mother arrived.

"My daughter! My daughter! Her name is Susie. Do you see her? She has red hair, with a green hair ribbon."

"What's your name?" Jonah shouted.

The woman stuttered. "Georgia Benton . . . but —"

"Take this child. Lay him down over there beside the other two, then come back."

"Susie! I need to find Susie!"

"Take the boy!" Jonah said, and thrust Travis into her arms. "I'll find your daughter."

Georgia Benton looked down at the child in her arms, then somehow pulled herself together.

"Well, my goodness, Travis Mize, you've gotten yourself all bunged up, haven't you, son? Don't cry, sweetie. It's gonna be all right."

She carried the boy over to where Jonah had laid the first two he'd found, the ones he'd seen from the road; then she ran back to the bus. As she ran, she saw her husband coming down in much the same way she had and said a silent prayer that he got down in one piece.

By now several cars were gathering up on the roadside, and in the distance, the sounds of approaching sirens could be heard. Jonah worked as fast as he could, assessing the seriousness of the injured against those that had escaped injury and were simply crying from the shock of the wreck.

He moved from seat to seat, helping the ones who weren't hurt to get out, while making sure that the ones who were still trapped weren't in immediate danger of dying.

It wasn't until he got to the front of the bus that he found the first fatality. The driver was dead, and there was nothing Jonah could do about that.

Sick to his stomach, he turned away and began renewing his search for a little red-headed girl named Susie, but she was nowhere to be found.

More rescuers had arrived, and they began piling into the bus with Jonah, asking what needed to be done.

"That girl's right arm is broken, and she has a cut on her head. Get her out next," he said, as he pointed to a child who was lying beneath the seats.

Two men quickly knelt to the task as another appeared at the back of the bus.

"Hand one to me!" the man yelled, then took the next child that was pulled free.

"What about Beau?" one of them asked, pointing at the driver.

Jonah shook his head.

The man flinched as if he'd been slapped. "Lord have mercy. He's my wife's uncle. This is bad."

Then Georgia appeared at the back of the bus again.

"Susie! Did you find Susie?"

"No, ma'am. Not yet," Jonah said.

When she realized there were no more children on the bus, she began to wail.

"Oh Lord, Lord, is she under the bus? Please God, don't let her be under it."

Jonah jumped past Georgia as he got out of the bus. He glanced toward the injured children, who had been carried a good distance away from the accident. The rescuers had taken off their own coats and put them over the cold and injured children while waiting for medical help to arrive.

At the moment, everyone there was being cared for. It was the missing child that had Jonah worried. He began to circle the wreck on his hands and knees, trying to see if anyone was trapped beneath. Just when he was beginning to fear the worst, a hawk circling overhead suddenly screeched. The sound echoed down the mountain.

Jonah heard.

He stood abruptly, then looked up just as the hawk screeched again.

Suddenly he turned and began running back up the way they'd come.

"Wait! Wait!" Georgia screamed. "You said you'd find my Susie. You promised me."

But Jonah wasn't listening to her. He was following the cry of the hawk leading him to the missing child.

One minute he was holding on to the underbrush in an effort to pull himself up, and the next thing he knew, he was looking down into the face of a little girl with a green hair ribbon in her red hair.

He fell to his knees, then pulled her out from under the mass of broken trees and scrub brush. Her face was a mass of cuts and bruises, and there were long, ugly gashes on her tiny little legs. The blue corduroy jumper she was wearing was black with her own blood.

Jonah's heart was pounding as he ran his fingers down the side of her neck, searching frantically for a pulse, and when he found it, he went weak with relief. It was faint and thready, but it was there, and it was all he needed. Unaware of the people gathering around him, he laid his hands on her body and closed his eyes.

Within moments, the air began to vibrate, then the trees, then the earth. An aura of white spilled from Jonah's body, down his arms and into the child, like water going over a falls.

Georgia's mother was still screaming and climbing, following the Indian who'd promised her a miracle. Then she saw her little girl, lying broken and bloody on the ground. Before she could scream her child's name, she felt a vibration around her and thought it was an earthquake — or the end of the world. But then she saw the light surround the man and her child, and her heart began to pound. She tried to move and fell to her knees instead. All she could think was that an angel was among them. She began to pray.

A paramedic was coming down the hillside dragging a stretcher, when he came upon the sight. He stopped in midstride as if he'd been nailed to the spot; he stared in disbelief, watching as the cuts on the little girl's face began to disappear. He saw the gashes on her legs closing, saw her eyelids begin to flutter and her chest begin to rise. He didn't know he was crying until the tears ran across his lips and he tasted their salt.

One after the other, people saw but didn't understand — not completely — not until the little girl opened her eyes and saw her mother kneeling a few feet away.

"Mommy . . . the bus broke."

Jonah picked up the child and laid her in her mother's arms. And while Georgia was praising God for the angel, Jonah headed back down the mountain to the other injured children.

An EMT was putting a brace around Travis Mize's neck when Jonah returned. Jonah knelt beside the medic and then touched his arm. "Please?"

The medic started to order Jonah out of the way, then found himself staring into eyes the color of a hot summer sunset. He felt an odd loss of focus, then rocked back on his heels.

Jonah slid between the man and the child, then laid his hands on the little boy's chest. "Travis?"

The little boy was wailing.

"Look at me, son. It's going to be all right."

Again the air vibrated, the trees quivered and the light enveloped them both. One man fell to his knees and began to pray, while others were convinced they were losing their minds.

After Travis sat up and announced that he'd lost his baseball glove, Jonah moved from him to another child, then another, calming, healing, doing what he'd been born to do. When the last child had been touched, calmed and healed, Jonah stood up, then looked around.

Sheriff Mize was holding Travis.

"Is he yours?" Jonah asked.

Mize couldn't speak. His face was pale, and his eyes held a wild, frightened expression as he clutched his little boy close to his chest.

"Did we get a head count?" Jonah asked.

Mize shuddered, swallowed twice around the knot in his throat, then took out his handkerchief and blew his nose loudly before he could pull himself together.

"Ten."

"Was that counting the driver?"

Mize couldn't quit staring at the Indian. He'd seen what he'd done with his own eyes and still couldn't wrap his mind around it.

"Uh . . . yeah, counting Beau."

"I'm sorry about him," Jonah said. "If they're dead, I can't help them." He looked back at the children, taking a mental head count. Eight. Nine counting Susie, who was still above them with her mother. They'd accounted for all of them.

"Then we have them all," Jonah said.

Mize's lips went slack. "God Almighty, man. Who are you? *What* are you?"

Jonah sighed. "You know who I am. I'm going to go now. Lucia will be worrying."

"Uh, no . . . someone told her you were here. She hitched a ride with Earl. I think she's up on the road waiting for you."

Jonah nodded, then quietly walked away.

As he started back up the incline toward the road, the rescuers stared. One reached out to touch his arm. Another backed away from him, yielding to his presence.

He wouldn't let himself think about the repercussions of what he'd just done. None of it mattered as long as the children were okay. All he wanted now was to get away from this place and go home.

When Jonah was fifteen minutes late, Luce had started to worry. Then, when a few more minutes came and went and she began to hear sirens, then saw people in cars driving hell-bent for leather out of town toward the mountain, she got scared.

Despite Harold's arguments, she got her coat and purse, and started walking. Something was wrong. She just needed to make sure Jonah was all right.

Halfway out of town, Deputy Farley saw her walking and picked her up on his way toward the scene. By the time she got there, she knew what had happened to the bus, just not what had happened to Jonah.

When she saw his truck, she panicked. She jumped out of the patrol car before it had stopped rolling and ran to the side of the mountain. When she looked down, all she could see was the back end of the school bus, and people running back and forth, carrying children in their arms.

But when she saw Jonah jump out of the back of the bus, she knew what was happening and that he was risking his life to make it happen. By healing the injured children in front of all those people, he was giving himself away.

But there was nothing she would do to change what he was. She sat down on the side of the road to wait. Jonah was doing what he'd been born to do. The rest would have to take care of itself.

A short while later, a couple of news vans pulled up. She saw them setting up cameras and interviewing first one person, then another, trying to piece together what had happened. When they shoved a camera into one weeping parent's face, she looked away in disgust, having come to the conclusion that reporters descended on tragedy like vultures on carrion.

An hour passed. The sun was only minutes away from setting when Luce saw a man with dark hair coming slowly up the slope.

She stood, willing him to look up, wanting him to know she was waiting. Then he did, and when she saw the look on his face, her breath caught on a sob.

Jonah saw her standing at the edge of the road, waiting — waiting for him. It was all he could do to keep walking, but he knew that if he got to Lucia, everything else would work out.

His mind was exhausted, his body on the verge of collapse. He'd never healed so many at one time, but there had been no choice. It had been all of them — or none of them. No way could he have chosen who should live and who should die.

His face felt stiff, his skin burned from the cold. When he looked down at himself, he realized he was covered in blood and there was a button missing from his shirt. Then he heard Lucia call out his name.

"Jonah."

He focused on her face and found the

strength to keep walking. Somehow he found himself standing before her. She opened her arms.

"My clothes . . . the blood . . . I'll get you all —"

"Hush," she said softly. "Just come here."

He took a step forward, letting her arms enfold him — letting the beat of her heart steady his own — and knew he was home.

"I'm sorry about the driver," she said.

Surprised that she understood the depths of his regret at not being able to save them all, he bit his lip to keep from weeping.

Unaware that a camera had been trained on his arrival and had captured their reunion, Jonah finally pulled away.

"Bridie is at Ida Mae's house. I need to get her before we can go home."

"Then let's go," she said.

Together they drove past the emergency vehicles and patrol cars, weaving through the onlookers who'd gathered at the sides of the road.

It was dark by the time they got Bridie in the truck and started back up the mountain.

At first Bridie was full of her day, and then she saw Jonah's face and the condition of his clothes. "Are you in one piece, boy?" she asked sharply.

"Yes, ma'am. I'm fine," Jonah said.

"Then what on earth . . . ?" Bridie muttered.

Luce glanced at Jonah, then patted Bridie's hand. "There was an accident. The school bus went over the mountain. Beau Davis was killed."

Bridie gasped, then muttered a soft prayer. "Lord, Lord, had he delivered all the kids?" she asked.

"There were nine still on the bus," Jonah said.

"Oh, no. What about . . . were they —"

"They're all okay," Jonah said.

Bridie shook her head. "That's a miracle. A plain miracle that none of the children were hurt."

Jonah just nodded. He didn't want to talk about it anymore.

Luce saw the exhaustion on his face and began talking to Bridie about her day with Ida Mae, so Jonah could have a few moments of peace.

After they finally delivered Bridie to her house and Jonah was satisfied that she was safely locked in for the night, he started back to the truck to tell Luce he still had chores to do. But she was already out and heading toward the back of the house.

"I did this plenty of times before you came," she said. "You just tend to Molly.

I'll get the chickens put up."

Jonah was thankful for Lucia's help, and since Molly's milk was slacking off, he was only milking her once a day. For that he was also thankful. It meant he didn't have to milk her tonight.

As soon as the animals were fed and housed, they headed back home. When they drove up to the cabin, Hobo was waiting for them on the porch. He bayed a welcome as they got out.

Jonah helped Lucia out of the truck; then they walked hand in hand into the cabin. Once inside, Luce began taking off Jonah's bloody clothes, dropping them right where he stood.

"I can —"

"No," she said, as he started to take off his shirt. "Let me."

He stood, unable to think. Unable to argue.

Somehow Luce knew not to talk. When she had him undressed, she led him into the bathroom, turned on the water in the old tub and then stepped back.

Jonah just stood there, numb to his surroundings.

"Jonah. Sweetheart."

He blinked, then realized Luce was talking to him and that there was water running in the tub.

"Get in, honey," she said softly. "You need to wash off all the dirt and blood. You'll sleep better if you do."

He looked down at his hands, then shuddered. "Oh. Yes. Thank you," he mumbled, then stepped into the tub as she shut the door behind her.

Luce quickly gathered up his clothes and threw them, coat and all, into the washing machine. As the water was filling, she went to the sink and washed her own hands, scrubbing them over and over, until there were no traces of the blood left on her, either.

She'd planned on cooking pork chops for their supper tonight, but she knew she would never get that much food down him tonight. Instead, she opened up a couple of cans of soup and began letting them heat while she started the coffee.

By the time everything was done, she went back to the bathroom. Jonah was clean, but he was standing in front of the mirror, staring at his own face in blank confusion.

"Jonah?"

He blinked, then turned and looked at her. For a moment Luce thought he didn't even recognize her; then he smiled.

"Lucia."

"Yes, darling . . . it's me. Here, I brought your old sweats for you to put on."

He stepped into them, then sat down on the lid of the toilet seat, as if the act of dressing had worn him out.

Luce grabbed a clean towel and began to dry his hair, rubbing the long black strands between the terry-cloth folds until they were almost dry.

Then she picked up her own hairbrush and began to brush through Jonah's hair, one long stroke after another, until his hair was smooth as silk against his skin.

"No one has ever done that for me before," he said, as she laid her hairbrush aside and wrapped her arms around his neck. When he laid his cheek against her breast, she gave him a fierce hug.

"Good," she muttered.

He heard the possessiveness in her voice and closed his eyes, savoring the knowledge that he was wanted — as much as he wanted her.

Luce felt his strength waning fast. He needed to be in bed.

"Come eat some soup, then get yourself in bed."

He didn't want to turn her loose. He hated to lose the contact of her warm body.

"Only if you come with me," he said.

"I'll always be with you," she said.

He ate the bowl of soup, grateful for the warmth spreading inside him, and took a couple of sips of coffee, then set it aside.

"Get in bed," Luce said. "I'll be there shortly."

After Jonah left the table, she quickly washed the dishes, laid some logs on the fire, fed Hobo, then locked up the house for the night.

When she got to her room, she set the alarm, then undressed quickly. She could see that he was already asleep and decided to take a quick shower.

A few minutes later she was back in her room. She pulled back the covers and crawled into bed.

Even though Jonah was asleep, his subconscious felt her presence. He reached for her, and when he felt her warmth, he pulled her to him, then sighed.

Slowly, slowly, Luce felt the tension in his body begin to dissipate. Then his arms went slack, and he slept.

THIRTEEN

The alarm went off in Luce's ear.

"I've got it," she muttered, although her eyes were still closed as she reached to shut it off.

Then Jonah's sleep-rough voice growled in her ear, "No . . . I've got it."

Without warning, he rolled her under him and proceeded to kiss every sweet inch of her body. By the time he got to the valley between her legs, her hands were fisted in his hair and she was begging for release.

But Jonah wasn't ready for it to be over. He rose up on both arms, then stared down at her face. Her hair was a tangle of dark, unruly curls, and her eyes were closed. He wasn't having any of that.

"Look at me," he demanded.

Luce opened her eyes.

"Yes. Just like that," he muttered, and slid inside her.

She groaned as he filled her.

When he started to move, she grabbed hold of his shoulders. Then he took her on the ride of her life.

As always, when she made love with this man, the first climax came and went within seconds. The aftershocks were still rolling through her in hard, jolting waves when he started again. He was like a drug in her system — one of which she could never get enough. Minutes later, when the second climax began, she would have sworn that her body was on fire. He was in every pore of her skin. Every muscle in her body was quivering. She was one giant ache. Then he slid his hands beneath her backside and lifted her up just as he thrust down.

She shattered, and as she did, one image after another spilled through her mind: of snow-capped mountains; dark night skies papered with the dancing lights of the aurora borealis; pale-gray pelts on fleet, four-legged wolves chasing elk down the slope of a mountain toward an ice-fed stream; the sound of wind against feathers, flapping, gliding, riding the air currents over a lush green valley far below.

When she felt Jonah stiffen, then heard the low, guttural moan rip up his throat, she knew what she'd given to him, as well.

It wasn't until she was coming down from

the ride, clasped tight within Jonah's embrace, that she thought to tell him what she'd seen.

Jonah listened, and his eyes widened with surprise.

"What is it? What did I see?"

"It was Alaska. My Alaska," he answered, then moved until he could see into her face. "While I find this connection between us remarkable, I suppose I'm not surprised. What you saw was what was in my mind. It's my home, and it's what I think of when we make love. You're home to me, Lucia. Wherever you are, that's where I belong."

Luce was moved by his words, but even more, by what she'd seen. "That place . . . that valley. It's real?"

He nodded. "It's called Snow Valley. It's where the wolf brought me. It's where I grew up."

Luce pulled out of his arms, then sat up. "Why didn't you ever go back?"

Jonah's eyes narrowed. "Bourdain."

She ran her fingers across his forehead until the frown lines were gone. "One day you'll take me there."

He sat up beside her, then pulled her into his lap. "Would you . . . could you . . . ?"

"What?" Luce asked.

"When this thing with Bourdain is over —

and it *will* be over — would you go there with me?"

Luce took his hand, then cupped it between her palms. "Do you know the Bible?" she asked.

"Some."

"The 'Song of Ruth'?"

Understanding came, and with it, his vision blurred.

Luce laid her hand in the middle of his chest. " 'Whither thou goest, my love.' "

Jonah swallowed past the knot in his throat and buried his face against the curve of her neck.

"Ah, Lucia . . . the last ten years of my life have been hell, but I would live them all over again if I knew it would bring me to you."

She couldn't speak for the emotion welling up inside her. All she could do was hold on to the hope that they would survive what the future had in store.

Caufield had been in Little Top for more than four days. The one local motel had been filled by the initial influx of press, but the problem had been solved by some enterprising residents, who'd taken advantage of the influx of media by renting out extra rooms and, in Caufield's case, a garage apartment once used by a mother-in-law who'd long since passed away. The setup was perfect. There were so many strangers in town, no one paid any attention to one more.

And, after all the fuss and bother, finding Jonah Gray Wolf had been unbelievably easy. Caufield couldn't help but wonder why, after all these years of hiding and running, Gray Wolf had decided to take a stand. The fact raised a niggle of concern, but not enough to panic over.

The finesse would come in taking Jonah in. After a bit of hobnobbing with a man named Shug, who ran a convenience store at the edge of town, Caufield learned there was a woman in Jonah's life, which began to explain why he was still here. Now, if Gray Wolf chose to balk, there was yet another screw to be turned, and its name was Lucia Andahar.

Bourdain had been on the phone nonstop ever since Caufield's arrival in Little Top. Every phone call had consisted of Bourdain demanding results and wanting to know what was taking so damn long. The man was there. Get it over with. The last conversation they'd had, Caufield had gotten tired of Bourdain's tirades and thrown out a challenge.

"Listen, Bourdain. Over the past ten years, how many men have you sent to do this job?"

Bourdain cursed beneath his breath. "That's not the point."

"You're wrong. That *is* the point. Before, you were calling the shots, and every time, they failed. I've read the file. I know what I'm up against. Now, either back off and let me do the job my way, or come down to Little Top and do it yourself. In fact, that's a damn good idea. Why don't you just pack your ass into that fancy limo you own, come on over to West Virginia and get your own damn hands dirty for a change?"

Bourdain flashed on the day they'd brought Gray Wolf into his home. He still had nightmares about that condor taking the man's head off with its talons, and the thousands of birds that had attacked.

He didn't want to face Gray Wolf again until he was certain he had the upper hand.

When the phone went dead in Caufield's ear, it was answer enough. There were things to be done that needed setups, not some steroid-packed mercenary attitude that could get a man killed.

Finesse.

It was all about finesse.

■ ■ ■ ■

And while Caufield was plotting how to claim a million-dollar bounty, the residents of Little Top were experiencing a revelation.

The Indian who lived with Luce Andahar up on the mountain was a healer. Not a Bible-thumping, laying-on-of-the-hands, "In the name of Jesus, you are healed," kind of healer.

Oh, no.

According to the witnesses who'd been helping at the bus wreck, he was more like an earth-trembling, light-enveloping, mesmerizing-miracle kind of healer. They were saying that when Jonah Gray Wolf had finished with one victim, he'd moved quietly to the next, and the next, until nine broken and bloody children had been put back together again.

Rocky Jones, one of the rescuers who'd been a witness to the healings, had been a blinding alcoholic for most of his life. That night, after it was over, he'd gone home, taken all the liquor bottles out of his cabinet, carried them to the sink and calmly emptied every one of them down the drain. It had been something he'd done without panic, and he hadn't taken or wanted a drink since. He swore the urge wasn't even in him anymore.

Dolly Woodliff, a woman who that very day had been diagnosed with breast cancer, had been standing behind the Indian when he'd healed Travis Mize, the sheriff's son.

She'd been on her way home, weeping as she drove, convinced she was going to die. Then she'd driven up on the wreck. After that, her personal fears had been put into perspective. But after witnessing the miracles, something within her had changed.

Like everyone else, she'd gone home that night, desperate to get rid of the bloody clothes she was wearing and wash away the horror of the event.

But when she stepped into the shower, her hands automatically went to the lump in her breast. The one she'd been feeling, then ignoring for the past six months. The one that Doc Bigelow had diagnosed that day as cancerous.

Only it was gone.

Horribly there this morning.

Miraculously missing tonight.

She'd made a flying trip back to Doc Bigelow's the next morning with the news, which he promptly told her was impossible. But after her insistence and then an ensuing fit of tears, he'd agreed to examine her again.

She'd held her breath as Bigelow began, needing to watch his face for the moment when understanding dawned. And she knew it would come. She also knew he was busy and cranky from nursing a head cold. She even forgave him for trying to tell her that her fears had let her imagination go into overdrive.

She knew what she knew.

And before he began the examination, Bigelow thought he knew things, too.

The lump would still be there, as would the small, healing scar where the needle biopsy had been taken. But to his surprise, it was gone. The breast was smooth and supple. No lump. No sign of a biopsy.

He looked, and he looked, then, thinking he'd somehow slipped and examined the wrong breast, removed the sheet from the other side of her chest and checked that one, too.

They were perfectly sound.

He took a deep breath then stepped back and looked at Dolly's face.

She didn't say it, but he saw the "I told you so" in her eyes.

At that point, Dolly got off the examining table, put her clothes back on and left without saying another word, leaving the doctor to figure the rest out on his own.

But word was getting around.

Everyone had a story to tell.

Everyone except Jonah. He wasn't talking to anyone.

After cautioning Lucia about the dangers of trusting anyone who was not a resident of the town, he drove her to work each morning and picked her up in the afternoon.

Due to the influx of media, who'd camped out all over the area, Harold decided to keep the diner open for the supper hour. Luce had been dreading the added work time until Harold assured her that he'd taken care of that and hired himself a second waitress to cover the new shift.

Her name was Dorothy, but she went by the name of Dorrie. Luce had met her for the first time two days earlier, as she was leaving to go home.

According to Harold, who'd gotten his information from Dorothy herself, she was a second cousin twice removed from the Dovell family, who used to own land up on the mountain, and had come to see the old family home, then decided to stay around for a while.

She was tall and skinny, with short black hair, small eyes, thin lips and leaning a bit too much toward the manly side for Harold's taste, but he figured her looks didn't matter all that much if she could do the job.

Dorrie was entering the back room as Luce was coming out.

"Hey, you must be Luce," Dorrie said, and stuck out her hand. "I'm Dorrie, the second shift." Then she smiled, revealing a set of unusually white teeth.

Luce suspected Dorrie was a victim of an overzealous dentist and a tooth-bleaching job gone bad, and tried not to stare.

"I'm Luce. Nice to meet you." Then she put on her coat and shouldered her purse. "Have a good evening," she added, while waving at Harold as she exited the diner.

Dorrie eyed Luce's curvy body without comment, then smoothed her hands down the front of her long-sleeved T-shirt, well aware that she was lacking in feminine endowments, and tied an apron around her waist. She gave herself one last look in the mirror hanging over a small sink, grinned widely to check her teeth, then wiped at the corners of her lips in satisfaction as she headed into the diner, thinking there was nothing like a nice, white smile.

And after the first day, Dorrie had proven her worth. According to Harold, she could carry four plates at a time to the table without a spill, and she had a good memory, which was a plus for figuring out who had ordered what.

Luce was happy Harold was satisfied, because then she didn't have to feel guilty for not wanting to work the extra hours.

A couple of days later, Luce noticed that Jonah was preoccupied as he dropped her off at work, but she thought nothing of it. She knew it had nothing to do with her. She'd heard him moaning and talking in his sleep, and realized that he was reliving some bad memories. All she was able to do was love him without question.

So when his goodbye kiss tasted of desperation, she held him just that little bit tighter as she told him goodbye.

The morning, which had started off busy, turned hectic. A news crew had set up shop in the diner and, despite her misgivings, was filming nonstop, getting footage as part of what they hoped would be a documentary on Mark William Ahern, along with interviewing everyone who came in and was willing to talk to them about the Indian who'd supposedly performed miracle healings.

Luce had taken note of the fact that, once Ahern had been arrested and identified as a serial killer, the media began referring to him by his full name, just like they did all the notorious criminals.

More than one reporter had tried to get her to talk about her relationship with Ahern, but she'd refused every time. Then they'd started digging at her about Jonah, whom she also refused to discuss. Harold had finally threatened them with eviction if they bothered her again. They didn't approach her personally after that, but she was well aware of how much footage they kept shooting with her in the frame.

By the time noon had come and gone, she was exhausted, both mentally and physically. And the closer it got to when Jonah would arrive, the more nervous she became.

For the past two afternoons, when it was nearing time for Luce to get off work, people had begun piling into the diner, hoping to catch a glimpse of the healer.

Today a woman, a stranger to the area, had walked into the diner carrying a baby in her arms. She'd chosen a table with a seat facing toward the door and begun watching the clock. Luce knew it was because of Jonah.

When three o'clock rolled around and she saw the black pickup pull up in front of the diner, she headed for the door, but the woman with the baby beat her out by a full thirty seconds. She already had Jonah cornered near the front of the truck by the time Luce got outside.

"Please, mister . . . my baby is sick. She was born with cystic fibrosis. The doctor says she's got it bad." Then her voice broke. "He says she won't live to see Christmas."

Immediately, every instinct Jonah had turned on. Christmas was less than two months away. This child wasn't any different than the children he'd pulled out of the bus. She was in just as much need — only younger. When the mother suddenly thrust the baby into his arms, he felt the gentle soul with a waning life and ached to make it right.

But another crowd was gathering.

He hesitated, then looked up. He couldn't do this again. Not like a circus event. This wasn't how it was supposed to be.

Before he could think what to do next, Luce was there, taking the baby out of his arms and whispering softly to the woman. "What's your name?" Luce asked.

"Eleanor," the other woman said. "And my girl's name is Brenda."

Luce looked up at Jonah. "Do you need a quiet place?"

"Please," he said, grateful that she understood.

Luce smiled at the mother. "Eleanor, why don't we all get inside, where it's warmer? The cold can't be good for the baby."

Thankful for the reprieve, Jonah followed Luce and the woman back inside the diner; then, after Luce's whispered request to Harold, they trooped up the back stairs to his home.

Once they got inside the solitude of the homey apartment, the thin, wheezing breath of her sick baby overwhelmed the mother, and she began to cry — deep, ugly sobs of despair.

Jonah felt everything she was feeling. Her loss of hope. Her fear for the child. The acceptance that she would most likely never see her daughter to a first day of school. Never see her marry. Never know the joy of being a grandmother to her daughter's children.

Unless he healed her child.

"Lucia."

She looked up.

"Give me the baby."

Luce laid the little girl in his arms.

Jonah took her to the sofa, then sat down with her in his arms. He unwrapped her from the blanket, then laid her lengthwise in his lap.

The little girl immediately began to beat the air with her hands, startled and uncomfortable by the lack of swaddling.

"Shh, shh," he said softly, and then laid his hand at the top of the baby's head.

Immediately, the little girl went still.

Luce heard a catch in the mother's breath. Instinctively, she clasped Eleanor's hands in her own, letting her know she wasn't alone.

Jonah could feel the baby's lungs laboring heavily in an effort to draw in enough air to infuse oxygen into her blood. The tiny heart beat valiantly, but Jonah knew the doctor was right. The little girl would not live to see her first Christmas unless he intervened.

He cupped the baby's tiny head, and as he did, the child's eyes suddenly focused, centering on his face with an intensity that was beyond her age.

"That's right, that's right. One small breath, then another, and another. I promise little girl, it's all going to be easy."

Then he stroked his finger down the side of her cheek until her eyes closed. At that point he picked her up and laid her against his chest, easing her tiny head sideways.

Her little rosebud of a mouth was making quiet sucking motions, and when Jonah put his hand on the middle of her back, the fingers of her left hand curled around the edge of his sweater, then tightened — as if she knew what was coming and was getting ready to hang on for the ride of her life.

Jonah inhaled slowly, then closed his eyes, letting every infirm facet of the child's body soak into his strength.

Luce found herself forgetting to breathe. When the air within Harold's home went still, then seemed to thicken, she knew what was coming next. Even though she expected it, she jumped when the dishes in Harold's cabinets began to rattle.

The mother gasped, and then she began to rock back and forth where she sat, moaning and praying, unable to tear her gaze from the man who held her child.

Luce knew Eleanor was scared, but there was no time to tell her that the end result would be worth the fright of her life.

Within seconds, light enveloped both man and child, pulsing, glowing brighter and brighter with each passing second, until both women were forced to look away.

Suddenly Eleanor slumped sideways, but Luce didn't let go. She didn't know how much time had passed, but when she realized it was over, Jonah was standing beside the window with the baby in his arms. She was laughing at him and patting both his cheeks with her hands.

She reached for the mother. "Eleanor. . . . Eleanor. Wake up."

The moment Eleanor came to, her gaze immediately went to the chair where Jonah had been sitting, but it was empty.

Then she heard her baby's laughter and looked toward the window. "Lord," she muttered, and staggered to her feet. "Lord, Lord," she said again, as she started toward the man who held her child.

When Jonah laid the baby in her arms, Eleanor put her hand on the baby's chest. The steady rhythm of the heartbeat was impossible to mistake, as was the warm pink of her daughter's soft skin. There was no pinched look about her lips. No gasping for air. The end-of-life look was gone from Brenda's eyes, replaced by a sparkle representing a lifetime of hope and expectation.

There were tears on Eleanor's face as she turned to Jonah. Twice she tried to speak, and both times words failed her.

Jonah felt her joy. It was enough. He laid his hand on the woman's shoulder. "It was good to meet you, Eleanor. Take your baby home."

Eleanor nodded wildly, then began to talk to herself and to her baby girl as she reached down to gather up their things. When she would have gone back down the stairs they'd come up, Luce stopped her.

"Let's take the back way. Then you can go home without being bothered by all those cameras and people."

"Yes, yes, all right," Eleanor said, as she settled her baby in her arms. She was halfway out the door when she paused to look back.

Jonah was standing with his back to the window, and from this distance and with the tears in her eyes, all she could see was his silhouette — a dark angel against the light. He would forever be the miracle she'd prayed for.

"God bless you," she said, and then stepped outside.

Luce glanced back at Jonah. "Are you coming?"

"You two go ahead. I'll be right behind you."

Luce nodded.

Together, the women made it down the back stairs and to Eleanor's car, which was parked down the street from the diner. Luce watched the baby being buckled into her car seat, then stood until Eleanor drove away. She turned to see if Jonah was following, then realized someone had seen their exit.

She looked back wildly at Jonah, who was standing at the top of the steps, fearing he would be trapped by a throng of people begging for the same thing he'd just given to a woman with a dying child.

He waved her on, and she didn't question the action; she just started walking down the street toward home.

Jonah's quiet exit had just become a thing of the past. After he'd sent Luce on her way, he hesitated at the top of the back stairs, figuring out his next move. Then it hit him.

He looked up at the sky, then closed his eyes. A few moments later, he ducked back inside the apartment and took the stairs that led back into the diner.

As he suspected, the room was packed. Word had obviously spread that another healing was taking place. These gatherings would only grow worse as time went on, but for the moment, there was nothing to be done except endure.

Steam from the heat of Harold's cooking was drifting from the kitchen and out into the dining room, while Dorrie, the new waitress, poured coffee and took orders as fast as she could write.

Jonah paused in the doorway. Through the plate-glass windows at the street, he could see Lucia walking down the sidewalk toward home. Somebody from one of the news crews suddenly bailed out of a parked van with a camera on his shoulder and aimed it in her direction.

Still, he waited.

Then he heard someone inside the diner give a shout. "For the love of God . . . would you look at that?"

Everyone turned to look, then jumped out of their chairs and crowded toward the windows. They were staring at an eagle that was soaring down Main Street, no more than thirty feet above the ground. The wingspread of the bird was as majestic as its demeanor. Back and forth it flew, soaring up, then floating down, riding the wind currents in glorious silence from one end of town to the other.

Outside, the cameraman was going crazy, angling for the best footage of the phenomenon, while the people inside Harold's diner began to spill out into the street for a closer look. Jonah started to head out with them, completely unobserved. As he moved toward the doorway, he suddenly felt the presence of a hunter. He knew the sensation far too well to mistake it for anything else.

He looked about him as people pushed out through the doorway and into the street, but he couldn't pinpoint the location. It wasn't a surprise that the hunter was already here; whoever it was, they would meet soon enough. For now, he just wanted to go home.

He paused for a second, gazing up into the sky just like everyone else. As he did, the eagle made one last pass, and as it flew over Jonah, it screamed.

Jonah headed for the truck. By the time he turned around and picked Luce up at the corner, the eagle had taken flight.

One minute it was there, and then it was gone. The crowd was ecstatic at what they'd seen. It was only after they began to file back into the diner that someone noticed Jonah's truck was gone. Then Harold went upstairs to check on Luce and came back with the news that no one was there.

No one had seen them leave. No one had known the woman who'd come in with the baby. She wasn't a local, so they had no way of knowing where she'd gone.

And while they knew the general vicinity of where Jonah would be going, no one would be following them out of town. After what Jonah had done for his son, Sheriff Tom Mize had put the fear of God in every resident and every member of the media, warning them all that if they intruded on that man's personal space, he would arrest the offenders and run the rest out of town.

For the moment, time — and Sheriff Mize — were on their side.

FOURTEEN

The ride up the mountain was quiet, even peaceful. The residue from the healing had left Jonah satisfied and Luce in awe. There was a part of her that didn't feel worthy of this man, but she loved him, in spite of all her misgivings. They were more than half-way home when she began to voice some of her concerns.

"Jonah."

"Yes?"

"What happens to you if you tie yourself to a mortal like me?"

Jonah laughed. "Hey, now, I'm good in bed, but surely I'm not that good."

She grinned back, then thumped him on the leg.

"I'm not talking about that. I'm talking about the other . . . you know . . . the miracles."

The smile on his face slid sideways. "Only God makes miracles, honey."

She frowned, then shook her head. "No. What you do is miraculous."

Then he sighed. "No. It's not, at least not in the way you're referring to it. That's what no one understands. What I do isn't miraculous . . . at least, not to me. It's just something I was born with. Something I've always been able to do. My father was a doctor. He could heal people. For some reason, my abilities are a few steps beyond what doctors do."

Luce rolled her eyes. "A few steps? Yeah, right. More like a few light-years. It's like you're not even of this world, Jonah. No one has ever been able to do what you do."

A shiver slid through his body like a sneak thief in the night. Not of this world? That didn't compute.

"You just keep on thinking I'm out of this world and we'll both be happy."

Luce laughed, and the moment passed.

"Hey, we're almost home," she said, as she pointed to the road leading to the cabin.

"I love the sound of those words," Jonah said, and took the turn in a flurry of dry leaves and flying gravel.

"What's the hurry?" Luce asked, as she grabbed onto the dash to keep from sliding.

"I'm hungry," Jonah said, as he hit the brakes and slammed the truck into Park.

"Hungry for you," he added, then growled beneath his breath as he pretended to nip at her earlobe.

By the time he was through, Luce was weak from laughing, and Hobo was barking wildly, trying to figure out what was going on inside the truck.

"Look what you made him do," Luce said, as she let Jonah lift her down from the truck.

"He's just jealous," Jonah said. "Before I came, he was the only man in your life." Then he pointed at the dog. "Get used to it, boy. She'll feed you and love you, but I sleep in her bed."

Hobo barked, then began running in circles, as if he were laughing with them.

The evening passed. Halloween was over. Thanksgiving was ahead. Jonah could only hope that when it came, they would still have something for which to be thankful. It wasn't until they had gone to bed and were almost asleep that Luce piped up with one last question for the day.

"Jonah?"

His eyelids fluttered as her voice called him back from where he'd gone.

"What?" he mumbled.

"Are you afraid?"

This sounded serious. He opened his eyes all the way and rolled over, taking her in his arms as he asked, "Afraid of what, honey?"

"The bounty hunters . . . and that man Bourdain. After all that's happened, he's certain to know where you are."

"I know."

Luce was shocked by how quickly he'd answered. "You've been thinking about this for some time, haven't you?"

"It's something I've lived with for more than ten years. It's become a way of life . . . running, I mean."

"The other day, we talked about me going with you, remember?"

He tightened his grip. "I'm not running anymore."

"What if they come?"

"They're already here," he said, remembering the knowing that had come to him when he was leaving the diner with all the customers. Somewhere in that crowd, the man who wanted to use Lucia to get to him had been there, watching.

Luce frowned and would have pulled herself out of his arms, but he wouldn't turn her loose.

"What do you mean, they're already here? Who are they? Why haven't you said anything? Why haven't they made a run at you?"

He didn't go into details with her about it. Trying to make people understand what he knew and how he knew it was too difficult.

"He has to be here. It stands to reason. But until he makes a move, I won't know anything."

"You can't just . . . sniff him out?"

He grinned. It seemed she'd taken his tracking abilities to a new high.

"Not if I don't know what he smells like first."

"Oh. Yeah. Right. Drat."

"It's all right," Jonah said. "Whoever it is, he can't hurt me. It's you he'll come after. That's what I know. That's what I fear."

Luce shuddered, then closed her eyes and clung to him as tightly as she could.

"I won't let that happen. I'll never let myself be alone with a man, even if I know him."

"That's good," Jonah said. He didn't want her to know how little her caution would mean when his tracker decided to make his move. "Now go to sleep."

"Okay," she said.

"I love you, Lucia. I will take care of you. Know that."

Luce sighed, then burrowed her nose a little deeper into his chest. "I love you, too," she said. "And I'm not afraid."

■ ■ ■ ■

Caufield fell onto the bed, exhausted in every bone. Stakeouts sucked. According to the rooster clock on the wall opposite the bed, it was midnight, but it would be three hours earlier in L.A. Time to check in with the boss. Time to tell him what was going down.

Bourdain was coming out of a restaurant when his cell phone rang. He saw who was calling and made his excuses to the people he'd just dined with, handed his ticket stub to the parking valet and stepped away to answer the call.

"Tell me it's good news," he said.

Caufield snorted. "Of course it's good news. Isn't that why you hired me?"

Bourdain's heart leaped. "You have him! Tell me you have him!"

"Hell, no, I don't have him. No one will ever be able to take him down. Haven't you figured that out yet? He cannot be taken."

Bourdain cursed, then realized where he was and stepped farther back into the landscaping, away from the front door of the restaurant.

"Then what are you trying to say?"

"He has a woman."

Bourdain stilled as understanding dawned. "Do you have her?"

"No, but I will."

Finally Bourdain began to believe it could happen.

"When? Tell me . . . no. Wait. I want to be there. Yes! Yes, I have to be there. Then, when the confrontation goes down, I can explain things to him. I can tell him about the riches he will have. The power that will be his for the taking."

Caufield rolled over on the bed and stared up at the ceiling, thinking back over the events of the past few days.

"Gray Wolf already has more power than you or I will ever see."

"I'm talking money! Fame! The world could be his."

"If he wanted that stuff, he could already have had it," Caufield said. "However . . . if you're so damn set on being here, then get your ass packed. This is Thursday. The only time she's ever away from Gray Wolf is when she's in town at work. I'll take her then and leave him to trail us."

"Don't leave too many clues," Bourdain said. "We don't want to make it too easy for him. I want him to worry about her just enough not to push me when we come face-to-face."

Caufield thought back over the stories going around about how Gray Wolf had caught the man who had been stalking his woman. Leaving Gray Wolf clues wasn't necessary — not when he could track like a damn bloodhound.

Bourdain was still rattling on, but Caufield was tired. It was time to end the conversation.

"Just get here by noon tomorrow or you're gonna miss all the fun."

"No. Wait! Why so soon?"

"Because the weatherman is predicting another snow, and I didn't bring my dogsled."

"Sarcasm does not become you," Bourdain muttered.

The line went dead in Caufield's ear.

Bourdain slipped his phone in his pocket, handed a twenty-dollar bill to the valet who'd just driven up with his car and then drove away, wheeling through the L.A. traffic like a madman. He didn't have any time to waste.

Later, after a quick check of the map, it was obvious that flying in to Little Top wasn't going to happen the normal way. There wasn't a landing strip between there and Charleston. In fact, there wasn't much between there and Charleston except mountains. It was too far to drive and get there in time, which left him with only one option.

He would take his private jet to Charleston, then charter a helicopter. It would be a hell of a trip, but he could get to Little Top by noon. Then, if the weather held and everything went according to plan, they would all be back in L.A. within a couple of days. If he could make Gray Wolf see reason.

No. Not if. *When.*

He picked up the phone. It was late, and he knew making calls at this time of night was going to cost him big-time, but it would be worth it.

The next morning dawned gray and dreary. There was a hint of more snow in the air. Jonah made a mental note to go by Middleton's Feed Store and get another load of feed when he took Luce to work.

Hobo was outside with his nose to the ground, checking for signs of all the nightly visitors they'd had while he'd been inside asleep.

Jonah reached for his coat, then changed his mind and walked out onto the porch without it. There was a part of him that reveled in the chill and dampness. Being comfortable with nature in all its phases was part of who he was.

Hobo barked once when he saw Jonah, then continued on his morning prowl. A squirrel scolded from a tall pine on the far side of the cabin. Hobo ran to investigate as Jonah stepped off the porch and walked into the yard.

He lifted his head, inhaling deeply of the cold mountain air, smelling the wood smoke from their fire, as well as a dozen other scents of the forest. He could tell without searching that no one had come to the cabin overnight except those on four feet. He looked up to see a lone eagle circling high overhead, scanning the landscape for a sign of movement from something hunt-worthy. Not the rabbits or the foxes — not even a tiny wood mouse who could hide in the smallest of spaces — would be safe from a raptor with that kind of eyesight and strength.

A cold blast of wind suddenly circled the cabin, blowing smoke into Jonah's eyes. He squinted against the sting, then turned his back to the force. As he did, he felt himself being watched.

Then he smiled to himself. He knew that scent.

"Good morning," he said softly.

The golden cougar walked out of the trees

toward Jonah with its head up and its tail low, signs of ease and friendship.

Hobo smelled the cougar, yipped once in panic, then bounded onto the porch.

"It's all right," Jonah said softly. "He means you no harm."

The cougar walked straight up to Jonah, and when Jonah lowered his hand, the big cat head-butted his palm, as if begging for a scratch.

"So . . . we meet again, Brother Cat," Jonah said, as he dug his fingernails through the pelt to that itchy spot just behind the cat's right ear. "Let's see what's bothering you there. Ah. A tick. Even in winter. That's no good."

An odd kind of snarl that sounded more like a gurgle came out of the big cat's mouth as Jonah pulled at the tick.

"Got it," he said, and held the tick down toward the cat's nose.

It sniffed Jonah's fingers, then, satisfied by what it smelled, lay down on Jonah's boots and rolled, until it was belly up.

Jonah squatted down beside it and began to scratch the cat's belly, talking to it as he would have to any human. Discussing the weather and family, and how successfully the cat's last hunt had gone.

It wasn't strange to Jonah that he knew all

the answers. Even though the cat didn't speak, Jonah heard him just the same.

Then suddenly the cougar was on its feet, sniffing the air. Jonah stepped back.

"It was good to see you, my friend. Hunt well. Just leave the big dog alone."

The cougar chuffed once, then was gone.

Jonah turned toward the porch, only to find Luce standing in the doorway, staring at him.

"I saw it, but I still don't believe it," she muttered.

Jonah grinned. "He had a tick he couldn't reach behind his ear. He just needed a little help."

Luce just shook her head.

As Jonah hurried up the steps, she added, "Hobo is inside. He may never speak to you again."

Jonah laughed. "Oh, sure he will. He knows my heart. He just doesn't approve of all my friends."

"That's the understatement of the day," Luce muttered. "Do you want breakfast?"

"No. I'll eat later. I think we need to leave now, or you're going to be late for work."

"I'm ready," she said.

"Let me wash my hands, and then I'll go get the truck."

Luce couldn't quit watching him. Even

after he'd stopped by the fireplace and made peace with Hobo, she kept staring off into space, remembering how the cougar had licked Jonah's fingers and rolled at his feet.

It was at times like these that she couldn't help but wonder exactly what kind of man this was to whom she had given her heart.

He was more than just mortal. He was more than just a man. And yet he walked among them with the same hopes and dreams, yearning for love and a place to call home.

He had her love. It remained to be seen where home might be, but she knew that wherever Jonah Gray Wolf went, she would follow.

Jonah drove up to the diner, but instead of just letting her out as usual, he parked, then killed the engine.

"Are you coming in?" she asked, surprised that he wasn't planning to drive on.

"I want to talk to Harold a minute," he said.

Luce sighed. "You don't have to —"

"Yes, I do," he said, and reached for her hand. "Come on. It won't take long, and I promise not to embarrass you."

Luce rolled her eyes, then got out and walked ahead of him into the diner with an extra twist to her step.

Jonah grinned as he watched her go, thinking that if Lucia was a bird, she would be like one of Bridie's little brown hens, the ones that ruffled up their feathers when he reached for their eggs. At the moment, Lucia's feathers were definitely ruffled. She just didn't understand the depths to which Bourdain would go. After what had happened to his father and the countless men Bourdain had sent after him over the past ten years, he knew Bourdain and his thugs would do anything for money.

Lucia had already disappeared into the back room when Jonah went in.

"Hey," Harold said, when he saw Jonah. "Come to eat some good cooking for a change, have you?"

Luce came out with her apron on and fire in her eyes.

"I heard that!" she said, and stuffed an order pad in her apron pocket.

Harold grinned, then winked.

Luce made a face, then began filling salt and pepper shakers, and making sure that sugar packets and creamers were on every table.

"I need to talk to you," Jonah said to Harold.

The older man waved him over. "Sure.

Have a seat." He poured Jonah a cup of coffee, then sat down beside him at the counter. "What's up?" he asked.

Jonah curled his fingers around the cup, then turned to face Harold.

"Lucia is still in danger."

Harold jerked. "What? Did Ahern escape? I was told that they took him out of town this morning."

"Really? I hadn't heard," Jonah said, then added, "Good, that means the media will go with him."

"Oh, I think they're already gone. Junie Sanders had been renting out her upstairs to a couple of them. I was talking to her last night, and she said they pulled out just after the evening news. You'd think they would have waited for daylight to drive."

"News waits for no man," Jonah muttered.

Harold nodded. "Yeah. Guess you're right about that. Now what's the deal with Lucia being in danger?"

"It has to do with me," Jonah said, ashamed to admit it.

Harold frowned. "I don't understand."

Jonah took a small sip of the coffee, then started to explain.

"There is a man who's been after me for many years. Ten years ago, he killed my father, trying to get to me."

326

"Lordy be," Harold muttered, then clapped Jonah gently on the back. "I'm real sorry for your loss, but I don't see how this puts Luce in trouble."

Jonah's gaze locked on Harold's eyes. "You know what I can do."

Harold swallowed, then nodded. "I've heard. It's hard to imagine, but I know the people who witnessed it. They aren't crazy, and they don't lie."

Jonah nodded. "Then, if you believe them, can you imagine why someone would want to control me? To have complete power over me and my abilities?"

"Oh. Yes. I see what you mean."

"So in loving Lucia, I've put her in danger."

"So, you telling me that you're leaving? I guess I can understand it, but I sure will hate to lose Luce."

"No. I won't drag Lucia into that kind of life, and I can't leave her behind. This is it. I'm not running anymore. We may not stay here permanently, but I'm not running from anyone again. They'll come for me again. In fact, I'm sure someone is already here in Little Top waiting for the opportune moment."

"Then you need to tell Sheriff Mize. I don't know whether you know it or not, but he's your new best friend."

Jonah almost smiled. "I could tell him, but what would I say? I don't know what the next hunter is going to look like. I don't know how or when it's going to happen, but when he makes his move, he'll go for Lucia, not me."

"Then I'm your man. As long as she's under this roof, she'll be safe. That I can promise you."

"No, you can't promise that. No one can. But look out for her just the same, will you?"

"Count on it," Harold said.

"I'm going to work now," Jonah said. "I'll be back later."

He got up and started toward the door, then turned around, looking for Lucia.

"Lucia . . ."

She came out of the kitchen, carrying a small brown bag.

"Two sausage biscuits — with grape jelly," she added, and handed him a cup of coffee to go.

Jonah arched an eyebrow. "My favorite! Thank you."

"You're welcome," Luce said, then stood on her tiptoes long enough to give him a quick kiss goodbye.

"Does this mean you're not mad at me anymore?" he asked.

"Probably," she said.

Jonah grinned. "See you this afternoon."

"Yes . . . see you," she said.

Luce stood at the window, watching him eat the biscuits as he drove toward Middleton's Feed Store.

Harold eyed her nervously.

She put her hands on her hips and glared. "I'm fine. Go make your gravy."

He escaped to the kitchen as Luce turned over the Closed sign on the door to Open.

With that, their morning began.

As Jonah worked his way around the feed lot, mending the fence, the chill in the air was even more prevalent than it had been earlier.

A small fox had come up to the barn, only to pause near where Jonah was working. His little black nose was twitching, as were the whiskers over his eyebrows.

Jonah frowned. "No chickens here for you, Brother Fox . . . and no mice, either. Try the next farm, please."

The fox stood for just a moment, then turned and slipped back into the forest the same way he'd come out.

Jonah nodded with satisfaction. Bridie's little brown hens and Brother Mouse were safe for one more day, at least.

329

A lone snowflake drifted past his nose as he tied off the last bit of broken wire; he tried not to let it concern him. It would be just like one of Bourdain's hired goons to take advantage of bad weather to make his play.

He dropped the wire cutters into the toolbox, then loaded up the scattered fencing equipment. He was in the truck and on his way back to the shed to unload when he heard a high-pitched scream, then saw Bridie come running out of the house with her dress on fire.

There was no time for shock to set in.

No time for remorse.

He had to get to her before her heart stopped beating.

The tires spun on the damp ground as he stomped the accelerator; then they finally caught traction, sending him toward the house at breakneck speed.

By the time he got there, Bridie was on the ground. Her legs were jerking as if she were having a seizure, and her tiny hands were beating at the air, as if trying to put out the flames. Even before he got out of the truck, he was sick to his stomach, thinking of the torture she was enduring.

Seconds later he was at her side, beating out the flames with his hands. After they were out, she lay moaning and shaking, begging to God to let her die.

"Not today, sweetheart," he said softly, then clenched his own hands, healing the blisters that had already started to form. Moments later, he laid his palms flat on Bridie.

Her eyes were rolling back in her head, and there was a fleck of bloody foam at the edge of her mouth.

"Bridie! Bridie! Look at me, honey! Look at me!"

Jonah's voice drew her from the edge of insanity to the intensity on his face. Then they locked gazes, and somehow the pain began to fade, like a bad memory in the middle of the night.

Jonah grasped her face with both hands as he willed her to a place where this horror did not exist. When she had ease, he began scanning her body for the extent of the damage. She had third-degree burns on her left leg and up the left side of her body to that same arm, and then up the left side of her neck.

She was going into shock. There wasn't a second to waste.

He laid his hands on her chest.

The silence on the farm was telling. Somehow the animals knew that their mistress was in terrible distress.

Jonah inhaled, letting his mind slide past the scent of burning cloth and flesh, and then he closed his eyes. Moments later the air thickened, charging with an energy not unlike the power of a lightning bolt being born within a storm.

Then the earth began to tremble.

One of the pumpkins on Bridie's front porch teetered, then rolled off the hay bale onto the ground, bursting open and scattering seeds as it fell.

Brother Mouse buried his little nose beneath his tail, while every living thing on Bridie's farm seemed to hold its breath.

Then the healing came, spilling from Jonah into Bridie in a flow of brilliance that pulsed with a rhythm matching that of Jonah's heart.

Nerve endings reattached. Blood veins that had exploded and fried became whole again, while layer after layer of burned flesh sealed over, healing completely, until Bridie Tuesday's skin was smooth and whole. The hair that had singed on her head became soft. The eyelashes that had been melted grew anew.

Bridie was still on the ground when the next flakes of snow began to fall, feeling as if she'd been born again under Jonah Gray

Wolf's hands.

Jonah knew when it was over, because he felt a surge building in her lungs. She opened her eyes at the same time that she took a deep breath. The scream hanging at the back of her throat never came out, as she found herself looking into Jonah's face.

"Am I dead?"

He picked her up in his arms. "No, dear, but you need to change clothes."

Her lower lip suddenly trembled, and her eyes filled with tears. "I caught my sleeve on fire."

"I know," Jonah said softly, as he carried her into the house, then down the hall to her room.

When he stood her up on her feet, she clasped her hands to her bosom to hold her sagging dress in place. She looked at Jonah once, then turned to stare at herself in the dresser mirror.

"I was on fire," she repeated, and kept staring at her blackened clothing and pale skin in disbelief.

She could see Jonah in the mirror as he stood behind her. His shirtsleeves were scorched, and one cuff was blackened. But his hands were as smooth as her skin.

"What did you do?" she asked.

"I put out the fire."

She looked down at her arms, then her hands, then her legs.

"I felt the fire. I smelled my own flesh a-burning, and yet there's not a blister on me."

"I told you . . . I put out the fire," he said softly. "Do you need help cleaning up?"

Bridie sat down on the side of the bed with a thump.

"Well, I should say I do," she said. "I'm too old to be settin' myself on fire." Then she sighed. "But I never thought I'd live to see something like this. Maybe you could hand me that blue-denim dress hanging on the inside of my closet door before you go?"

"Yes, ma'am," Jonah said. He handed her the dress. "Do you need anything else?"

"No."

Jonah started to leave, when Bridie suddenly called out, "Jonah!"

He turned. "Yes?"

"God has blessed you highly."

"Yes, ma'am. That He has."

"I'm proud to know you," she added.

A slow smile spread across his face. "Well. Thank you . . . and I'm proud to know you, too."

Bridie made a face. "Land sakes . . . I haven't done a single thing in my whole lifetime that would hold a candle to what you can do."

Jonah shook his head. "Oh, but that's not true. You make the best custard pies I've ever eaten."

Bridie managed a grin. "Well, there *is* that."

"You get changed. I'm going to clean up the kitchen," Jonah said.

Bridie's lip trembled. "I guess I made a big mess of the noon meal."

"Never mind," Jonah said. "After what just happened, I think you're due some special attention. How about we go down into Little Top and let Harold feed us today?"

Bridie sagged. "I don't know if I'm up to that."

"I think you are."

She sighed. "I guess we could eat our dinner down at Harold's. Maybe I could even stay with Ida Mae for a spell until it's time for Luce to get off work."

"I think that's a fine idea," Jonah said.

Bridie nodded, then glanced out the window and frowned. "It's started to snow."

"Then you better bundle up," Jonah said, and left her to change clothes, while he tended to the burned food, and the water all over the floor. Obviously she tried to put out the fire herself before running out of the house.

A short while later, Jonah loaded her up and they started toward town. Bridie was silent. Jonah could tell something was on her mind, but he had something on his, as well.

"Bridie."

"Yes?"

"Have you ever thought about moving to town?"

She frowned, then clasped her hands into fists and jammed them into her lap.

"Lord, no. My Franklin put me up on that mountain. I reckon I'll be there when I go to meet him."

"You almost went to meet him today," Jonah muttered.

She glared. "What's that got to do with me moving?"

"If I hadn't been there, how long do you think it would have been before somebody found your body?"

Bridie gasped. Her face went from flushed to pale.

Jonah sighed. "I'm not trying to scare you, but —"

"Yes, you are, and it's working. I reckon I'd like to be buried with all my parts."

"If you lived in Little Top, you wouldn't spend your days alone."

"I'm not alone. You're here," she argued.

"But I won't always be here."

Bridie's expression sagged. "You're leaving? But I thought —"

"Not now . . . but maybe in the spring."

"I was kind of hoping you would get attached enough to Luce to stay. I don't have any children, you know, and I've been planning all along to leave my place to her."

Jonah smiled. "She would be honored to know you think of her that highly. But I can't stay permanently here, and you know why."

"No, I don't. I don't understand why —"

"Do you know how many people have seen what I can do?"

She grew still.

"Pretty soon I won't be able to drive down Main Street without somebody stopping and turning around to follow me . . . wanting to be healed . . . wanting someone to change their life for them. There's a man who's been after me for years, wanting to use my powers to his own advantage."

"Lord have mercy," she muttered.

"Exactly. It's not that I don't want to stay. It's just that I can't . . . not and lead any kind of a normal life. Lucia doesn't deserve that kind of turmoil."

"You aren't going to leave her behind when you go, are you?"

"Never."

"Okay, then," Bridie said. "So whatever you decide to do, I'm still leaving my place to her."

"Why don't you sell it and move into town? Spend the time you have left helping Ida Mae make quilts and going to the library anytime you want, and having Harold fix your lunch every now and then."

"I don't know," Bridie said, but Jonah had planted a very fertile seed. The idea of being able to do all that without worrying how it was going to happen was tempting.

"I know you don't, but think about it. Okay?"

She sighed. "I'll think on it, but I won't make any promises."

"Good enough," Jonah said, then he pointed. "Ida Mae is at Shug's getting her truck gassed up. Want to invite her to have lunch with us?"

Delight spread across Bridie's face at the spur-of-the-moment idea.

"Why, I think that would be a fine idea."

"Good," Jonah said, and slowed down before turning off the road and pulling in at the station. He honked the horn.

Ida Mae saw them, waved, then hurried over. A few minutes later, Jonah was chauffeuring the two best friends into town.

FIFTEEN

Luce was more than surprised when she saw Jonah bringing Bridie and Ida Mae into the diner. She topped off the glass of iced tea Dr. Bigelow was drinking, then headed toward the door.

"What a nice surprise," she said, as Jonah leaned down and kissed her cheek.

Bridie's eyes were a little too bright. Luce suspected tears.

"Is everything all right?" Luce asked.

"It is now," Jonah said. "I'll tell you about it later."

Luce nodded. "Good enough. Would you rather sit at a booth or at a table?"

Bridie and Ida Mae opted for a table. Jonah followed behind them as they talked their way through the room. When he held a chair out for Bridie to be seated, she lifted her chin like royalty and primly sat herself down. Ida Mae giggled when Jonah did the same for her.

Luce grinned. They were having themselves a day at Jonah's expense, but he didn't seem to care. She couldn't help but wonder what had happened to get Bridie off the mountain, and when she noticed Jonah keeping a close eye on her, as well, she began to worry. Still, whatever it was had obviously passed. She would learn about it soon enough. She gave them a few minutes to go through the menus and hurried back to the other customers.

Jonah knew the two old women were discussing the merits of meat loaf as opposed to a piece of fried ham steak, but he was more focused on Lucia.

Her cheeks were as red as the plaid shirt she was wearing, and she moved among the booths and tables with a skill born of many years at the job, always smiling, laughing, teasing with the people she served.

He wondered how she would fare in a place where the neighbors were few and the mountains were many — where the sun never fully set in the summer, and the nights were six months long.

But the longer he loved Lucia, the more he thought about Alaska. He'd never allowed himself to dream about it before he'd met her. Now it was always at the back of his mind.

Behind him, the door bell jangled as someone entered the diner. He glanced up as the newcomers walked past their table; then every instinct he had went on alert.

There were two men, both tall, and obviously workout fanatics, because their bodies were so heavily muscled that they walked like robots. One was wearing hunting gear; the other was in denim and leather. They scanned the room for a few seconds before one pointed out Lucia to the other. They grinned and nodded, then headed for a back booth.

Jonah couldn't help but wonder if these were the latest of Bourdain's hunters.

When Lucia left glasses of water and menus at the men's booth, they tried to strike up a conversation with her, but she was obviously having none of it. She was polite, but distant.

Luce was on her way back to take their orders when the doorbell jangled again, only this time it was Dorrie, the second-shift waitress.

Luce saw her and waved. "Are you lost?" she said, as Dorrie slid into a seat at the next table over from Jonah and the women.

Dorrie grinned, flashing her snow-white teeth. "Nope. Just shopping." She held up a couple of sacks, then put them on the floor by her feet. "I'm starved, and the snow is getting heavy. I just want something warm in my belly before I go home."

"Harold made chili," Luce said, then turned to Bridie and Ida Mae. "Girls . . . have you decided what you want to eat?"

"Meat loaf with all the trimmings," they said in unison.

Luce made a note of their orders, then turned to Jonah. "How about you? Are you having meat loaf, too?"

"What did those men say to you?" he asked.

Luce glanced up at the strangers, then caught them watching her and quickly looked away.

"They just asked if there were any good hunting places around here. I asked them what they were hunting, but they changed the subject."

Jonah frowned. "Stay away from them."

Luce sighed. "I have to wait on them, Jonah. It's my job. Now, do you want meat loaf or what?"

"No, I think I'd rather have some of that chili you mentioned."

"Me, too," Dorrie said from the next table, then grinned at Jonah when he glanced her way. "Hi. How you doin'? You're new around here, aren't you?"

"Sort of," Jonah said, and then looked away.

It was obvious she was simply trying to make conversation, because everyone and their hound dog knew who he was. And it was certain that she knew. She worked in the same place that Lucia worked, for heaven's sake.

Luce turned in their orders. A few minutes later she was delivering chili and meat loaf to both tables, as well as bowls of chili to the two hunters.

She was serving the last bowl when one of the hunters reached for her arm. She flinched, and as she did, the bowl of chili went flying. Crockery smashed and chili splattered — all over the table, the floor and the hunter's pants legs.

"Damn it, woman! Look what you did!" he yelled, and quickly stood up, brushing at the mess on his clothes with a napkin.

"I'm sorry," Luce said. "But you startled me. You shouldn't have grabbed my arm."

"Hell. Can't a man be friendly?"

His tone was defiant. Jonah was pissed.

He stood up.

Luce glared.

He hesitated; then, when she went to the back room to get a mop and cleaning supplies, he sat back down.

343

"Poor thing," Dorrie said, and shoved her chili aside. "I'm gonna give her a hand. The sooner those two get out of here, the better off we'll all be."

She got up and hurried to the back room.

Bridie and Ida Mae fell into a whispered conversation about the rudeness of the younger generation, while Jonah kept watching the men.

Harold carried another bowl of chili out and helped the men move to another booth, and the uproar settled. It took a few moments for Jonah to realize that Lucia still hadn't come back with the mop. His first thought was that she was still in the back room, upset, maybe crying. He didn't know how she would feel if it seemed he was interfering with her job, so he stayed seated for a little while longer.

But the chili was congealing, and neither Luce nor Dorrie had yet to show their faces. Finally Jonah stood up. He had waited as long as his conscience would allow.

"Excuse me, ladies," he said, and headed for the back room.

The hunters gave him a curious stare as he approached. The closer he got to them, the slower he walked. By the time he passed them by, they were looking down at their food with serious intent.

Then he walked into the back room. "Hey, Lucia . . . do you need any —"

The place was freezing, and there was no one in sight. Then he realized the back door was ajar and moved to close it. As he did, he saw a set of footprints in the snow already on the ground, and what appeared to be drag marks beside them.

A frown settled on his forehead as he shut the door and turned around. The door to the ladies' bathroom was open. He glanced in. There was no one in sight. He was about to go check the kitchen when he saw three small red drops near the toe of his boot.

His heart stopped as he squatted down, swept a fingertip through the drops, then lifted it to his nose.

Blood!

He groaned as the hair crawled at the back of his neck. Lucia was gone, and so was Dorrie.

He spun and dashed to the back door, then yanked it wide open.

One set of footprints. One set of drag marks.

Damn it to hell! Bourdain had tricked him big-time. All these years, and this was the first time he'd ever sent a woman after him. He'd been blindsided. Dorrie, or whoever the hell she was, had taken Lucia, and he'd never seen it coming.

He started back inside, then realized he'd been hearing the sounds of an approaching helicopter. That was when it hit him.

They were taking her away, just like they'd taken *him* when they'd kidnapped him from Alaska.

Now they would use her for bait. He knew Bourdain well enough to know that he would sacrifice anything and anyone to get what he wanted. And he wanted Jonah.

Just as he started out the door, Harold walked in.

"Hey, what's going on?"

"It was Dorrie! She took Lucia. Call the sheriff. Tell him to stop her SUV and not to let that helicopter take off!"

Then he bolted out the back door.

Snow was coming down heavily now — huge, wet flakes the size of duck down that melted on his clothes almost as fast as they landed. He already knew that Lucia was unconscious, or she would be screaming at the top of her voice. But it didn't matter. Her scent was with him always, and it was guiding him now. All he had to do was follow it to get to her.

Bourdain landed at the edge of town in an open field. It was as close as he could get.

He'd just received a phone call from Dorrie Caufield. She had the woman and was coming in fast.

Bourdain jumped out of the chopper and began pacing, watching for Caufield to show. The snow was falling faster now, and the pilot was yelling at him that they had to leave now or forget it. But he wasn't leaving. Not without Jonah Gray Wolf.

He rubbed at the scars on his chest — the ones left behind by the grizzly that had gutted him. He didn't know that Jonah Gray Wolf's healing skills were far greater than they had been. He didn't leave scars anymore.

Then Bourdain's cell phone rang.

Caufield was shouting at the other end. "Someone called the sheriff. I can't get to you. I'm going up the mountain to the cabin where Gray Wolf's been staying. The front yard is large enough to land a chopper. We'll reconnoiter there."

"No! No!" Bourdain yelled. "Don't get into his territory. You'll never get out!"

"Shut up and listen!" Caufield screamed. "I'm not going to run an armed roadblock for you *or* for a million dollars. If you don't want to play this my way, then I'm letting the bitch go and getting the hell out while the getting is good!"

Bourdain cursed. Everything was spinning out of control. He didn't want to face Gray Wolf like this, but this might be the last chance he would ever have to get this close.

"How do I find this cabin?"

"Go north up the mountain from town. You'll see a front porch and a piece of a roof. The cabin is built inside a cave, but the clearing in front is big . . . plenty big. Are you with me?"

"Yes. Just don't lose the woman."

The line went dead in Bourdain's ear. He dropped the phone back in his pocket and vaulted into the chopper.

"Up the mountain to the north, and hurry!"

The pilot shook his head. "No way! The air currents will be hell between those peaks, and with the blowing snow, visibility will be minimal, at best."

Bourdain pulled a handgun from his pocket.

"Up now, or I swear to God, I'll shoot you where you sit and take my chances."

The pilot paled, then gritted his teeth and revved the engine. The blades began turning, faster and faster, until the chopper began to rise. Just as it lifted off, a patrol car appeared on the adjoining road.

Bourdain slapped his leg and laughed.

They'd beaten the cops. The rush was a high better than if he'd taken a hit of cocaine. The adrenaline shooting through his veins was like nothing he'd ever experienced. Below, he could see a stick figure of a man getting out of the patrol car and looking up as he talked into a handheld radio. But he was too late. They were beyond the reach of the local authorities.

Bourdain sneered. No Barney Fife of a sheriff was going to take him down. Ignoring the scene below, he began to focus on the mountain looming before them. Just when he thought they were going to crash, the chopper went up, grazing the tips of the tree limbs with the skids, and then they were free.

"Where are we going?" the pilot asked.

"Look for a clearing about halfway up. There will be a small covered porch with a large clearing in front of it. Caufield's SUV should be there, as well. It's black. Should be easily visible from here."

"Open your eyes, you asshole. Nothing is easily visible from here," the pilot snapped.

Bourdain stared through the windshield, then glanced down. He could still see enough to get where he needed to go.

Sheriff Mize was on the radio to Earl Farley.

"They lifted off from Pushman's field and are headed north. What's the location on the black SUV?"

"I don't know, Sheriff. One minute it was coming down Delaware Avenue, and then it took a sharp left. There's nothing but a dead end down there. I kept thinking the driver would realize it and come back out, but nothing happened. When I drove down there to check it out, it was gone. From the tracks in the snow, looks like they went into four-wheel drive and drove out through Harris's backyard. Melvin is gonna be real pissed. Made ruts at least a foot deep."

"I don't give a damn about the ruts in Melvin Harris's yard. Just find that SUV," Mize snapped, and jumped back in the patrol car and turned toward town.

There was only one road that went north out of town, and it went straight up the mountain. So either Luce Andahar's kidnapper was lying low somewhere in town, waiting to skip out when no one was looking, or she'd made a big mistake. There was nothing up the mountain but the end of the road.

Between one breath and the next, Luce woke up screaming Jonah's name. There was blood in her mouth, and the blinding ache at the back of her neck was so severe that she knew she was going to throw up.

When she began to gag, Dorrie, better known to her acquaintances as D.J., started cursing.

"Don't you fucking throw up in my car!" she yelled. "Do you hear me? Swallow it, or you'll be swallowing your damned teeth."

"Then you shouldn't have hit me," Luce muttered, and rolled over on her side just as the contents of her stomach spewed out on the back of the seat.

"Fuck! Fuck!" D.J. yelled, and began pounding her fist on the steering wheel as they flew up the road.

The snow was falling so heavily that it was all the windshield wipers could do to keep a clear view, and the curves on the road were getting slick. Twice, the SUV had fishtailed before she'd been able to regain control.

Nothing was going as planned, and it was all that damned Bourdain's fault. He'd just *had* to be here. Couldn't let her do the job her own way. Hell no. Big man with the money thought he knew it all. If she wasn't careful, he was going to get them killed.

D.J. had only been past the cabin twice, but she knew she couldn't get lost. There was only one road. It took you up, and it brought you back. Trouble was, that meant that if Bourdain didn't show, they were trapped.

Luce heard Dorrie muttering, but wisely stayed still. Her mind was racing, trying to figure out where they were going and how she could possibly get free.

She knew that Jonah couldn't be far behind them. He would have noticed quickly when she hadn't come back with the mop. She wondered who'd cleaned up the mess, then knew she was losing it. Spilled chili was the least of her worries.

After a while, she began to focus on what she was hearing. The engine was whining — obviously pulling hard. She knew they were on an incline, because she kept rolling to the back of the SUV. Even though she'd been blindfolded, something made her think that they were driving up a mountain, which made no sense. There was nowhere to go once you were up but back down again.

Then the SUV hit a pothole, and Luce groaned. The top of her head felt as if it were going to explode. Once again she felt nausea stir. Moments later, she rolled on her side and retched a second time.

Caufield cursed some more, then accelerated through the next curve.

Jonah had been running through the back streets of Little Top, trying to get to where the chopper had set down. He'd figured Dorrie would be trying to make the connection and get out of town fast. When he heard the siren on Mize's patrol car, then saw the chopper take off, he dropped to his knees in despair. They had her. He was too late. God only knew where they were taking her, but he knew it would be fast and far away.

Fear shattered what was left of his control. He rocked back on his heels and screamed. When they heard the cry, it struck fear in the hearts of those who lived nearest. Some thought it was an animal; others feared it was the death throes of a man in mortal pain.

And it was. For Jonah, losing Lucia was as painful as being pierced through the heart. He had been running ever since he left the diner, and he had been lost for most of that time. The snowfall was muting and mingling so many scents that he couldn't stay focused. He was scared — as scared as he'd ever been in his life. He'd promised Lucia he would protect her, and now, five minutes after they'd taken her, he had no idea where they'd gone.

He crawled to his feet, but he didn't know where to go. He couldn't bear to go back to their cabin. Her ghost would be everywhere.

But he couldn't just walk away from Little Top, because Bourdain had to know where to find him, so he could make his deal.

Snow had blanketed most of his hair, and the back of his coat was covered in a mix of icy slush. He swiped his hands across his face, as if trying to clear his mind, then began to scan the area. He needed to get his bearings, but all he could see were faint images of houses and trees.

Then, suddenly, a wolf walked out of the snow.

Jonah stopped. He hadn't known there were wolves anywhere in the state. He hadn't seen any before, and he wondered if this one was even real.

The wolf watched him without making a sound.

"Do you know where she is?" he asked.

The wolf howled, and the sound woke a sense of homecoming in him so strong that tears came to his eyes. But his question had been answered.

He started to head for the diner to get his truck, then realized he was closer to the mountain than town. He turned toward the trees and started running. He'd run up this mountain once to help Lucia save her dog. This time, he was running to save *her.*

■ ■ ■ ■

D.J. wheeled into the yard at the old cabin site and pulled her SUV up as close to the porch as she could get. The chopper was going to need the entire clearing to set down, and she wanted to be ready.

She had jumped out on the run and started toward the back of her car when a huge brown-and-white dog came out of nowhere. One minute she was standing; the next thing she knew, she was flat on her back and fighting for her life.

The dog's teeth sank into her wrist, and she screamed in pain as she heard bones break. Blind with pain and scared half out of her mind, she knew she was only going to get one chance to save herself before it was too late. When the dog lunged again, she put her forearm between its jaws and her face as she dug into her pocket with her free hand.

The cold, smooth feel of steel beneath her fingers was a godsend. She dragged the gun up and out of her pocket just as the dog went for her throat. Once again she blocked the lunge with her arm, and once again the animal's teeth sank through muscle and tendons, shredding them, along with her clothing.

The pain was so intense that she thought she would faint, but it was now or never. She saw the fangs, saw eyes red with rage, then pushed her pistol into the big dog's chest and pulled the trigger. Over and over. Until the gun was empty and the dog was lying flat on top of her.

"Damn, damn, oh, damn," she mumbled, as she struggled to get out from beneath its weight.

She managed to pull herself upright by leaning against the bumper, but when she finally stood, her head was reeling from shock and pain.

Something warm was running down the top of her hand. When she looked down, she saw it was blood. Her blood. Coloring the snow beneath her feet.

Furious that she'd been caught unprepared, she yanked the hatch open and, with her good arm, grabbed Luce by the hair and dragged her out backwards, while Luce screamed and cursed Dorrie's name.

D.J. yanked Luce up onto her feet, pulled and dragged her past the dog's body to the porch steps, then shoved her backward.

Luce fell hard, raking her back against the second and third steps, before she rolled over onto her side and sobbed.

Hobo was dead. She'd heard the fight. She'd heard the shots. It was the silence that told the rest.

Somewhere in the distance, she thought she heard a helicopter, then told herself she was crazy. No one could fly in this kind of weather.

She didn't know exactly where Dorrie was, but she could hear her moaning and cursing somewhere off to her right. She rolled over until she was sitting up, then scooted to the steps before she found her footing.

She knew it was futile, but waiting to die wasn't in Luce Andahar's makeup. Even though her hands were tied behind her back and she was blindfolded, she bolted off the porch and made a break for the forest, screaming Jonah's name.

Running was the last damn thing D. J. Caufield would have expected the fool woman to do. She was bloodied and blindfolded and still acting like she had a chance.

D.J. started to shoot, just to put the bitch out of her misery, then realized she'd emptied her gun into the dog. She started to reload, then remembered that they needed the woman alive to get to Gray Wolf. Shit. It wasn't enough that her damn dog had nearly torn off her arm. Now she was going to have to chase her down.

Cursing at the top of her lungs, she shoved her pistol in her pocket and took off across the yard, shouting Luce's name.

Sixteen

Jonah was halfway up the mountain when a cougar jumped out in front of him. It snarled, then screamed, before disappearing into the snowfall.

Jonah kept on running, thankful for the update. At least he knew Lucia was alive and on the mountain. But there was another problem. One he hadn't expected.

The chopper. It hadn't left the area. It was somewhere above him, lost in the blizzard. He didn't know what the hell was happening, but he knew he was about to find out.

A burst of fear sent him into overdrive as he began to sprint, leaping over fallen logs, dodging thickets of underbrush, all the while keeping her face in his mind.

Before he knew it, he was at the creek. He cleared it in one bound and kept on going, taking heart in the knowledge that from here, it wasn't far to the cabin. The snow was ankle-deep and still falling, and the wind was beginning to blow. He couldn't imagine what it was like up in that chopper, lost in a swirl of wind and white. Whoever was up there had to be out of his mind.

Then he heard Lucia scream. She was calling his name — screaming it, choking through sobs — and from the sound of her voice, she was running.

With one last superhuman push, he burst out of the trees and into the clearing. He saw her, hands tied behind her back, blindfolded and bloody, running in the wrong direction.

He felt her fear and confusion, then a searing, piercing pain, and knew she was on the verge of a breakdown. Something bad had happened — something — oh, God. *Hobo.* That bitch had killed Hobo.

"Lucia!"

He said her name, no louder than if he had been standing beside her, but he knew that she sensed his presence when she turned in his direction.

"Jonah? Jonah?" she cried, and even though the sound was swallowed up by the storm, he heard her.

"I'm here."

She staggered, then fell to her knees.

He bolted forward, then increased his speed when he saw Dorrie coming at Lucia from the other side of the clearing. One of her arms was hanging limp against her side and her clothing was shredded and bloody, but it was nothing compared to what he wanted to do to her. Enraged by what Bourdain and his hired killer had done, he lengthened his stride. They wouldn't put their hands on Luce again.

Suddenly, there was a blinding whoosh of air and snow, and the whap-whap sound of rotor blades. The chopper was over their heads and setting down without care for who was beneath it. The cockpit was swaying from side to side as the pilot fought with the wind currents, trying to keep the chopper upright.

Lucia was right beneath the skids, trying to stand up and run, but she was too weak.

Jonah looked up. The chopper kept descending and was only a few yards above her head. He made a dive for her midsection, catching her in a flying tackle, then rolling them away just in time.

Her breath was hot against his neck, and he could feel her shaking.

"Jonah! Jonah! Dorrie . . . it was Dorrie. Not a man . . . a woman. They tricked us."

"I know, baby . . . I know. It's all right now. They can't hurt you again."

"Yes, they can!" D.J. shouted.

Jonah looked up through the flying snow. Dorrie was standing over them with a gun pointed in his face, and behind her, the chopper door was opening.

A man jumped out, then strode toward them, oblivious to the backwash from the chopper blasting his hair and clothes. The ten years since Jonah had seen him had turned his hair from dark to white. But his eyes were still the same — cold and greedy — and he was smiling.

Major Bourdain.

Their gazes met. Bourdain sneered, his expression challenging and victorious. Then Jonah turned his back to the blast of snow and wind, shielding Lucia as he helped her to stand. The wind was whipping his hair into his eyes and across his face, as he took off her blindfold, then untied her hands.

"Leave her alone and turn around!" Bourdain called.

Lucia was shaking so hard she could barely stand. Jonah whispered gently against her ear, then began to pull on the tendrils of her hair that had become caught in the blood drying on her face.

The fact that Jonah Gray Wolf was ignoring him enraged Bourdain as nothing else could. How dare the son of a bitch act as if nothing was wrong?

He pulled a pistol and jabbed the barrel into the middle of Jonah's back to punctuate his words. "Don't turn your back on me!"

Jonah tossed the blindfold away, then laid his hand on Lucia's head. It came away bloody. The look he gave Dorrie as he turned was colder than the snow falling down around their heads.

"You shouldn't have hurt her."

A shiver ran up D. J. Caufield's spine. The warning in his voice was unmistakable, but she couldn't bring herself to move. Her legs felt heavy, and the world was beginning to spin. She didn't know if it was her or the wind from the chopper blades throwing her off balance, but either way, she was going down.

"Shut up! Just shut the hell up!" Bourdain said. "All you have to do is lay your hands on her and she'll be good as new."

But Jonah didn't acknowledge him, and when Caufield suddenly dropped to her knees, Bourdain felt himself losing control. Before Bourdain knew what was happening, Jonah was staring through the snow, into the cockpit, directly at the pilot's face.

The pilot had been unable to see much of anything, and then all of a sudden a big Indian seemed to appear out of nowhere, watching him, blaming him. He frowned. Where had that emotion come from? He hadn't done anything to the man. Suddenly he felt the skin tingling on his body, then beginning to sting before morphing into a hot, burning sensation. In a panic, he revved the rotors and lifted straight up into the air.

Bourdain turned around in shock, then ran a few steps after the copter, screaming in frustration. "Come back! Damn you, you sorry bastard . . . come back!"

He fired a shot up into the sky, but it was useless. All he could do was watch as his only means of escape disappeared. His shoulders slumped as he turned around, and it dawned on him that making amends with Jonah Gray Wolf might be the difference between life and death. He began to babble, desperate to make the man understand.

"Jonah . . . son . . . I can make you rich beyond your wildest dreams. Your power would be beyond measure. People will bow at your feet and honor your name as no one has been honored before you."

Jonah didn't pay any attention to Bourdain as he pulled Lucia into his arms. He steadied her until she was leaning against his chest with her head against his heartbeat. She was sick with pain, and weak from the loss of blood. No matter what happened afterward, he wasn't letting her suffer another minute.

He closed his eyes.

Bourdain felt the air thicken, and the snowfall softened when the wind began to calm.

"Wait!" Bourdain shouted, and pointed his gun, but the act was futile. He wouldn't shoot. He couldn't. "Don't! Not now! Let's talk this out," he pleaded.

The earth began to tremble beneath Bourdain's feet. Earthquake? In the winter? Did such things happen? He didn't know, but he didn't want to be caught in a natural disaster.

Bourdain looked for Caufield, but she was on her knees in the snow, struggling to get up.

"Caufield! Go get your car. We're leaving. Now!"

D.J. rolled over onto her back and stared down at her hand. Blood continued to roll out from under her coat sleeve, staining the snow beside her leg. She heard Bourdain's order, but she didn't have the energy to move.

When the ground continued to tremble so hard that the snow shook off the tree branches, Bourdain dove toward Caufield and started digging through her pockets for her keys.

"Your keys! Where are you car keys?"

"Get off me," she mumbled, as she shoved him off her chest. "They're still in the car."

Bourdain leaped to his feet, but then he paused, stunned by the sight of an aura beginning to emanate from Jonah's body. The older man's eyes widened, and his lips went slack. He'd never seen this before. If this was what Jonah had done to him that had saved his life, he was amazed. It was beautiful — so beautiful. His eyes filmed with tears as his heart swelled in his chest.

Mesmerized by the sight, he watched as the light grew in such measure that it began to flow from Jonah to Lucia, then pulse throughout her body.

Caufield felt the peace and forgiveness within it. She wanted to be closer — needed to find the blessing that she sensed was in it. But when she tried to crawl toward the light, she fell to her side. In despair, she began to weep.

The light was around them and within them; then suddenly it was over. Lucia was aware of nothing but Jonah's arms around her, then a weight lifting from her body. When she heard Jonah's voice, she looked up.

"Lucia . . ."

She couldn't take her gaze from his face. His eyes were glittering as he brushed his lips across her forehead, then ran the edge of his thumb along her lip.

"Know that you are well."

Bourdain couldn't believe this. It was as if he wasn't even there.

"Damn it, Gray Wolf. Step aside."

Jonah cupped Lucia's face, making sure she looked at no one but him.

"Go to the cabin."

She walked out of his arms and started across the yard without looking back.

Bourdain swung his pistol up and took aim at her back.

Jonah stepped into his line of fire.

Bourdain's hand wavered. But he was still the one holding the gun.

"You come with me — now — or I'll kill her where she stands."

Suddenly, D. J. Caufield began to shriek. Her struggles increased a hundredfold as she tried to get up, but it was no use. She pointed at Bourdain.

"Behind you! Behind you!" she screamed.

Bourdain turned, and a warm stream of urine spilled down the inside of his leg.

Four cougars crouched behind them. They were silent, unblinking, their tails twitching, their eyes fixed on Jonah's face.

"Oh, Jesus," D.J. whispered, and then looked at Jonah in disbelief. She'd read all the reports, but she hadn't understood. Not really. Not until now.

"Come on, Gray Wolf . . . do something," she begged.

Jonah looked at her then, and felt no empathy for her wounds or for her fear.

"I told you, you shouldn't have hurt Lucia," he said, and turned his back on both of them.

Bourdain began to beg. "You can't leave. I'll kill her."

Jonah pointed. "You better quit worrying about Lucia and worry about them."

The cougars snarled.

Bourdain tried to shoot, but the gun wouldn't fire. He hit it against the side of his leg, then pulled the trigger again and again, but it was dead metal in his hand.

"Call them off! Call them off!" Bourdain begged. "If you do, we'll talk. Anything you want. It's yours. Just name it."

There was a long moment of silence, then Jonah's eyes narrowed.

"Anything?"

Bourdain was near tears as he began to laugh. He'd known it all along. All they needed to do was talk face-to-face.

"Yes. Yes. Anything. Name it, and it's yours."

"You know what I want?" Jonah asked.

"No. What?"

"I want you to die."

The smile slid off Bourdain's face as the reality of Jonah's words soaked in.

"But you're a healer. You don't kill people," he mumbled.

"Oh, yeah, right. That's what *you* do, isn't it?" Jonah said.

The cougars snarled. One screamed a warning that sent Caufield into hysterics. She didn't understand it. It was her arm that was injured. What was wrong with her legs?

Bourdain didn't have the guts to look over his shoulder again. He didn't want to see them and know what their presence meant.

"Oh, God. Oh, Jesus. Don't. I'm begging you. Don't," Bourdain cried.

"Shut up," Jonah said. "Did my father beg for his life? Did he? Did he beg for mercy before your hired guns put a bullet in his head?"

Bourdain flung the gun at Jonah's head and started running toward Caufield's car. The cats took him down in two leaps. One bite and Bourdain's neck was broken. He never made a sound.

Caufield took her gun out of her pocket and put it in her mouth. If she was going to die, she was going out on her own terms. But the chambers clicked without firing, and she remembered again that she'd emptied the gun into the dog and never reloaded.

She was sitting in the snow, sobbing and begging and trying to reload her gun with one hand, when the cougars hit. Like Bourdain, she was gone in seconds.

The cougars chuffed softly.

"Thank you, my brothers," Jonah said.

Suddenly the distant sound of sirens could be heard.

The cougars' ears flattened. They hissed, then slipped away, swallowed up by the trees and the snow.

Jonah didn't spare the bodies a second glance. They'd chosen their own fate, while he'd been trying to deal with his own.

Sheriff Mize's patrol car was coming up the driveway, followed by Earl's.

Jonah's shoulders slumped as he turned away from the carnage and headed for the cabin.

The sirens were in his ears now, swallowing the sound of his breath and the wail of the wind.

He looked up.

Lucia was standing in the doorway as both patrol cars slid to a stop, sending snow spraying into the air.

Jonah kept on moving, needing to feel her in his arms. It wasn't until he was holding her that the world settled back on its axis.

Behind him, he could hear the Sheriff and his deputy talking. Within moments, their time together was going to be limited until Mize was satisfied with what had gone down.

Lucia took him by the hand. "Jonah?"

"Yes?"

"Is it over now?"

He sighed wearily, then managed a smile as he cupped the side of her face.

"No, my love . . . it's just beginning."

EPILOGUE

Spring had come to the high country. Tiny flowers were poking their heads through small crusts of lingering snow, while the birds that had gone south were returning in full force. The sunshine was new and still weak, but warm against a man's face.

It was on just such a day that Harve Dubois began circling the Snow Valley hunting camp in his old Bell Jet chopper, returning from Seattle with the first of the season's visitors.

Much had changed in the ten years since Jonah had been gone. It wasn't just hunters who came to the camp now. Artists and photographers had caught on to the beauty of this tiny part of Alaska, and reservations were filling up faster each year, which suited old Silas Parker, the camp owner, just fine.

Word around the camp was that Harve was bringing in someone special, and all kinds of theories abounded, from the possibility of a nature photographer from *National Geographic* to a psychic who wanted to investigate her pet theory regarding the life cycles of people who were exposed to the aurora borealis.

Small children were running about, chasing a dog who had run away with their kite.

A woman was standing in the doorway of her home, shading her eyes against the skyline as she watched Harve begin his descent. A middle-aged man stepped out of his toolshed and then leaned his ax against the woodpile to watch.

It was always a point of curiosity to see what kind of people would pass through their lives each year. It didn't matter to the Inuit, because they had been here first. For them, Alaska wasn't a place to visit.

It was home.

But as they watched, something else began to happen on the hillside above the valley.

Something that brought old Silas up out of his chair on the porch and had him running out into the road.

Something that made Marie Tlingtik put down her laundry and walk to the edge of her yard with her hand over her heart.

Something that made Wilson Umluck's face break into a huge, happy smile.

There were wolves — at least twenty,

maybe thirty, of them — coming out of the trees at a lope, yipping and howling in what sounded like joy, like the sound of small children who'd been let out to play.

It was then that Silas knew who was in Harve's chopper.

He started down the dirt road toward the landing pad. It occurred to him as he hobbled along that he should have brought his cane. Then he rounded the corner of the last cabin, and when he saw a tall Indian man standing beside the chopper, with long black hair hanging loose about his face and shoulders so broad they stretched the fabric on his shirt, he began to cry. Huge, gulping sobs that burned his throat. He hadn't believed he would ever see him again — at least not in this lifetime. But here he was. He'd come home.

The wolves were running now, at breakneck speed, spilling down the hillside in fluid motion, with their heads up and their tongues hanging, still yipping, calling back and forth to each other as they ran to greet the man.

From the moment Harve had flown them in to Alaskan territory, to this moment, when Jonah stepped out of the chopper, he'd felt different. Lighter. Free. Knowing he had the possibility of a home, now, and a future.

A future with Lucia.

Bridie Tuesday had long since been settled into a house down in Little Top, and Jonah had been satisfied in knowing she would never be alone again.

At the thought, he turned toward the chopper. Lucia was standing inside, waiting for him to help her out. He put his arms around her waist and lifted her down.

She was smiling. It was all he needed to see.

Lucia was stunned by the majesty of the mountains and the beauty of the low valley between them. She'd already made a life-time friend of Harve Dubois and was anxious to meet the rest of the people from Jonah's home. She didn't know that Jonah had already set one surprise in place for her.

Something he'd had Harve do before he'd come to pick them up.

Something that would settle them into a perfect rhythm as they began the rest of their lives, living in one of Silas's new cabins.

Lucia couldn't quit looking at the vista and the valley, knowing that this place was going to be their home. Then, as she looked up toward the mountain slope, the smile slid off her face. In a different place, and without this man at her side, she would have been scared out of her mind. But she was *here,* and so was Jonah.

And so were they.

"Look," she said, pointing over Jonah's shoulder.

He turned, and as he did, a smile broke across his face. He threw his head back in a laugh that turned into a howl, and then he started toward them at a lope.

Lucia watched in awe as man and pack met, and Jonah went down in a tangle of legs and tails. She could hear him laughing from where she stood as the wolves licked and sniffed and yipped and howled.

"Oh my," she whispered, as Harve Dubois sidled close and put his arm around her shoulder.

"He's a pistol, ain't he?" Harve said.

Lucia sighed. "Actually, Harve, that's something of an understatement."

Finally Jonah pushed his way out of the pack, stood and began brushing himself off. The wolves behaved as if they didn't want to leave, but then he laid his hands on their heads as he walked among them, and Lucia heard the promise that he made.

"I am here. I am home. I will never leave you again."

It seemed to be enough. Within moments they were gone, running back up the slope and then disappearing into the trees.

Silas Parker was puffing hard as he finally reached the landing pad.

Jonah saw him and was struck by what the passage of time had done while he was gone.

Silas Parker had turned into an old man. His hair was shoulder-length and as white as new snow. His belly was round, and his knees had started to bow from the pain of age and arthritis. But he was still Silas — looking at him in awe, just as they said he'd done on Jonah's first arrival.

The story was an old one. One Jonah had heard all his life. When the she-wolf had brought him into the camp, then left him in the dirt, it was Silas Parker who had picked him up and carried him to safety.

And now here he was again, the first member of Snow Valley to come to welcome him back.

His heart was full with emotion as Silas came toward him. Then, over Silas's shoulder, he saw people spilling out of houses and calling his name. Some were waving. Some were crying. But they were all coming down to welcome him, just as the wolf pack had done.

Silas took him in his arms and then hugged him fiercely.

"Welcome home, son. Welcome home. I didn't think we were ever gonna see you again."

Jonah's vision blurred as he hugged the old man back. Then he remembered Lucia and reached for her.

She clasped his hand as he pulled her to him.

"Silas. This is my wife, Lucia. Lucia, this is Silas. He taught me how to fish."

Silas beamed as he eyed the small, dark-eyed woman.

"Pleased to meet you," he said.

"Oh, no. The pleasure is all mine," Lucia said, and then set her place in Silas's heart forever when she gave him a hug.

"Look," Silas said. "They're all coming to welcome you home."

A small dog ran ahead of the people in a race of its own. It was brown and white, with a black patch of fur over its left eye, giving it a whimsical expression.

Luce's heart tugged at the sight. Losing Hobo the way she had still gave her nightmares, and she missed the big dog's crazy tricks.

When the little pup came to a stop at her feet, with its tongue hanging out and one ear cocked as if waiting for the punch line of a joke, Lucia was hooked.

She dropped to her knees, then held out her hand. "Well, hello, little fellow. I'm very glad to meet you."

Jonah glanced over at Harve, who nodded.

Jonah knelt beside Lucia. "His name is Howdy."

Lucia smiled. "Really? So . . . howdy, Howdy."

The pup barked, then jumped up and licked her chin before she could dodge the attack.

"I have it on good authority that the little guy is in need of a home," Jonah said.

Luce rocked back on her heels as her eyes filled with tears. "Oh, Jonah."

He picked up the pup as Lucia stood, then put him in her arms.

But the crowd was growing closer, and Luce could tell how touched Jonah was by their exuberance. She cuddled the pup under her chin as she nudged Jonah along.

"Go," she said. "The least you can do is meet them halfway."

Jonah laughed, then kissed her soundly before he started to run.

The crowd was shouting now, calling to him in their native language, yipping like the wolf pack to signal their joy, crying out his name until it was an anthem echoing back from the hills.

"Gray Wolf. Gray Wolf."

"The healer is home."

We hope you have enjoyed this Large Print book. Other Thorndike, Wheeler, and Chivers Press Large Print books are available at your library or directly from the publishers.

For information about current and upcoming titles, please call or write, without obligation, to:

Publisher
Thorndike Press
295 Kennedy Memorial Drive
Waterville, ME 04901
Tel. (800) 223-1244

or visit our Web site at:

http://gale.cengage.com/thorndike

OR

Chivers Large Print
published by BBC Audiobooks Ltd
St James House, The Square
Lower Bristol Road
Bath BA2 3SB
England
Tel. +44(0) 800 136919
email: bbcaudiobooks@bbc.co.uk
www.bbcaudiobooks.co.uk

All our Large Print titles are designed for easy reading, and all our books are made to last.